THE CUSTODIAN
Breaking the Circle

By
C A Middleton

WORDS MATTER
PUBLISHING
OUR WORDS CHANGE THE WORLD

Words Matter Publishing
P.O. Box 1190
Decatur, IL 62525
www.wordsmatterpublishing.com

Cover design by Amina Abu El Hawa

ISBN: 978-1-958000-02-1

Library of Congress Catalog Card Number: 2022943870

Dedication

Again, as in the first, I dedicate this to Mary. She started the whole thing off by saving my bath and a pan of boiling spuds.

Acknowledgements

I'd like to fank (in Yorkshire we have little use for the "TH") Tammy and Shannon at Words Matter Publishing for the never-ending work. But most of all, my dog, Trixie, for her mentoring the second Custodian and my bestie for her patience and cups of morning tea.

Huge FANKS to Amina Abu El Hawa for such a ridiculously emotive cover and for the epitome of a patient ear. You have outdone yourself.

TABLE OF CONTENT

Part One

Chapter One

There is a castle built on the wilder part of the Yorkshire coast made from human skulls. It looms atop a fragile rock. The raging sea batters the east side. The chill wind howls and whistles along the many smiling jaws and black, empty eye sockets. A sinister song of death.

The architect built the castle as a macabre folly. Now his great-great-grandson sleeps inside the main hall, upright in the lord's seat at the far-end of a long and extravagant dining table. I step through the two huge double doors- ajar as if a welcome to enter. The light from the many candelabra shines along the tanned leather hanging on the cold stone walls. I assume, by the shape, they are the skulls' skins.

Why am I here?

A letter sent by the great-great-grandson, a Lord Jonathon Markham, no less.

Dear Sir,

I understand you are a man without fear of the otherworldly. I have news regarding the mysteries of Broughton Road you may want to hear. Come post-haste to my folly on Black Rock. I will leave the west side servants' entrance unlocked and will await you in the main hall. Come alone and, despite the scene that will greet you, without fear.

Yours sincerely,
Lord M.

Chapter Two

The Custodian awoke from a dream with a start, inside his usual bed, the bath, and sucked in oxygen as if he needed the chemical's energy to yawn. He cast his eyes around the bright, sunlit room. The decorators had used cheap emulsion on the surrounding walls. For reasons beyond him, he would have given anything to smell the paint's aroma. Little did he know, certain such scents had pleased him in his former life. He grunted. If asked, however, he couldn't even describe what paint smelled like anymore.

Fragmented images of the previous night's dream filtered to the front of his mind, saddening him. He wished he could remember the name of the angel in the dream, never mind what she wanted to tell him. Every night the beautiful and kind lady appeared to him, yet she always left him feeling depleted and lost for a short time the morning after.

The sound of the keys rattling in the front door startled him. He shot to a sitting position before hopping out of the tub with a quiet grace unassociated with someone of his scrawny stature. It took time and practice for him to become a master of his fragile form and he had time in abundance. He rushed to the landing banister, his nerves jangling, as the door opened and two living humans entered. He recognised the male, but like everything else in his world, his memories tickled the back of his mind without pushing forward to identify themselves. The raven-haired young lady, with the brown aura The Custodian had come to regard as one denoting fear, caused no such tickle.

"As you can see," the man began, in what seemed an almost rehearsed speech The Custodian felt sure he had heard before, "The flat's been renovated throughout. If you'd like to follow me." He flashed a practised smile and led the lady up towards the landing. The Custodian liked the look of the lady. Probably because he only ever saw sweaty labourers and they had stopped visiting quite a while back. "As you can see, a completely new bathroom has been installed which even includes a jacuzzi bath." The lady turned to check out the bathroom. "Take your time, Miss Richardson. I'll wait in the kitchen." The estate agent bowed slightly towards The Custodian, creating a confused frown from the recipient, and headed towards the kitchen.

Miss Richardson gave The Custodian little time to mull over the strange bow because she appeared from the bathroom and scampered, like a nervous mouse, to the kitchen. Despite her twitchy demeanour, The Custodian warmed to her. Not in a romantic way. He saved such feelings for the lady who haunted every dream he had endured since first waking inside the flat. The Custodian followed Miss Richardson into the kitchen, careful not to stand in the way. Nothing nauseates a person in limbo more than looking at the pumping, beating, squishy insides of the living when they inadvertently stroll through him.

"As you can see, we have recently added a new back door with a lovely balcony you can grow herbs or flowers on. The steps lead down to a reinforced gate with a secure lock. Not that we have much in the way of robberies around here," The estate agent assured her with another one of those well-rehearsed smiles.

The Custodian cringed as he remembered the mess the builders made when they battered down the wall where once a wide window sat, replaced it with a smaller window and added the new PVC door. The Custodian forced himself into the corner cupboards as the tour continued. The living made their way into the lounge and then up another short set of stairs to the third floor and into one of the two rooms The Custodian, for reasons beyond him, dreaded visiting. The feelings emanating from the master bedroom, if he ever willed the bravery to attempt to enter, stirred up the coldest fear he had ever suffered. The irrational fiery ice pumped up his legs, swirled into his stomach like acid and on to his head until the panic forced the young man to spin upon his heels and sent him scampering back to the lounge. Therefore, he waited on the middle step and watched with envious eyes as the estate agent showed Miss Richardson the room beyond the white gloss-painted door.

To those of flesh, the room seemed no different to any other room converted from an attic space. Three wooden beams ran perpendicular to a dormer window facing a cloudy Yorkshire sky. A fitted wardrobe and dressing table were set into the left wall. Miss Richardson looked happy with the room as they exited and headed to the second, smaller bedroom.

"And you can use this room as an office or a walk-in wardrobe," the estate agent twittered. "Have you any questions, Miss Richardson?" he asked as they made their way towards a panicked Custodian, who turned and bolted back to the lounge where safety whispered calm words into his ethereal ears.

"Erm, no," Miss Richardson replied with a shy shrug. "Well, erm, I have the funds to buy straight away. How quickly can things be completed?"

"I can get back to the office and get straight on with it if you have time to follow me and sign. I know the owners will be more than happy to complete. All paperwork should be signed and sealed in a matter of days."

The Custodian had never seen such joy in another man's eyes than the glint in the estate agent's. Miss Richardson looked at her wristwatch with nothing but worry darkening hers.

"Yes, I think I have time. But I must hurry. I need to be back in Surrey for six," she said.

"Then we have no time to waste," the estate agent simpered.

"Bye, then," The Custodian said to the closing door, seconds later as they left him to his habitual silence.

Chapter Three

Lydia Gardner, nee Anderson, who used Richardson to buy the flat, left Yorkshire in a panic. If she failed to arrive home in time, she would meet the wrath of her wife. That is why she drove to the other end of the country to find a new home. She could take no more of the hell in which her life dwelled. Lydia fought back the tears as she, along with a steady stream of other vehicles, joined the M1 and the three-hour journey down the motorway until it met the circular M25. Lydia allowed herself to hope she may just pull off her plan when she joined the London Orbital Motorway after finding the traffic flowing like a polluted river rather than the usual jams most people come to expect. She only had to complete this first task without it ending in her wearing a bruise or a limb-cast of one description or another. Around Birmingham, she even began to ruminate on whether she could stand the next few days in her wife's company it would take to finalise buying the flat.

"It's only a few days," she began like a mantra. "I am Lydia Richardson. It's only a few days. I can do this."

Lydia had gone by three names in her life, so would not find Richardson too difficult to get used to. Before taking

Julia's name on the day of the wedding for, as her new wife said, professional purposes, though Lydia later came to understand Julia only wanted another way to dominate her, Lydia also went by her penname, Lydia Surräge. She chose the name for no other reason than it sounded like the county of her birth and also because she liked its mellifluousness. Lydia now used Richardson because it sounded so ordinary. She needed its banality as a shield. Because she knew the impossibility of living under her maiden or pen name. Both would make it too easy for Julia to find her. And if she found her, Julia would no doubt finish off the torture with Lydia's death.

Lydia recalled those first two years when her wife actually treated her well. They dated a year before declaring their love during a civil service in Las Vegas, and Lydia had never felt happier. Julia loved and cared for her like no man or woman before had ever done. And that included her parents. They stopped talking to her shortly after she told them, knees already shaking, seated on the couch of their home, about her relationship with Julia. Not that they bothered with her much before the news.

"Is this some kind of sick joke?" her father, former police Chief Superintendent at the Met, hissed as he stood and towered over her. "Are you seriously telling me you have suddenly decided to become a lesbian and we will never get grandchildren?"

"But, Dad, there are other ways. I can still have a child."

"What? From some unknown pervert in a sperm bank who needs the money to keep his drug habit? Over my dead body, young lady."

"But, it's not…"

"And who will carry this seed? You or your dungaree-wearing, skin-head girlfriend? Because it will never be yours if she carries it. I'll tell you that for nothing, young lady," her father sneered.

"Julia is a barrister who specialises in helping battered wives and girlfriends, actually, Dad," Lydia replied and stood for the first time in her life to face off with him. "And she has long hair and never wears dungarees. That's the sort of dinosaur thinking that keeps good people from coming out to their parents."

All the while, her mother sat meek and mild in her favourite chair.

"COMING OUT," her father bellowed back. His usual way of winning any argument. If he failed with logic, out came the bull. This time, unfortunately for him, Lydia's anger kept her upright. "YOU'VE LIVED WITH BOYS AND NOW YOU'VE DECIDED YOU LIKE WOMEN. IT'S A FAD AND A PHASE."

"I'm not gay, Dad. I'm bi and I've always known it but just been too damned afraid to say it."

"Bi?" He sniggered. His amusement lowering his voice. "Have you heard this nonsense, Jennifer? Your daughter's a bi-sexual." Her mother shrugged in response. Forever the mute. "There's no such bloody thing."

"There is and I am one," Lydia replied, angry but relieved to unburden her lifelong secret. The argument carried on for another half an hour before Lydia stormed out of the family home, telling them, "If you can't accept what I am, this discussion and our relationship is over. You know where I am if you change your mind and wish to support your daughter in her decisions."

"And you know where we are when you come to your damned senses," Her father hissed back before slamming the front door in her face.

Nobody ever described their alienation as Julia's doing. Her friends soon following suit took a little longer and had Julia's M.O. written all over it. You see, Julia created arguments out of silence to push everyone away. Telling Lydia her men friends only wanted one thing and wailing if she did anything other than acquiesce to her demands.

"You're going to leave me, aren't you?" was one of Julia's favourites. If that ploy didn't work, Julia promised to kill herself if Lydia left her. And when that scheme ran dry and Lydia replied by screaming, "GO ON, THEN! DO IT!" Julia's threats to harm herself turned to threats to hurt her wife until she broke Lydia's spirit entirely. The fun-loving woman who loved to dance almost as much as she lived for writing withdrew until only a frozen lump remained where once beat a joyful heart. Her writing turned from jolly children's stories to dark and macabre horror, though luckily, they sold.

Then, three years after marrying Julia, Lydia began researching a story she planned which centred around the famous Pendle witch trials. Later, she came across an obscure book in her favourite little shop by a writer of ghost sightings, a certain Irving Stofferson, who connected the trials with multiple suicides inside a flat in the little North Yorkshire town of Burrstone. At first, the idea amused her. She even googled the building and, when she learned the flat was up for sale, her plans moved on to leaving Julia for good, hoping such a distance would make finding her almost impossible. She loved the idea of writing in the atmosphere of so many myths and legends and she would only be a short drive from the site of the witch trials, Pendle Hill. The notion of a ghost inhabiting the flat also amused her. She had never believed in such nonsense. So, with one eye on whether the flat sold, she changed her name by deed poll to Lydia Richardson, opened a secret bank account and syphoned parts of her residual cheques into the new account, telling Julia there had been little or no sales for months. Obviously, the beatings increased due to the lack of Lydia's contributions, but with a prize at the end of the pain, she bore the bruises like medals. Next, she bought a burner phone so Julia wouldn't see the estate agent's number on the phone records she demanded to see every month and hid it in the garage. A year passed and the flat remained for sale. And then one bright Monday in June, at six-thirty in the morning, Lydia fed Julia her breakfast like a dutiful wife, watched her leave for the train to London, put the dinner in the slow-cooker, and drove to pretty Yorkshire to fall in love with the funny little flat. Something soothed her battered soul as soon as she entered. The place felt like home, and she knew before seeing the kitchen she had to buy it immediately.

Now, as she exited the horrendously clogged M25 and headed towards Woking, as the clock showed 5:55, her mind and stomach bubbled with fear and anxiety. If Julia arrived home before her, the beatings would become severe. The last time it happened, Julia broke Lydia's arm.

"And you say anything other than you fell down the stairs and I will break your other one, you hear?" Julia snarled as she drove her sobbing wife to the hospital.

The nurse questioned her injury, as Lydia's records showed similar admissions in the past, but Julia won her over with a soft smile and tales of her job championing real abuse. Lydia wondered if she had arrived with a man whether things would have ended much differently.

Lydia squeaked in panic as she pulled into their drive and her mobile phone erupted into life. Julia's name appeared on the screen. She switched off the engine and bolted to the front door. If Julia suspected Lydia had driven the car at such an hour, even though the evening bells clanged in the local church, the beating would begin without a doubt. The phone played its awful tune of doom. Lydia reached a shaky hand into her bag and pulled out the keys, only to drop them on the doorstep. She squealed again as she bent down, scooped them up and fumbled the key into the lock. The phone rang on, scraping at every nerve. Just as her head felt ready to explode, she opened the door and answered the phone, trying to keep her voice level.

"I'm sorry, Julia, I was in the toilet," she blurted.

"That's okay, silly," Julia replied in a sweet tone she always used if other people stood close enough to hear the conversation. "I just rang to let you know I will be a little late because of the bloody train. Okay, sweetheart? I didn't want you worrying."

"Okay. Er, thank you. Dinner will be ready when you get back," Lydia said after calming enough to notice the smell of the slow-cooked beef bourguignon waft towards her nostrils.

"Awww, that's lovely of you, darling. Okay, speak soon. Love you."

"Erm, love you too," Lydia lied. The words tasted like burnt dung on her tongue.

Lydia spent the time before Julia arrived home driving into the garage and then making sure everything in the house sat in its rightful place as judged by the all-powerful Julia.

An hour, later her stomach turned at the sound of the front door opening and then banging shut.

"I'm home," Julia called, all sweetness now dropped from her voice. "I hope you managed to at least reach a thousand words today? I don't go out at the arse-crack of dawn every day and slog my brains out for you to lie around the house like some kind of kept whore," Julia called as she hung her coat in the hallway.

"Erm, not quite. I'm sorry," Lydia squeaked. "I've hit a bit of a block. I did make you a lovely dinner, though, my love."

Julia didn't reply with words, but Lydia prayed she wouldn't walk into the lounge before entering the kitchen. She waited, wringing her soaked hands. Her stomach roiled. *Please, please, please,* she begged inside her mind. She couldn't see from her position by the stove where Julia stood. Three seconds later, as Chopin's Marcha Funèbre, her anthem of torture, began its sombre march, Lydia's bladder felt ready to explode. She cowered, involuntarily, like a child before a grizzly, into the corner of the kitchen before Julia even stepped one foot into view.

"Please," she cried, "Please, Julia. I'm so sorry."

Chapter Four

Clifford Manor, set eight miles outside of Burrstone, North Yorkshire, is an impressive eighteenth-century building erected, unlike most at the time, not on the blood of slaves and the antiquities of fallen countries. This building hides a much seedier past. The impressive building sits at the top of a long tree-lined drive, separated from the lower classes with its high walls and fifteen-foot wrought-iron gate crowned with the phoenix crest of the family who founded the estate. If we snuck inside and crept past the Sumerian artifacts and along to the entrance of the main hall, we would hear the low mumbling of a continuous chant. Inside the hall, with the scent of honeysuckle hanging sweet in the air, dressed in red robes, legs crossed, sit The Thirteen. With hands resting palms-up on thighs and heads bowed, they invoke their lord before a huge marble altar. A gigantic gold-framed mirror sits on the wall behind it. Two giant orange candles stand either side of the mirror, their flames dancing in an unseen breeze. A massive tome, The Secrets of Solomon, lays open on a golden bookstand in the centre. As you can see, this is not their first invocation. Long before the builders laid the first stone for the elegant walls around them, The Thirteen have met to invoke and pay homage to only one demon.

"Ahvalen esen Clauneck kiar," They repeat as one.

Such an invocation should take weeks and months to the novice. The Thirteen, though, have a long-standing special relationship with the demon of wealth.

The glass of the mirror begins to swirl with dancing fog. As if seeing this, and remember their eyes are closed, The Thirteen chant louder and louder in an ecstatic trance. They sway as they call their benefactor.

The fog spills from the mirror now and pirouettes like a child ballerina around the summoning room, only decorated with the austere portraits of those who came first. And just as the fog tightens around the group of devotees, a man of around six-feet-nine, wearing a gold cloak and black shoes of the finest leather, strides out of the mirror and stands before them.

"Thirteen," he announces with a deep and cultured voice. "Look at me." As one, The Thirteen remove their cowls and face the demon. The man in the centre of The Thirteen is none other than the estate agent. "You call me from a dinner in my honour. This better be good." He smiled but the words carried cold-steel menace.

"Lord Clauneck, please forgive us," the estate agent said with a bow of reverence. "We have your next soul."

"Really? They're coming quicker every time, aren't they?" Clauneck smiled. His eyes turned red with joyful anticipation. "Male or female? Actually, scratch that. The way everyone up here's changing their sexual identification these days, I wouldn't be surprised if it claims to be a damned antelope." He sniggered at his own joke. His sycophantic disciples joined in. "So, I best get in touch with upstairs. They will be surprised. While I'm debasing myself with the white-lighters, you begin the preparations in the location. How long before the next soul takes residence?"

"A week?" The estate agent replied in almost a question.

"You don't seem too sure," Clauneck sniggered.

"Well, I, erm, wasn't certain if I was moving her too fast, my lord."

"Have you done your due diligence?"

"Yes, lord. She comes from violence and subterfuge. Her heart is pure yet broken. Just as you like. She has nobody but her tormentor to miss her. She has changed her name so nobody but those the world classes as conspiracy theorists will come sniffing. And we know their kind are never taken seriously."

"A broken soul. Ooh, one of my favourites. So, make the doorway preparation and she should be ours in no more than two months. Anything else? I have several extremely dirty girls and a roast hog to devour, and I need not remind you how much I dislike either cold."

"Erm, just the matter of the payment, your lordship," the estate agent said hesitantly.

Clauneck's face turned purple. The human likeness twisted into a monstrous grotesque mask. Two golden horns grew and twisted from his skull. He threw off his robe and two giant bat-like wings spread from his back. The room froze in fear.

"Don't be so bloody vulgar," He growled as he loomed over the quivering estate agent. The agent gulped as the demon's index talon stretched out to trace a line across his throat. "It'll be where it always is." Before The Thirteen uttered another word, or even a sigh of relief, Clauneck turned on his heels and picked up his shimmering robe. "Tatty-bye," he called out cheerfully before entering the mirror and disappearing.

CHAPTER FIVE

Lydia awoke in stabbing pain several times during the night. The broken rib she had suffered the night before vented its fury each time. Once, at around three in the morning, she found herself, curled into a ball, sobbing in her sleep.

"If you don't quit your snivelling," Julia hissed, "I will cut out your tongue and feed it to you for breakfast."

Lydia pursed her trembling lips and held her breath until she gained control. Her left side burned with pain and she needed to change positions to relieve it but knew doing so with Julia half-awake wouldn't ease anything. She waited in agony until Julia's breathing became slow and steady, alongside her usual slight growl, indicating sleep had taken her. Even then, Lydia only made small, careful movements until she lay on her back. The new position did not eradicate the pain but it thankfully eased the intensity.

To move her mind away from her ribs, Lydia planned the next day. A case of finding joys inside dark holes.

I have three hours before the alarm goes off, she thought. *Then I see her off, pack some essentials, drive the car to the second-hand dealership on Marx Road, get a taxi to the Ford dealership on Carlisle Avenue, use my new ID papers to buy another car and drive to Yorkshire. Simple. Not too complicated. Then I'll be free.*

With a warmer feeling tickling her mind, she fell into a less uncomfortable sleep.

"Morning sweetheart," Julia cooed, her face hovering over Lydia's like a smiling spectre readying to dislocate its jawbones and swallow her head whole. "I've brought you breakfast."

"Wha'," Lydia mumbled, confused. "But, what time is it?"

"It's nearly nine o'clock, sleepy-head," Julia smiled as she laid a tray containing Lydia's favourites on the bed. A pot of tea; scrambled egg with triangles of toast stacked next to them, and not underneath, so as not to cause the bread to become soggy; a bowl full of sliced watermelon and strawberries with a dollop of Greek yoghurt and honey; and even a plum-coloured rose from the garden in a tiny vase. Yet, instead of filling Lydia with love, the gift only made her more anxious. "As it's our anniversary next week, I have decided to take the day off and focus on you, my sweet. Lovely, eh?"

"But…" Lydia began, shuffling and wincing up the bed to sit.

"I know, it's little off the cuff for me, but you deserve it for putting up with me," Julia said and sat at the edge, taking Lydia's shaking hand. "And it's also to make up for last night. After today, I'm going to find help."

Lydia had heard similar speeches several times before, so she nodded like a compliant child.

"You don't believe me, do you?" Julia asked.

"Yes," Lydia lied.

"I know I've said it before, Lyd, but I promise I'm going to get help."

Another thing you've said before, Lydia thought, yet said, "Okay. Thank you."

"Good. Now that's settled, I'm going to let you eat breakfast. Then I am going to go shopping and make you a beautiful dinner, How does that sound?"

"That sounds really nice, thank you," Lydia replied as she sat propped up in bed inside her déjà vu bubble.

"Good. Now you eat up, my love." Julia patted her wife's hand and skipped away to dress.

"Like I believe you," Lydia mumbled.

"Sorry," Julia began, popping her head around the door, startling Lydia "Did you say something, sweetheart?"

"I said, I can't wait for tonight," Lydia replied, as fast as a rumour can spread.

"Aww. Me neither."

Idiot, Lydia thought. *Think, Lydia, you idiot. Think.* Lydia felt her cheeks burning from shame. Over the last year, she had perfected living inside her head and there she sat on the verge of escape, forgetting and allowing her traitorous tongue to take command. She heard the shower spray hitting the bathroom tiles. *Now, can I really afford another day in this hellhole? Even if she's trying to be nice, it will only take one slip-up for her to turn. I know, but what if she really means to get help? Grow up, Lydia. How many times has she said the same shit and then snapped hours later? You've got to go today.* Living in one's head gives you many perspectives. *But how? I won't have time to drive to the second-hand dealership, sort all the paperwork and then do the same again before she finishes shopping. The plan was predicated on her being at work all bloody day. Then, sod the plan. Drive into town, ditch the car and the phone and get a train. There's one every half hour.* Lydia looked at the clock on her phone. It read, 09:09. A sequence some believe is an angel number.

She took it as a sign for no other reason than a push in a better direction. *I can do this,* she urged. The shower turned off. Lydia gulped. *Relax. If she sees you anxious, she'll suspect something,* Lydia told herself and took a deep breath. The inhalation sent a searing pain from her rib to make her wince.

"Awww," Julia cooed as she appeared with a towel wrapped around her long, slim body. A body Lydia once worshipped and now despised. "You okay, honey?"

"It's okay. Just my side."

"I'll get some paracetamol when I'm out," Julia replied and turned to dress.

"Thank you." Lydia suppressed a snarl just in case her wife turned around.

"That's okay. You make sure you eat your breakfast, sweetheart. You'll need your strength."

You couldn't be more correct, Lydia thought.

She picked at the food but each bite tasted like poison in her mouth. Julia stayed in the room to dress and apply her make-up and every second in her presence felt like a day for Lydia. Until, one long hour later, Julia kissed her wife on her forehead and said, "Right, I shouldn't be long. But you know how the traffic can be?" She picked up the tray of half-eaten food, "I hope you'll have a better appetite for later. I'm going to cook all your faves. You'll like that, won't you?"

"Yes, thank you," Lydia replied and attempted a smile.

"Good. You take your time getting dressed, sweetheart. There's no rush. I'll leave the pots in the sink for when you're ready." And with that, Julia strode out of the room.

Lydia wasted no time. She slowly slid out of the bed, each tiny movement causing her to suck in breath, and tiptoed to the wardrobe.

"I'm going, sweetheart," Julia called from the hallway. "Love you!"

Lydia replied with the same through cringed lips. But, not saying it may have resulted in Julia storming back up the stairs. She heard the front door bang shut and took a slow inhalation to focus. She needed only her laptop, the burner phone, the new and old identification, and her new and old bank cards.

Before the weaker side of her persuaded her otherwise, she left her contract phone so Julia could not follow her, along with her wedding ring, on the kitchen surface near the dirty pots. She then hobbled outside, drove into Woking, and parked in the train station's car park, praying she would not see Julia's silver Audi. Her mind and body both spun sickeningly with both the worry and the pain every time the traffic lights forced her to stop, but she arrived without seeing her wife. The rain, as if mirroring her mood, began to pound the open parking area. Lydia sighed and shuffled out of the car, pulling the hood of her coat over her head. The rain gave her reason to cover her face from CCTV and she thanked a lord she never believed in for the help.

"Excuse me," a nervous and tired voice asked, startling an already jittery Lydia. She turned to find a filthy and bearded homeless man, already drenched with rain, dripping before her. "I'm sorry, I don't mean to frighten you, but do you have any change, please? I haven't eaten for days."

An idea struck Lydia. "Can you drive?"

"Yes, I used to drive tanks and lorries in the army," the man replied with a confused frown.

"Good. I can give you fifty quid to drive this as far as you can. It's mine but I'm trying to get away from an abusive marriage."

"Then, in that case, I'll do it for free," the ex-soldier told her and stood an inch taller than a second previous, as if receiving this new mission gave his life purpose.

"Bless you," Lydia smiled and then winced. "I still want to pay you." She opened her purse and pulled out the full fifty pounds she kept hidden for emergency purposes, such as escape taxis or moments just like this. "I want you to take this and my heartfelt thanks. It's diesel, but you shouldn't need to fill it for a while, as I only filled the tank the other day. Actually!" She exclaimed as an idea struck her. "Could you please go into the glove compartment. There, you'll find the paperwork. There should also be a pen. I hope."

The man rushed into the car and produced both. The look on his exhausted face as he watched this attractive stranger lean into the cover of the car to sign it over to him would make a great newspaper clipping. The tears he shed flowed with genuine thanks.

"How can I ever repay you?" This man who signed his name as Roger Tyke sobbed.

"When you get back on your feet, buy one of my books, Roger." She smiled and stroked his arm. "You are doing me a greater service than I am for you, believe me."

And with that, Lydia, her heart ready to explode with hope, excitement and a cruise ship full of nauseating nerves rushed to the train station, bought a ticket and, three minutes later, boarded the train to Waterloo Station, London.

Chapter Six

A day earlier, The Custodian sighed as the new visitors left him to his silence. He struggled to understand why the estate agent bowed in his direction.

"I probably imagined it," he said aloud and winced. He hated how his voice sounded, as if he had his head wedged in a kitchen paper cardboard tube. One of the decorators who painted the flat's walls had brought his young son one rainy day and the boy seemed fascinated with the way it made his voice sound as he giggled down the cardboard core. "Try sounding like that all the time," The Custodian grumbled to the oblivious lad during that moment.

Most of the time, The Custodian kept his thoughts inside his mind. Now and again, they slipped out.

He slouched into what some called the living room. The name amused him when he first heard another workman use the word.

"I'll make a start in the living room, Alex," Inky, a scary-looking beast with scribbles and drawings all over his face, neck and arms, called to a smaller, quieter man who it turned out was his boss.

"Aye, all right," Alex replied from the kitchen.

The Custodian, not long in his post, rushed, confused, into the room, wandering what made it living. He hadn't seen anything to justify such a title. On arrival, he watched, disappointed, as Inky, the only living being in the room, flipped open a paint tin and began covering the ceiling in white gloss. The disappointment lasted only a few moments.

Well, at least I now know what to call it, the young spirit shrugged. Well, he did, until a work-lady, a rather pretty woman, who ruined her first impression by cursing more than the men, called it a lounge. The Custodian gave up wondering why the world used so many words for one square room. Although, he stuck to lounge as it made more sense to someone of lesser substance who spent more time than anyone else within its walls.

With the memory of the workers fading inside his mind, The Custodian perched on the window overlooking the main road and the train line beyond. The perch made him feel close to something he just could not put his finger on. Like the name of the girl he dreamed about every night without fail. With another sigh, he looked down at the street below. He then frowned as he noticed a gentleman wearing a rather dapper slate-grey brimmed hat staring up at the window in which The Custodian sat. The man carried a black notepad in one hand and a pen in the other.

"Are you okay, my friend?" A booming voice belonging to the owner of a little shop situated to the right of the flat called out. The locals all called him Mr K.

"Yes, thank you," the hat-wearer replied.

"I know you, eh?" Mr K asked in his thick eastern European accent. "You are the ghostie man off the television, yes? I see you. Are you looking for the spirits again?"

"Kind of, yes. I believe the upstairs flat is for sale?"

"I do not know," Mr K shrugged. "They have not put up a sign, but the people were doing the working in it until maybe a few weeks ago."

"Hmm." The hat-wearer scratched his chin as if thinking. "Did you ever meet the last owner? Erm," he consulted his notepad, "a Michael Parker?"

"Oh, yes. A nice boy," Mr K replied in a sad tone. "He always came to my shop for that and this. Very polite. So sad. He liked Queen."

"The queen? A fan of the royals, eh?" Hat-wearer said and made a note.

"No. No. The band, Queen. Always had them coming in his ears."

"Ah. The band. Okay. Did he strike you as depressed enough to kill himself?"

"He never struck me once. A nice boy, see? And also, was very happy on the last day. So sad. He wore good mask."

"A good mask?"

"You know, to hide his pains."

"Ah, yes, I see. Did he have any friends?" Hat-wearer asked after making more notes.

"Not that I see. But my shop only open until seven at the night. So, who knows, eh? He did work in the supermarket. Maybe they can help."

"Thank you, I'll try them. Tell me, is that the front room?"

Both men turned to look up at the window in which The Custodian sat. He suddenly felt naked in their gaze.

"Yes. So sad," Mr K repeated. "So very sad."

Chapter Seven

"Well, isn't that fortunate? I was just about to call you, Miss Richardson," the estate agent cooed on the other end of the call.

"Good news, I hope?" Lydia asked. She gave in to the itch of calling as the train left King's Cross and headed for Leeds.

"Oh, very good. The owner has signed. We're just waiting for the tedious solicitor stuff and you can move right in."

"Oh, that's excellent. Thank you. I was actually calling to tell you I'm travelling up to Yorkshire and have booked a room at an hotel called the Bon Suite."

"Great choice, Miss Richardson. It's on the outskirts of town and has a spa. You'll love it."

The call soon ended. Lydia sighed and looked out of the window from her table seat. The busy streets of London soon sped by, replaced by fields, trees, and tranquillity. For the first time that morning, Lydia believed she had done it. She had escaped Julia. She sighed again. As if a huge straw bale she had lugged for days had dropped from her shoulders. Ten minutes earlier, however, found her rushing through the streets of London in search of her bank. Her stomach aching with nerves. Her side on fire as she entered the automatic doors. The clerk cast a suspicious eye when Lydia asked for the contents of her bank in the form of a cheque, only to hand it back to her to deposit it in the Richardson account. Lydia thanked the stars the clerk did not have the experience to question her. Either that or she just cared little for her job.

Now, though, Lydia allowed herself to believe a new life awaited. She looked at the time on the telephone. *She will have found the phone and wedding ring by now,* Lydia thought, surprised at the little wave of guilt splashing inside her heart. "Sod her," she mumbled and then looked around the carriage. Nobody appeared to notice. Most sat typing on laptops or watching films with their headphones stuffed into their ears. *Whatever happened to just sitting and reading,* Lydia thought, the author inside her disgusted. She looked back at the time. *Two and a half hours to Leeds. Twenty minutes to wait for the train to Burrstone. I should arrive in Burrstone around quarter to four. Enough time to pick up some clothes and maybe enjoy a spa.*

She closed her eyes and drifted along on a contented boat. She dreamt of summers long past with friends who giggled and danced. Until a dark cloud grew to wipe away the smiles.

"YOU CAN'T ESCAPE ME," the cloud with Julia's voice screamed. Hands formed from the centre of the gyre and rushed out for Lydia's neck.

"Arrrggghhh!" Lydia cried and grasped her side as the pain in her rib flared into life.

"I'm sorry, Madam, I didn't mean to startle you, but we've arrived in Leeds," a huge, bear-like train conductor assured Lydia. Despite his size, there appeared a gentleness behind his hooded eyes.

"Sorry," Lydia replied, blinking away the sleep. "I didn't mean to drop off."

"That's okay. It happens," the conductor smiled. "No harm done."

Lydia thanked him and scurried out of the train, gripping her side, and onto the empty platform one, wondering how long she'd slept. Surely there should still be some other travellers stumbling off alongside her. She looked at her telephone.

"My god," she groaned. She only had eight minutes before the next train. "Somebody could've woken me sooner," she mumbled before scurrying towards a sign pointing out platform 6a.

On arrival, she found the train already waiting with its automatic doors open and inviting. A surprised Lydia stepped into the rather plush, air-conditioned carriage. *Beats our local trains,* she thought, recalling the dingy, graffiti covered lumps of unloved steel clacking up and down the tracks. She took an empty seat opposite a womble of an old lady clutching her bag to her chest. The lady smiled warmly across. Another experience alien to Lydia. Nobody smiled on London-bound trains unless they had lost a screw. She smiled back regardless.

"Welcome. This is the fourteen-fifty-six train to Burrstone," a recorded message boomed from the train's speakers. "Stopping at Shipley, Saltaire, Bingley, Crossflats, Keighley, Steeton and Silsden, Cononley and arriving in Burrstone for fifteen-thirty-nine."

Lydia mused over the quaint town names, looking forward to seeing what they looked like.

Soon enough, the train quietly left the station. Lydia swallowed three paracetamols before staring out of the large window, impressed at how developed Leeds looked. She always carried visions of a deprived northern city, rife with prostitution and football hooligans, but what she saw made her want to come back and have a proper look. This splendid view of tall towers and wonderful architecture, however, soon passed into the back-to-back Victorian housing associated with the poor mill families as the train sped on. This then faded to trees, rivers, and canals. The train stopped at the various stations obviously built on the sweat and depravity of nineteen-century mill workers. Lydia still vowed to spend a little time in each after she had settled in Burrstone. She used to enjoy travelling to new towns. They all had their own culture within a culture if you spoke to the locals. Julia only liked to travel if a white, sandy beach waited at the end of the aeroplane flight. So, Lydia lost her wandering spirit. Now she felt the urge to explore return, she yearned to drink a local beer in a clicky, little town, where the natives cast a suspicious eye until they knew you. She spent most of her university years clasping her student rail pass, a pack full of jam sandwiches on her back, travelling the length and breadth of the UK. From Banff to Bangor; Scarborough to Southend. She sighed as the memories filled her mind.

"The next and final stop will be Burrstone," the speakers announced. "Please make sure to take all your belongings and have a great day."

Lydia stood and followed a young couple as they exited on to a little concrete platform leading towards the station entrance. She found the station quaint, with its overhanging Victorian, white-painted steel and glass roof, held up with ornate posts. The automatic main doors opening as she walked towards them surprised her, though. They didn't seem to fit in with the rest of the nostalgia.

"Excuse me?" Lydia asked a gangly train guard. "Which way do I walk to the town centre?"

"Your best bet, love," the guard began, "is to cross the car park and just follow the main road to the right. It'll lead you all the way there."

"Thank you," Lydia replied and shuffled to the door. The

pain in her side had started to burn once again. She decided the long seated moments helped little with the discomfort.

The sun beamed down between two large and picturesque clouds as Lydia crossed the tiny car park. Her spirit felt light for the first time in too long as she reached the busy main road, looking left and right.

I recognise this road, she thought. To the left, the road passed under a stone bridge and the right led past a local supermarket. *I do know this. The flat's just down there,* she thought with glee as she looked beyond the bridge. *I remember passing it the other day.* She itched to prove her theory correct but knew she had little time to pick up some clothes, so headed right. She passed the supermarket with its huge, packed car park, over a little stone bridge spanning a murky-looking canal and on to a quaint town centre set with cobblestones on either side for, as the sign read, "**Market day: Wednesday and Saturday. No Parking!**" Lydia couldn't wait to see what the market brought. She enjoyed their eclectic air.

After purchasing three outfits, a bathing suit and several pairs of underwear, Lydia took a taxi to Bon Suite on the outskirts of Burrstone.

"Are you being staying long in the Burrstone?" The driver, whose badge stated him as Mohammed Rafiq, asked in broken English.

"Yes," Lydia replied. "I'm buying a flat here, but it won't be ready for a few days so I'm staying at the hotel. Have you been here long, Mohammed?"

"Twenty minutes," Mohammed smiled through the rear-view mirror.

"No," Lydia frowned, "Erm, I mean how long have you lived in Burrstone?"

"Twenty minutes," he repeated before announcing,

"Hotel here," as he pulled the car to a stop under a large terrace overhanging the entrance to the stone-built hotel.

A bemused Lydia climbed out of the car with her bags and paid the strange driver.

"Enjoy the staying of in here," Mohammed called out before screeching out of the entrance and back down the road to Burrstone.

Lydia shrugged, turned to take in Bon Suite and approved. She stepped along the red carpet leading towards the main entrance. The grandeur of the hotel surprised the typical southern soul of Lydia a little, with its wide staircase and plush sofas. She always lightly teased an old university friend, Simon Weatherby, from Yorkshire, whenever new technology appeared on the market. "Do they have Sky up there yet? Or are your lot still stuck with three channels?"

Julia took it a step further during the last night Lydia would enjoy Simon's company by insinuating northerners lived in caves and slept with their own family. Simon took it in good spirits until he later saw bruises on Lydia's arms in the shape of fingers.

"Is she hurting you, Lyd?" he asked in a whisper as Julia trotted to the toilet.

"Noooo," Lydia lied. "Don't be silly. I did this to myself in my sleep. I had a nightmare and woke up gripping my arm. Mad, eh?"

"I'm not sure I believe you, old cock. You know you can stay with me any time you want."

Lydia placed a hand on his knee. "Thank you, but I did it to myself. Do you think I'd let someone hurt me, Si? Really?"

"What's going on here, then?" Julia asked, obviously trying to keep her voice even and cheery. "I always suspected you carried a little torch for my Lydia, Simon."

"It's not like that, Jules," Lydia told her, feeling like a beachcomber with her leg trapped between two rocks just as the tide begins to rise.

"I was concerned about the bruises on her arm, but if Lydia says she did it to herself then there's nowt to worry about," Simon said.

"Yet, you don't deny having feelings for Lydia," Julia continued sounding every bit the barrister.

"Why should I?" Simon shrugged. "Of course, I have feelings for Lyd. She's one of my oldest and best friends. But not feelings like you're insinuating. For one, I'm bloody married, and Claire also loves Lyd to bits. Are you now going to suggest we both want some sort of debauched threesome?"

"Your words, Simon. Not mine."

"Please stop. Both of you. There's nothing sinister going on here," Lydia begged, tears beginning to well.

Shortly after that incident, the ties with one of her closest friends faded and broke, leaving Lydia confused and hurt. Now she had left Julia, Lydia looked forward to reuniting with her friend Simon and the others. Yet, she knew she would have to give it time. Because having her friends watched would be the first thing Julia would do.

"Baby steps," Lydia mumbled as she shuffled, laden with bags, into the foyer of the plush northern hotel.

Ten minutes later, Lydia laid the clothes on the bed and frowned at the room offered to her. The corner room, with one window facing the car park and two others overlooking the pleasant scenery of a canal and fields full of lambs and sheep, contained a bed with a garish silver crushed velvet headboard with matching sofa and chairs sitting on a slate grey carpet. The designers had painted three walls with magnolia and papered one with a grey feather effect, giving it a less than pleasing appearance.

"It certainly doesn't rival Mal Maison or The Dakota," Lydia muttered. "But, it's a bed for a few days and it doesn't contain Julia."

She turned to inspect the bathroom. Lydia always believed the bathroom really defined her stay in a hotel.

"Nice," she told the large mirror as her eyes swept across the deep bath and the monsoon shower surrounded with fine Yorkshire stone. "Very nice indeed."

The mobile phone erupting into life on the bed startled her. She rushed to the bedroom and, heart thrashing inside her broken rib cage, swept the phone off the bed. "The estate agent," she sighed and wondered why on all the dunes of the Sahara she would consider Julia the caller. "Hello?" She asked after tapping the device.

"Miss Richardson, it's Daniel from Greyson, Sutcliffe and Milner. I have good news," the estate agent began in his usual chirpy manner. "All the papers are signed and you can move in tomorrow. Congratulations."

"Wow! That's fast. Thank you."

"I know. I can't ever recall a property moving from for sale to sold so fast. So, can we say we meet at the office at eleven in the morning? That way, you can take your time and eat a good breakfast. It is, after all, the most important meal of the day."

"That sounds brilliant. Thank you again," Lydia replied.

"Absolutely our pleasure. Okay, well, I'll see you tomorrow. Enjoy your night," Daniel said and cut the line.

Lydia, jaw swinging loose, slumped onto the bed and stared at the telephone in disbelief.

Later, wearing a new, sleeveless, flowery summer dress and high heels she wished she hadn't bought as they seemed to exacerbate the pain in her ribs when she walked, Lydia entered the restaurant. The nerves fluttered inside her stomach. The last time she had eaten alone in a restaurant was way before Julia.

I've made a mistake, she wittered inside her mind. *What will people think?*

"Good evening, madam," a tall, handsome, young maître d' appeared and asked. "Are you staying with us?"

"Erm, yes," Lydia replied, trying to keep her tongue in check. "Erm, room 208."

"Thank you." The maître d' consulted an electronic tablet he carried. "Miss Richardson? I only ask for the table size, are you dining alone this evening?"

"Erm, yes," Lydia replied in almost a whisper.

"That's good. I love dining alone," the maître d' smiled. "Saves all the boring small talk. Now, if you'd like to follow me, I have the perfect table."

Lydia smiled back and followed, in her mind, his model arse in the tightest of black fitted trousers across the dining room to a table looking out to a wonderful sunny evening.

"How will this do, Miss Richardson?" the maître d' asked.

"It's perfect. Thank you," Lydia simpered.

"Good. Your waitress will be over in a moment. Enjoy your evening," he said, bowed slightly at the waist, and strode away.

If only you were on the menu, Lydia thought and turned from staring at his posterior to the view outside.

Sadly, the waitress was not her type at all. The food tasted fine, though.

Chapter Eight

Daily life for the Custodian grew surprisingly easy over time, despite the consistent banality of one view and the same walls in which he paced. Boredom had not yet kicked in. Even still, the most exciting part of each day usually involved Mr K arriving and leaving. The Custodian never knew the times he came and went, as he did not have the luxury of a clock. However, even in the darkness of the winter months when the length of time between morning and night flashed by, nothing really changed. He welcomed visitors and the dramas of the outside world. Such as the time a couple who appeared to have rubber legs and equally floppy but acerbic tongues staggered by in the street below swearing and railing at one another. Or the less caustic time when the local youngsters enjoyed a water fight under the rays of a bright, cloudless day. Their giggling screams, although a little more muffled than outside, bounced around the empty flat and filled The Custodian's spirit with joy.

Other than those small pockets of activity, the world around The Custodian remained the same. He awoke in the bath after dreaming about the same beautiful angel urging him never to forget the thing he failed to remember, and then spent the day wandering around the flat. Well, most of the flat. For reasons beyond him, the main bedroom, the stairs leading down to the flat's exit door, and the newly fitted back door filled him with freezing, irrational fear if he stepped too close. So, he stayed clear of each.

Then, shortly after the visit from the lady and the estate agent, on a night when the full moon frowned down from a pitch-black sky, just as The Custodian prepared to enter the bath for his rest, he heard the main door shut and noises floating up through the floorboards of the lounge. Nothing excessive or riotous. First, he heard mumbling. Adult mumbling. As if the people down there had stopped by to exchange pleasantries. Then, the mumbling became a litany. Over and over the new guests chanted.

"Can you please say something different?" The Custodian grumbled after at least the third hour.

And, do you know, they did. The chanting stopped and the low murmuring of general conversation replaced it. Shortly after that, The Custodian heard the main door to the building close with a bang. He shot to the window as thirteen hooded figures climbed into four separate cars he never heard arrive and drove away.

"Maybe they're swingers," The Custodian mused, not quite understanding what "swingers" are but remembering one of the builders mentioning such a select club. A group that, according to the grinning builder named Crumpy, involved keys in a bowl, sweat and moaning. "It would account for the weird chanting, I suppose," The Custodian added before sliding back into the bath.

Chapter Nine

Lydia's mind felt like porridge. Despite the comfortable mattress, she awoke several times in tears, screaming in fear, or gripping her throbbing ribs. Each time, Julia's face loomed towards her, eyes burning with furious rage and hatred.

At nine o'clock, Lydia stumbled down to breakfast, yawning constantly, her nerves exposed.

I should be happy now, she told herself, feeling anything but.

A grumpy, middle-aged waitress met her at the entrance to the dining area, took her room number and escorted Lydia to a table in the centre of the already crowded room. She felt naked with so many eyes surrounding her.

"Tea or coffee?" The waitress grumbled.

"Erm, tea, please," Lydia replied, wondering how such an unpleasant woman had acquired the job.

"Okay. The buffet is over there whenever you're ready," the waitress nodded to a large spread and walked away before Lydia had time to ask anything.

Lydia, eyes cast to the wooden floor, traipsed over to the buffet and despite her stomach reeling from exhaustion and worry, scooped a little scrambled eggs and bacon on to a warm plate before scurrying back to her table. Once there, she found the waitress was at least efficient if nothing else, because two pots sat steaming on the table. One filled with brewing tea and the other boiled water. She placed her plate on the table and shuffled into her chair.

"We'll have to hurry if we want to get a look at the abbey, Brin?" Lydia heard an elderly Australian lady behind her say as she picked up her fork.

"It doesn't open until ten, Alice," A male replied, sounding like he spoke through a mouthful of food. "Relax. Remember, this is supposed to be a bloody holiday."

"Yes, but that's your second plate of food and you know you'll take forever on the dunny after all that."

Classy, Lydia mused as the first reluctant fork of scrambled egg entered her mouth. The creaminess pushed her to a second forkful.

"Granny?" A little Scottish girl from another table asked. "Can we go on the river in a boat?"

"They're called barges on canals, dear. And, aye, we will be going on a barge. Now eat all of your breakfast like a good girl. You'll need your strength."

"Can I leave the black pudding, Granny? I dinna like the taste."

"Aye, lass," a gruff male voice replied. "They're an acquired taste. Give it me, eh? Yer Gramps'll eat it fer yer."

"You watch yoursel', Conor," the elderly lady cut in. "You ken your cholesterol is high."

"Och, a little bit of black pudding isna gonna make a difference, my sweet," the old man replied.

"Aye, but it's porridge for you, the morrow, ye ken," the lady told her husband.

"Eeeh, yer granny is bossy, is she no, Rose?" Conor sniggered. The little girl hidden from Lydia giggled along with her grandad.

Listening to their conversation eased Lydia's mind for a spell. Concentrating on the conversations of others whenever Julia allowed her out of the house always took her away from her own hell.

Soon enough, Lydia swallowed the last of her meagre breakfast and, eyes still on the floor, made her way back to her room. She threw herself on to the bed and flicked through YouTube for her favourite meditation video. Without which, she knew she wouldn't have survived the last few years. After pressing play, she leaned back against the pillow and allowed the gentle guru's voice and the ethereal mixture of pipe music and whale song to wash over her as she took in deep inhalations.

Twenty minutes later, Lydia felt ready to at least square-up to the upcoming day. Although, she still wondered why the excitement of new home life did little to thrill her.

An hour later, the taxi driver called Sajid, a much quieter man than the first one she had met on arrival, dropped her off outside the offices of Greyson, Sutcliffe and Milner. Its classy wooden-framed windows looked slightly out of place sitting between a charity shop and a Gregg's bakery. She paid the driver and entered the office.

"Miss Richardson," Daniel announced from the other end of the mahogany-walled room. Each wall contained rows of glossy photographs showing expensive properties. "So good to see you. Your stay at Bon Suite was relaxing, I trust?"

"It was lovely, thank you. I booked for two nights, so I'm looking forward to trying out their spa."

"Ah, yes. I have a membership. The steam room is great for the old pores. Right, shall we finalise the sale?"

It took very little time for Lydia to dot all the I's and cross the T's. When finished, Daniel presented her with a little basket of, as he called them, goodies to enjoy in her new home. And this little basket must have cost them a small fortune as Lydia knew Angel champagne, even a 0.75-litre bottle, cost over a hundred pounds. The small box of chocolates by Pierre Marcolini cost no less. On top of that, there sat Laura Mercier Crème Brulee Honey Bubble Bath and a bottle of Molton Brown Rhubarb and Rose Shower Gel.

"This is amazing," a shocked Lydia exclaimed. "Thank you so much."

"Our pleasure. We've never had a faster sale. So, you go back to your hotel, or your new home, and enjoy a relaxing evening."

"Well, I think I need some furniture first. So, the hotel it is."

"Oh, you may also be needing this." Daniel rushed back to his desk, returned with a smile and slipped a laminated sheet into the basket. "A full list of all the good furniture and white goods retailers nearby. It should save you trawling the internet."

"Bless you," Lydia gushed. "That's very kind."

"We aim to please," Daniel smiled.

Lydia thanked him again for all his help, though refused him ordering her a taxi. "I feel like a stroll. But, thank you for everything."

She shook his hand, hiding the revulsion of feeling his sopping-wet palm, and left the office, sighing as she looked up and down the high street. This time with a sense of calm. She dug into the basket. Not for the expensive gifts. The simple Yale keys in the small brown envelope, one for the main door and the second for her flat, meant more to her than the gifts.

"My new life," she said out loud, startling a passing elderly lady. "Sorry, I was thinking aloud. I've just moved here, you see."

"Don't you worry, lovey," the old woman told Lydia. "I always talk to myself. It's the only time I get any sense. Congratulations on your move. It's lovely around here. We were voted happiest place to live, you know?"

"I didn't know that."

"Oh, yes. The cameras from the BBC came and everything. My granddaughter, Kelly, was on telly, just behind the Mayor, she was. Anyway, must dash. My programme starts soon. Good luck."

Without another word, the old lady walked on. Lydia wondered, for a brief moment, what her programme was, before heading up the high street towards the town hall. There she found a flock of elderly, either sitting on the benches that lined the front of the stone building or tottering this way and that.

Lydia took a seat on the end of a bench, content to watch the traffic and the tourists pass by. Another thing she hadn't done for so long it made her feet itch. And then she saw her. Lydia's heart stopped. The world around her froze. Because, around sixty metres down the other side of road, in front of the library, a tall, blonde woman, wearing dark glasses, and a suit only a professional woman competing with men would wear, strode between the traffic and headed Lydia's way.

No. No. No, Lydia screamed inside her mind. *She can't have found me so soon. She can't.*

The blonde lady's stride widened with some purpose. Lydia saw the woman grin. Lydia's stomach swirled and swam. Her breakfast threatened to vomit forth. Her heart beat so fast now it felt like a rat in her chest scrabbling to free itself.

Please, please, please. Lydia sobbed inside. The Julia of Lydia's nightmare had only thirty metres, at best, before she would stand within striking distance of the now frozen but shaking Lydia. *Surely, she wouldn't hurt me in front of witnesses,* Lydia told herself, her eyes darting left and right for a hero. *Surely, she wouldn't.* She also knew if Julia did, the elderly people milling around her would have no strength to save her from the onslaught Julia would rain down.

Ten metres and the red lipstick grin on Julia's face widened to a fully grown smile. A tall man in a Saville Rowe suit met her by a deluxe chocolate shop on the corner and the two embraced. He took the lady's sunglasses off to reveal, although similar in appearance, this woman was not Julia. The relief within Lydia swam from her spinning mind to her whirling stomach which forced her, staggering, towards the alley behind the chocolate shop. Clasping her left hand over her rebellious mouth and the other grasping the hamper, Lydia slalomed between the dithering tourists and slipped into the alley to heave for all her worth.

"Holy shit," an unseen teenaged girl announced. "Are you okay, hun?" Lydia felt a hand stroke her back and flinched. "It's okay, hun," The girl cooed. "I'm here to help. I'll go get you a glass of water. I'll be right back." Lydia heard her scamper away.

The pain in her sides burned like magma as she vomited forth great chunks of breakfast by the back door of the chocolate shop. By the time the need to vomit had tempered, the girl presented a still bent over Lydia with a glass of water.

"Are you preggers or summat?" the girl, Lydia now saw as a sweet-faced red-head with a nose piercing, asked. "My sister spewed all day, every day when she was preggers."

"Thank you," Lydia said and sipped the cool water. "No. Not pregnant. Just a little unwell."

"You sound posh," the girl said. "Are you from Ilkley? I'm Sam."

"Nice to meet you, Sam. No, I'm from Surrey. Thank you for the water. It's very kind of you."

"My nan says to help everyone because you never know when you might need it. Though now I say it out loud, it sounds a bit selfish really," Sam shrugged. "So, you just visiting?"

"No. I've just bought a flat up here."

"Cool. My sister's just bought a flat too. She wants me to live with her. But, I think she only wants me to so I can look after little Tommy, her baby. Which I wouldn't mind because he's a proper cutey. But, I wouldn't want to look after him all the time. Anyway, leave your glass by the back door when you feel better. I've got to go now. Hope you feel better. See ya." And, with a quick smile, Sam rushed back into the shop.

This new peace didn't suit Lydia. Sam's happy rambling blocked the dark thoughts lurking at the back of her mind like wraiths. The blonde lady in sunglasses flashed behind Lydia's eyes. Her hands began shaking. She threw the last of the water down her throat, told her thoughts to, "Fuck off," and slumped down the high street to the taxi stand. She dared not look up from the pavement in case she imagined another Julia. The peace of the hotel room called her. She needed to meditate and shower. Lydia thanked the stars she had booked two days.

An hour and a half later, Lydia, a little calmer after her meditation and freshen-up, sat in yet another taxi as it headed towards Broughton Road. When they passed the train station and headed underneath a narrow but high road bridge, she knew her assumptions on arrival were correct. Within a minute the driver stopped outside her new home. She thanked the driver, paid him, and stood, basket of goodies in hand, on the pavement looking up to the first-floor window.

"Good afternoon," a giant of a man with an eastern European accent called out from a shop doorway to the left of the flat's entrance. "Are you okay?"

"Yes, thank you," Lydia smiled. "I've just bought the flat upstairs."

"Really? They never put up a for sale sign. Humph. Well, it is neither or not, as they say. So, welcomes to the Burrstone, my dear. Voted happiest town in the UK, eh?"

"So, I hear. Thank you."

"I am the Mr K, eh? I own this little shop. So, if you needed anything from Mr K, all you do is shout down and Mr K will throw up all over you. Yes."

"Erm," the imagery brought back the morning's hell. "Thank you," Lydia said, nevertheless. "I will remember that."

"You do. I have to go now. Cash In the Attic is on television. It makes me laugh. Goodbye." Mr K turned and disappeared into his shop.

Lydia frowned and shrugged, the usual response to first meeting Mr K, and strode forward to unlock the front door to her new home.

Chapter Ten

Little did Lydia know, The Custodian watched her arrive and fidgeted with excitement on the windowsill when she told Mr K that she'd bought the flat.

"No more talking to myself," he twittered when he heard the key rattle in the flat's front door. After hearing the door bang shut, he could stand no more and skipped to greet Lydia. He, sensed, however, by her aura, conflict radiating from her.

He watched her sigh as she reached the top step and slump, carrying her little basket of goodies, into the kitchen. Once there, she just stood by the sink, staring through the window at the stone, terraced houses beyond. The Custodian watched her from behind and wished he could hug her. No more so than when she turned and he saw the tears dribbling down her cheeks.

"Stupid idiot," she griped and wiped the saltwater from her face. "I'm free and all I'm worried about is how she feels. Bloody ridiculous."

She slouched to the bathroom and threw a quick swill of cold water from the basin tap over her face. Her reflection in the mirror looked jaded. "Christ almighty, I look a hundred years old," Lydia muttered as she kneaded the dark skin around her eyes. "God damn it," she cursed again as she looked for a towel and realised the only thing she had to dry her face was toilet roll. So, she mopped her face with two-ply and slumped down the stairs and left The Custodian to his usual silence.

For the full hour of her absence, The Custodian paced between the kitchen and lounge, desperately trying to think of something he could do to make her smile. For a while he attempted to pluck out the bubble bath and soaps to carry them into the bathroom. He even formed a plan to run her a bath. Sadly, however, he had not mastered moving objects yet. He found so much as nudging an open door impossible.

When she returned, it pleased him to see her aura a little lighter. Not shining with vibrant colours. Just not swimming with browns and blacks as she lugged several full carrier bags up the stairs.

"Hello," The Custodian said as he followed her into the kitchen and watched as she dropped the bags and rifled through them. He eagerly waited to see what she'd bought. There turned out to be nothing more exciting than a kettle, cups, a set of cutlery, a box of kitchen knives, a pad and pen, and food. "Nothing for me, then," he sniggered.

Watching Lydia make herself a cup of tea strangely made him want one. That never happened when the workmen and women sat around, drinking out of flasks or sipping from cans. When brewed, Lydia took her steaming cup into the lounge, along with the pad and pen, and sat in the middle of the room. Her action intrigued The Custodian, who wanted to sit opposite her, yet decided on his usual perch.

"Right," Lydia announced and, in between sips, made little sketches of the layout of the room and the furniture she thought would look great within it. "Ooh," she announced, surprising The Custodian. She ran back into the kitchen and returned seconds later with a laminated sheet. The Custodian, ever nosy, peered over her shoulder and saw lots of names with eleven numbers opposite them.

"Country Flair," he read. "Thirty-one Swadford Street. What on Earth is that?" He asked, and, of course, received no answer. Well, not verbally, anyway. Lydia typed the name into her telephone and the furniture and furnishings that flicked across her screen answered his question. "Ah, you're buying furniture!" He exclaimed. "I've seen other people using those mobile phone things, but they only checked the news or looked at nude people rolling around with each other."

For the next hour, she clicked on various pieces of furniture from the names on the list before yawning and lying back on the carpet.

"I can do this." She told the ceiling. "I can really do this."

"Of course, you can," The Custodian added. "I'm here. We'll be like a super team."

Lydia humphed as if almost scoffing at his words, grabbed for her phone and called a taxi. Within ten minutes she, along with some of the items in the basket, left the flat and climbed into the back of a large blue car.

The Custodian watched her disappear up the road. He sighed and turned back to the room. The pad and pen still lay on the carpet. His struggles with moving objects earlier entered his thoughts.

"It would be funny to see her face if I moved them on to the windowsill. And it's not like I've anything better to do tonight." He shrugged and hunkered down to prod the two objects for all his worth. Yet, his worth was not good enough. He retired to his bath later that night more frustrated than ever before.

Chapter Eleven

On the other side of town, Lydia's evening fared no better. Her attempts to relax in her bath before going down to dinner proved a perfect time for Mr Id to appear and grind the egos, both super and normal, to a fidgeting, irritated froth of fine-smelling bubbles. She only spent around twenty minutes in the water before climbing out and stomping to the bed to meditate. Mr Id, however nattered behind her closed eyes until she fell asleep and woke fifteen minutes later with a scream of alarm. She struggled to remember any nightmare images to frighten her awake, but Lydia felt fearful nonetheless as she sat up in bed and shivered in her damp towel. She reached for her telephone to check the time. Only an hour and a half before dinner and the last thing she needed was seeing other people. Lydia decided on room service, though didn't expect much. She pulled open the drawer next to the bed and fished out the menu.

"Humph," Lydia exclaimed in some surprise. Yes, the menu contained the usual assortment of sandwiches, ranging from the vintage prawn in Marie Rose and beef with horseradish, but they also offered quite a sophisticated three course menu. Some of the dishes sounded a little cryptic. For instance, Lydia had no idea what would arrive if she ordered the Heirloom Carrots, Fig & buttermilk with Almond Brittle, but she wanted to try it. So, she did. Lydia called the reception and pre-ordered Beef Bourguignon, Roast Shallots, Creamed Mash, Red Wine Jus, and a sweet of Chocolate Mousse, Hobnob, Hazelnut, Orange Sorbet & Salted Caramel. The latter again intriguing Lydia due to its less than clear description.

After passing her order down the phone to a chirpy receptionist, Lydia reached for the television control, yet paused before pressing the "on" button.

What if Julia's called a press conference to try and find me? the ridiculous Mr Id whispered into her inner ears. And for the briefest moment she pondered the scenario. Until her logical little Miss Ego coughed and said, *there's no way Julia would make this public and run the risk of ruining her career if the truth came out. You know her. She will hire people to find me by focusing on the people I know. So, carry on doing what I'm doing.*

The hard but fair face of Harriet "Harry" Breeden-Soames then entered Lydia's thoughts. The one person she needed to talk to. "And probably top of Julia's list for whichever private investigator she hires," Lydia told her reflection in the silent television screen. She turned to her telephone, sitting on the bedside table. "I'll do it tomorrow."

The next day, up, dressed and full of a hearty breakfast, Lydia checked out a full two hours before needed. Yet another new experience for her because Julia always insisted on waiting until the last second before leaving an hotel with her bag full of freebies. Lydia found this kind of behaviour cheap but never said it for fear of a new bruise. At twenty past nine, she exited the taxi on Broughton Road and sucked in a deep breath.

"Good morning!" Mr K called from his shop doorway. "I hope you have more things than that. If not, I have some nice furniture you can have." He pointed to a weathered deckchair. "I use it in the garden, but furniture is furniture. Yes?"

"Thank you, but I'm having some delivered over the next few days. By the way, I'm Lydia Richardson."

"And very nice to meet with you, Lydia Richardson. Speak later, eh? You maybe meet my wife. She make good food."

"Yes. That would be lovely," Lydia smiled and walked towards the door. "Bye then."

Upstairs, The Custodian, still trying to knock the pen off the sill, listened to Mr K and Lydia's conversation, not looking forward to the arrival of more people. More people in the flat meant they forced him into tight corners to avoid seeing their insides if they passed through him. His fears were proved reality two hours later when a Country Flair lorry and a Burrstone Electricals van arrived at near enough the same time. Men carrying a king-sized divan passed others who had just lugged something called a washing machine up the steep steps. The lounge went from a space-filled heaven to one cluttered with a three-piece suite and a man drilling a large flat-screen television into the chimney wall.

"What on Earth does that do?" The Custodian asked nobody as he peered over the workman's left shoulder. "Is it like a really bad mirror? Because I can only just see your reflection in it."

"How's it going?" Lydia asked over the workman's right shoulder.

"Good. Should have it sorted in five minutes. Do you have co-ax?" The man asked.

"Damn. No. I forgot all about that," Lydia replied.

The Custodian frowned from one face in the screen to the next. He had no idea what they meant.

"No worries. I have a few spares in the back of the van. I should have one long enough to reach the box," The workman told Lydia.

"Thank goodness for that. How much are they?" She said and reached for her handbag.

"On the house," the workman smiled. "Call it a moving in present." The workman stepped back, scaring the unprepared Custodian, who shot to his left. "Be back in a mo'."

"Bless you," Lydia cooed. "That's very kind. Thank you."

"Pleasure. Just give us a good review after and we're all square," The man winked and strolled out of the room.

"Done," Lydia called back. She turned to sit on the sofa and looked at the television from such an angle, frowning.

"What are you doing?" The Custodian asked, also frowning.

Lydia stood and pushed the sofa back a few inches before returning to the couch to stare up at the television with a thoughtful look. "That should do it," she murmured.

"Do what?" The Custodian asked, more confused than ever.

"Here we go," the television workman announced as he entered the lounge, followed by two men each carrying a bedside table. The television man carried a coil of white cable and brandished it like a trophy for Lydia to see.

"That's fantastic. Thank you," Lydia replied.

"Do you want these up in the main bedroom, love?" a blond-haired man carrying the first of the bedside tables asked.

"Yes, please," Lydia. "That'd be brilliant."

"No probs," Blondie replied and led the way for him and his colleague as they traipsed up the short stairs to the master bedroom.

"Thank you," Lydia replied. She watched the burly television workman plug the cable into the television and then into a small white box in the corner of the room. "When I post the review, who do I say you are?"

"Tony, single, and house-trained," Tony replied with a grin.

"I'll give you ten out of ten for subtlety and enterprise," Lydia replied with a grin. "However, I'm sorry, I've just got out of a rather messy relationship."

"Hey, no worries," Tony shrugged. "Can't blame a bloke for trying. I bet whoever messed up's regretting it now." He smiled across, stood and held out his hand. "Remote, please."

"Phew," Lydia sniggered, "For a minute there, I thought you were about to ask for my hand in marriage."

"I'm forward but not that bloody forward," Tony laughed.

Lydia smiled and passed the remote. Tony turned to the screen and flicked it on.

"Whoa!" The Custodian exclaimed and settled on his perch. "That's cool. Like one of them telephone things but bigger."

After a few moments of Tony finding all of the available channels, he passed Lydia the remote. "You're all set," he told her. "And, if you find yourself bored and fancy a drink, you know where to find me."

"I do. Thank you for your help, Tony," Lydia replied, flattered but not that flattered.

For the next hour, The Custodian mostly watched daytime television, which followed folk buying houses or repairing them. Other than that, he entertained himself by trying to move a rolled up ball of packaging tape. Lydia spent most of the time in the master bedroom, making the bed so she could sit on the edge and stare out of the window at the passing clouds. The Custodian watched the flecks of greys and blacks within her aura, which he recognised as sadness, from halfway up the small flight of stairs before returning to the ball of tape when some new task caught her attention. However, people came and went, and still the only time the ball moved was when a workman knocked it off the windowsill with his backside.

"Hey!" The Custodian complained. "I was playing with that."

By the time the sun's summer rays left long shadows along Broughton Road on the third day, the house looked amazing and Lydia stood alone in the lounge doorway, drained. The Custodian sat on his perch. The only things on the windowsill were the pad and pen, and he did not put them there. The only sounds were the passing cars growling through the open window behind The Custodian and children giggling somewhere down the street.

The Custodian felt powerless to hold back the tears welling in her pretty eyes.

"Hey, don't cry," he called to Lydia, his own heart breaking for her. She slid down the wall by the door and crouched as the tears turned into sobs. "Hey," The Custodian cooed. As he stood, his hand brushed the pen. He watched with wide eyes as it rolled to the floor.

Lydia ceased her sobbing. "Is there anyone there?"

"YES," The Custodian exclaimed, excited. "YES. I'M HERE."

"It was the wind, you silly cow," Lydia scowled, even though there was no wind to blame. She wiped the tears from her cheeks, pushed herself to her feet, walked over to where she didn't know The Custodian stood, picked up the pen and placed it back on to the sill before traipsing upstairs.

"It wasn't the wind," The Custodian told her back. "Watch." He turned and wafted the pen. Nothing. He tried again… and again. "I swear to bloody God, I moved it," he moaned and swiped for the pen with more force. The sound of her renewed sobbing coming from the bedroom stopped his next attempt. "Please don't cry," he called to her. Her sadness tore through him. He stood as if to go to her, his soul in pieces, and this time his hand struck the pad and sent that flapping to the carpet. The Custodian stopped and looked from his hand to the pad. He frowned as he watched a neon blue light sparking from his palm fade. He swiped for the pen. It sat still on the sill as if mocking him. "Blue light, move the pen," he told his hand before swatting at the ballpoint. Nothing. "AAARRGGHH," he growled, almost ready to join Lydia in her salty misery.

Chapter Twelve

The next few days saw reflected emotions in both residents of 67A Broughton Road. Both rose from broken sleep consisting of dark dreams. Lydia's dreams veered from feelings of fleeting joy when in the company of old friends to images of alienation and fear that woke her with screams wedged in the back of her throat. The Custodian opened his eyes with images of the angel with no name and yearned for her touch.

They then both slouched around the flat or slumped, one on the sill, the other on the sofa, watching nothing in particular. The Custodian had never felt so empty inside. The sullen burden, like Sisyphus and the rock, had become so common to Lydia it bordered on the mundane. The only thing missing was Julia's threats and follow throughs. Now and again, as she half-dozed on the sofa to some shows about life on a children's ward, or antiques, Lydia woke with a start to the voice of her wife screaming into her inner ear. Her actions startled The Custodian, who wondered what had frightened his housemate.

On the fifth day, shortly after her favourite breakfast of soft cheese on toast, sprinkled with za'atar, a dish she once enjoyed with Palestinian friends, long before Julia, Lydia's eyes opened for the first time since she had officially moved into the flat. Because, on the screen, after an advertisement for over-fifties life insurance, came a segment on the Pendle witch trials. The whole thing did not fit Lydia's understanding of the story, and seemed a little too sensationalist for her taste, but it did pull her from underneath her black cloud. From there, her mind began ticking to the other reason for moving to Burrstone, besides escaping Julia.

"The story," Lydia exclaimed before remembering she hadn't called Harry.

"Sorry?" The Custodian asked.

As he moved closer, he saw Lydia blink as if waking for the first time in years, turn down the volume of the television, reach for her telephone and laptop, turn on the computer, wait for the damn thing to warm up, hunted out a number alongside the name Harry and tapped it into the telephone. While she waited for Harry to answer, Lydia tapped the speaker icon. The Custodian, intrigued, sat on the side of the sofa.

Lydia drummed her fingers on the side of the couch. Both nervous and excited to speak to someone from her former life.

"Harry here. Who's this?" Harry asked in her usual abrupt manner. The Custodian sat up straight on hearing her voice booming from Lydia's telephone.

"Harry, it's me, Lydia," Lydia replied in almost a whisper.

"Lydia, my old saltshaker. How in the name of God's right toe are you, my love?"

Harriet "Harry" Breeden-Soames was Lydia's literary agent and had been for years. To most, she came across as brash and loud. Lydia loved her for it.

"Erm… I have some news," Lydia told Harry.

"Well, spit it out, old cocker," Harry began. "What's with all this wilting wallflower bullshit. It's me, Harry-poohs."

"I've left Julia."

"Who's Julia?" The Custodian asked.

"Well about bloody time, my old, spangled banner," Harry began, "About time. And you calling me because you want a proper woman in your life and not some manipulative horse-dangler?"

"Not quite," Lydia said after laughing for the first time in too long. "God, I've missed you, Harry."

"Of course, you have, my little fruit pickle. I'm little miss missable. On a serious note, if there ever is one, are you okay and what happened?"

"Well, it's all a bit difficult to say but…"

"Has she hit you?" Harry asked, her voice turning stern.

"Hmmm-hmm."

"NO!" The Custodian exclaimed and noticed the faint blue light on his hand briefly flare up.

"The cock-smuggling bitch!" Harry growled. "Not you, John," she told someone in the background. "Mention the word cock and you immediately think I'm talking about you. Go get me a nice pot of coffee and I'll forget the whole bloody thing. Right, back to you, Lydia, my pretty pumpernickel. Where are you? Are you safe? Is she under arrest? And do you want me to take her damned hypocritical head?"

"Well, I've moved. It's best I don't tell you where just yet. I'm safe and just about to start work on a new story. I've been planning this for a while, you see. I just couldn't take any more."

"Why didn't you tell me earlier or go to the police? You've never been one to take shit, my old monkey-chops."

"I didn't say anything or go to the police because she threatened to kill me if I did and has many private investigators, and goodness what else, on her payroll. I couldn't risk her harming you or any of the friends I've lost because of her."

Just saying the words opened the pressure valves to the years of abuse. "I c-c-couldn't t-talk to…" she sobbed.

The Custodian moved closer to her, feeling her pain.

"Hey!" Harry cooed. "Hey, baby-cakes. Hey. I'm so sorry. I didn't know you were going through this. I figured she was a manipulative bitch from that time I met her but not this. A fucking barrister hiding under the cowl of helping battered women is a batterer herself. It would make a damn good story if nothing else, eh?"

"I'm not bloody writing it," Lydia told Harry and tried to laugh but it only sounded strangled.

"So, what's your plan, my little sugar-muffin?"

"Well, she's bound to call you…"

"Then she can flick herself off until Lucan comes out of hiding, my old flower-kerchief," Harry scoffed. "She'll get sweet F.A. out of me. With glazed cherries on it."

"Thank you. She always said her investigators can uncover even the most invisible evidence, so, the next time I ring you will be from another sim card. And I'll only call you on your mobile."

"Wow, all Bond, Jenny Bond, stuff, eh?" Harry sniggered. "Love it. Why don't you just go to the police, my little star petal?"

"You've said it yourself. She's manipulative. She'll say I'm lying. Who are they going to believe? Me, a storyteller, or a barrister who protects beaten women and has done more pro-bono work for those who can't afford her than anyone else in the UK?"

"I see your point. But, you can't hide forever."

"I won't. I just need to find the old me again and then I'll bounce back. I just need time, Harry."

"I'll help," The Custodian told her.

"Enough said. Holy Saint John's tennis plimsoles, she's done a number on you, hasn't she, my beauty?" Harry said.

"A little bit," replied Lydia.

"Well, not anymore. Your pal Harry's here for you."

"And me," The Custodian added.

Lydia soon ended with promises to call Harry's mobile every day to assure her all was well, and sighed. Her whole spirit felt lighter for sharing her problem with another. Her eyes flicked to the silent television, showing some kind of garden restoration show. That would be one thing she would miss. She loved her garden in…

"No," she snapped at herself, startling The Custodian.

"What?" He asked.

"You can't think like that." She stood and strolled to the window, sending The Custodian into a skittering panic as he danced around like a frightened puppy to avoid her. He watched as Lydia stared out over the railway lines and to the hills beyond. "That can be my garden as I research the witches," she told her faint reflection. "I'll need a car."

"You need to give me a little flipping warning before bolting this way and that," The Custodian griped. "If I had a heart, you just stopped it beating."

So, the next day, she bought a little car. Nothing too fancy. Although, Lydia did fall in love with the little red Mini as soon as the tall, slim saleswoman showed her.

Before she left for the car showroom in the taxi, the Custodian saw, for the first time since her arrival, flashes of yellow in her aura, telling him of a new optimism. Seeing the flashes pleased him. Although, the notion of Lydia's ex arriving and hurting her angered him and occupied more of his thoughts since finding out about her the day before. This spurred him to learn faster to move and lift things.

So, after Lydia left the flat, he returned to his old favourite of trying to prod the open lounge door into movement. The exercise did not start well. He suffered less nausea than passing through a human but watching most of hand disappear through the bare wooden panel on his side of the door and waggle still made him a little queasy.

"Why can't I do it again?" The Custodian moaned and stomped back to his perch, where he glared down at his hands. "How the hell did I do it?" He took a deep inhalation for no apparent reason than some ingrained habit then thought about the day it happened. "Lydia was upset. I didn't like to see her cry, so it upset me. I stood and knocked the pad to the carpet and then saw the funny blue sparkles. I've tried loads of times before and never seen that light. Maybe it only works when I'm upset for someone!" He exclaimed to the empty room.

The Custodian, filled with new purpose, rushed back to the door. He thought about her pain and jabbed the door with more force. Horror replaced purpose as most of his arm shot through the wood. He tried again. Same result. And again. And again. And… "ARRRGGHHH," he shrieked full of pure rage and whacked the door shut. "I DID IT. I REALLY BLOODY DID IT," he hollered in excitement and shot a look at his hands. The sparkly blue light began fading. "NO," he panicked and punched the door, knocking the panel out to land on the landing carpet beyond. "Oops," he squeaked.

The Custodian stood for a few minutes, staring through the hole he had created until a car pulling up outside the flat distracted him. He rushed over to the window, hoping Lydia had not arrived home via her usual taxi. On seeing her, he shrieked in fear. This time, she exited a new car, all content and calm.

"NO," The Custodian yelled, before rushing back to the scene of his crime. In his fear, he rushed through the door and tried to pick up the battered panel from the carpet. But he failed to create the blue light or grab purchase. "PLEASE, PLEASE, PLEASE," he screamed. The panel, however, showed no concern for his panic.

He heard Lydia rattle her key in the door and entered after shouting "Hello" to Mr K. The Custodian, dismissing all logic, stood in front of the door as if in some ridiculous way he would block her from seeing the hole. He knew this also failed after Lydia reached the top of the stairs, turned on to the landing and froze in fear.

"Hello?" she called out, looking through The Custodian.

"I'm really sorry," The Custodian told her, dropping his forehead to the floor.

Lydia stood, all colour lost from her face and her aura turning brown with fear. She turned, bolted down the stairs and left the flat, calling for Mr K. The Custodian sprinted to the window in hope to hear the conversation.

"No. I hear and see nobody near your flat, Lydia," Mr K told Lydia. "Are the front and back doors broken too?"

"I haven't checked the back, but the front was fine," Lydia replied, breathing heavy.

"You want I check the flat?"

"But what if they are still there?"

"Then they better leave, quick-smart, or Mr K will make wiping their bottoms hard from then on." He offered a quick smile, patted Lydia on the back as some kind of reassurance that nearly sent her sprawling and strode towards the entrance. The Custodian turned to the landing. Mr K must have taken the steps five at a time because he reached The Custodian's position remarkably fast. The shopkeeper's eyes warned any intruder to run quicker than he. The Custodian nearly did just that. Mr K turned into the kitchen. The Custodian soon heard him try the back door. He then entered the lounge looking confused.

"If anyone upstairs, you better run out. Only warning I give," Mr K called as he shot up to the second floor and checked both rooms. He strode slowly back down, shaking his huge head. "Lydia, all is clear." He stopped at the lounge door and inspected the damage. "No human has been here," he told Lydia as she appeared on the landing.

"What do you mean?" She asked, frowning.

"I mean, back door locked, front door locked. This door broken. No human broken it. Not unless they have key or are invisibles." He shrugged.

"What do you think could have done it?" Lydia asked.

"I'm not sure," Mr K conceded. He picked the panel off the carpet. "Did you maybe bang the door hard as you leave the house?"

"No. I remember leaving it open."

"Weird, eh? Maybe the Velni," he mused.

"The Velni? What does that mean?

"They are mischievous, little demons. Nothing more. Just say hello and goodbye to them and they will leave you alone, yes?"

The Custodian had little need to read Lydia's aura to see the amusement flickering within her eyes. Yet, despite her cynicism towards Mr K's belief, she said hello and goodbye every time she arrived or left the flat from that moment on. This pleased The Custodian, as he then could pretend he had a new friend.

Chapter Thirteen

Over the following few days, The Custodian decided to wait for Lydia to leave before practicing his new obsession. He did try as she slept the night after he had broken the door panel, making progress with a teaspoon Lydia left by the sink. However, in his exuberance, he flicked the piece of cutlery into the air and it clattered noisily into the sink, causing Lydia to rush downstairs in a panic.

"Sorry," he told her as she, brandishing a hammer, ran around the house to check the locks.

"If there is a bloody Velni, or whatever you're called, pissing about, can you please bugger off," she snapped before returning to bed.

So, when Lydia drove away in her little red Mini the next morning, after a grumpy "Goodbye," The Custodian shivered with excitement to get a chance to carry on with his quest.

Lydia felt a certain relief to get out of the flat. The sun shone across and over the Kelly-green fields and hills surrounding little Burrstone as she headed out of Yorkshire towards Lancashire and a village called Roughlee. Soon enough, she dawdled behind farm traffic and the proverbial Sunday drivers but did not mind. The rolling hills and fields bouncing with sheep, cattle and horses, capped by an almost ice-blue, cloudless sky, calmed her mind.

Meanwhile, back at the flat, The Custodian felt far from calm. He stood by the sofa cringing. You see, as soon Lydia had left, he decided, in all his wisdom, to swipe at a sofa cushion, thinking he could not possibly do any damage with such a soft furnishing. The first three attempts saw him glad of his ethereal form as he swung, missed, and spun around like a drunk at a fair. The fourth time, he added a little more aggression and still nothing moved. The next five attempts ended the same but his aggression increased. The tenth time was the charm as he let vent a scream of frustration and swiped like a mother at a disobedient child's rear-end. That time he felt the connection, saw the blue sparkles, and watched the soft, square cushion shoot into the air, hit a rather pleasant painting of a sunset, knock it off the wall and send it crashing to the floor.

"NO!" he screamed in fear.

Lydia's hour and a half in Roughlee passed pleasantly. The home of Alice Nutter, one of the supposed Pendle Witches, and the only one to come from money, offered her nothing more than Lydia had already read on the subject. Although, Nutter's brass and Corten steel statue saddened Lydia as much as she assumed the sculptor intended. Her downcast expression and shackled hands conveyed nothing of her witchy legend. After a stroll up and down the pretty stream and a contemplative stare into the busy, little waterfall, Lydia headed back to her car and on to Barley. She hoped this next village, with its sculpture park dedicated to the Pendle witch trials, would present her with a little more detail.

She parked her car in the gravel car park, snatched her jacket out of the boot, as darker clouds now swam the blue sky like schools of fish, and headed to Aitken Wood where the sculpture trail was set. The first two pieces she came across, Magic Chair and Boggart, set within the birch and beech trees, reminded her of the old picture books her grandma kept on her bookshelves. They struck her as whimsical. Others, like the avant-garde piece, Wishing Widow, made little sense to her. She always struggled to understand such abstract art. Nevertheless, she stood before, in her opinion, the strange, lumpy shit-covered bi-pedal structure and tried to find meaning.

"I don't get it either," a male voice told her.

Startled, Lydia turned to face a middle-aged man in either a black fedora, or a tiny Stetson, trimmed with a belt of tanned leather, and wearing a long dark coat, even though the weather hardly warranted something so heavy. His smile seemed somehow familiar, though.

"I'm sorry?" Lydia asked.

"By the way your head is cocked to the left, I'm guessing you don't get this piece any more than I. Though, I could be wrong, of course," The man told her and shrugged. "My name is Irving Stofferson." He held out a hand.

"Ah," she exclaimed, "I thought I knew you. You're the ghostie man."

"I hope I'm much more than just a ghostie man," Stofferson smiled. "As serendipity appears to have played her hand in our meeting; don't you think?"

"How do you mean?"

"I'm investigating a group of the Pendle witches' ancestors and hoped to bump into you at some point in the future. Here you are having a nice jaunt around their manor on the same day as my visit."

"I'm not just having a nice jaunt," Lydia told him.

"I'm planning a story about the witches, from a different perspective, and came to see if there was anything they missed on the internet."

"A fellow writer. Cool. Any luck?"

"Not so far. Er, why would you want to bump into me?" Lydia asked, his comment only just dawning on her.

"You live at 67 Broughton Road, yes?" Stofferson asked.

"Yes. Have you been stalking me?" Lydia asked, an image of Julia loomed at the back of her mind causing a frozen lump to grow in her stomach.

"No. No. Stalking the house. You see, I believe there is a strange connection and an even weirder story for you to mull over that connects certain ancestors of the Nutters, Redferns, Whittles and Greys. Or as you know them, cunningly masquerading as Greyson, Sutcliffe and Milner, and the many deaths connected with the fortune they've amassed."

"You're implying all those suicides you mentioned in your book are due to the ancestors of some of the accused?"

"Oh, I'm not implying anything. I can go through the whole sordid story. As told to me by a former member of their coven, or The Thirteen, as they call themselves."

"I'm sorry, this is a great story, but too far-fetched for reality." Lydia backed away. The man sounded obsessed and she didn't feel strong enough to confront his ridiculous notions in the middle of a less than populated wooded area. "I really must go. All the best."

"I'm sorry if I've frightened you," Stofferson said with a small bow.

"No. No. Not frightened me. I'm just hungry and need a nice pint of vodka."

"Can I just ask one thing before you go?" Stofferson added yet didn't wait for a reply. "Have you noticed any strange occurrences in the flat since you've moved in?"

"No. Nothing," Lydia lied. "All's super."

"Well, if anything does concern you, or even amuse you, here is my number."

"Thanks," Lydia said and snatched the proffered business card, stuffed it into her jean pocket and attempted to stop herself sprinting as she left Stofferson by the bobbly legs of the Wishing Widow.

Inside the flat, The Custodian fared no better than earlier. After about ten minutes of pacing the front room, repeating several choruses of his now favourite song, "No, no, no, no, no, no," he stopped and realised panicking would not help him. So, he slumped cross-legged behind the sofa and cleared his mind to calm himself. He enjoyed it so much he spent a good hour revelling in the peace. He then opened his eyes, turned his hands palms up and focused on them. For no other reason than why not. After at least half an hour of just studying the creases and his digits, he imagined the blue sparks. Nothing happened. And the same occurred over another thirty minutes. His actions changed nothing, however. The cushion and painting he knocked to the floor sat staring, accusing him of his crime.

"I can't reverse it, can I?" He mused in a dreamy kind of a way.

He again returned his concentration to his palms. Another half an hour passed. And then Lydia's face jumped into his mind. He watched the tears form in her eyes and pour down her cheeks. He felt the wave of despair, he recalled a similar feeling once, long ago. It tore at the inside of his chest like another time he only saw in the flashes of dreams. Those dreams where his nameless angel whispered her last words before fading forever. Now, he had no need to look down to know the blue sparkles danced upon his palms and fingers. Pushing his excitement deep down, he stood as sedately as a royal and walked over to the fallen picture frame, bent over it, felt the frame in both hands and lifted it back to the nail to which it hung earlier.

The scream vented behind him did not help the situation at all. So, startled, The Custodian dropped the picture back to the floor.

"Hello?" Lydia asked in almost a whisper. Her jacket and handbag lay dropped by her feet.

"I'm sorry," The Custodian turned and told her. "Not that you can hear me, but I was only putting it back. I suppose seeing a painting floating in the air must be quite frightening."

"Hello?" Lydia asked again, now wondering if she really saw a man trying to hook the painting on to the wall. "Is there anyone there? Show yourself."

"I'm sorry, I can't." He said as Lydia stuffed her left hand into her jeans pocket and pulled out a card. Then, without taking her wide, frightened eyes from the painting, she reached down to her bag, pulled out her keys and telephone before backing out of the room, slowly pulling the door closed behind her as she went. The confused and sorrowful Custodian saw, through the hole in the door he had created, her backing all the way to the stairs. "You don't have to go. I won't hurt you," he said as she bolted down to the exit. "Well, that went well," he shrugged and reached for the painting once again.

Outside in her car, Lydia sat in the driver's seat looking up at the front window of the flat. She pinched Stofferson's business card between the index finger and thumb of her left hand as she gripped the telephone in her right. Seeing the man holding the painting before disappearing shocked her more than she realised possible.

"What the frig's happened to me?" she muttered. Lydia was the tomboy who her friends, boys or girls, sent into abandoned buildings or churchyards first. "Now I'm frightened of bloody ghosts?"

She recalled the initiation rites of newcomers to the little village of Safford's Cross where she grew up. The little stone-built hamlet was older than some countries, having been mentioned in the Doomsday Book. The time-pitted church sat in the centre, only marginally younger. Some of the gravestones' inscriptions had weathered away to just dents in the stone slabs. But best of all, for the younger Lydia, rumours mentioned the ghost of a priest killed during the English Reformation by Henry VIII's troops, who wandered through the churchyard on cold winter nights only to disappear when he left the far-end gate. Lydia and her friends told every new child to the village this legend and demanded they walk the full length of the footpath to prove their worth. Anyone not willing would never have the acceptance of the rest. Most reluctantly took the test. However, what they didn't know was that Lydia snuck in via the back gate and climbed into a macabre coffin-shaped flowerpot, empty due to winter's deathly fingers. There she lay in wait for the nervous initiate to frighten them witless by sitting bolt-up right on their approach.

"And now I'm scared?" The older her grumbled. "Actually, I've sort of known there was something in the house but haven't been scared. Screw you," she berated herself. "Who wouldn't be shocked if they walked in to see some idiot moving their pictures?" This realisation fuelled her resolve. She rang the number on the card.

"Hello," mumbled Stofferson on replying. He sounded as if she had woken him from a snooze.

"Sorry to disturb you, I met you at the Pendle Sculpture Trail earlier."

"Ah, yes. 67 Broughton Road."

"Lydia Richardson."

"What can I do for you, Miss Richardson?"

"Well, I may have told a little porky earlier," Lydia told Stofferson. "I have noticed some weird things happening. Erm, in fact, I've just walked in on one and I've nobody else I can talk to."

"Really? Colour me intrigued. What did you see?"

"I walked in to find a man moving a painting in the front room. He heard me scream and disappeared, dropping the painting. Before that, I came home to find a panel in the living-room door smashed out but no signs of anyone breaking in. There's been other things but today I actually saw someone."

"I'm guessing none of it a threat to you?"

"Well, no. Why would you assume that?"

"Because there is a pattern I was going to speak to you about earlier, but I understand some strange dude with a silly hat just popping up to chat might worry some people. Yes?" Stofferson asked with humour waving around the words' edges.

"A bit," Lydia laughed. A giggle that made her feel so much lighter.

"I apologise for the abruptness. I just couldn't believe I'd bumped into you and became a little eager."

"So, it was just a coincidence?"

"Absolutely. I promise. Now, what's your plan? Do you want me to come in with you and speak to Michael?"

"Michael?"

"An educated guess. The person who owned the flat before you was a young man called Michael. I met him once. Nice young man," Stofferson told her.

"What did he look like?" Lydia asked.

"Oh, about five feet eleven, slim, dark hair, blue eyes, quite pale looking. He had a kind air about him. Familiar?"

"Fairly familiar bearing in mind the larger percentage of British men have brown hair and blue eyes."

"True," Stofferson conceded. "Without seeming too forward, we could book a day and I could see for myself and also tell you about the flat's rather interesting history. Say, next Wednesday?"

"How about now? I don't fancy waiting around to make sure he's a nice little ghostie."

"Fair point," Stofferson replied. "I'll be there in twenty minutes."

"I'll put the kettle on," Lydia replied. She signed off, leaned back in her seat and sighed.

"Did you lock yourself out of flat?" Mr K called from his shop doorway.

Chapter Fourteen

"Oh, yes, Michael did talk of the spirits?" Mr K told Lydia.

Lydia followed Mr K into his shop and asked about the former owner of her flat for two reasons. One, to check Stofferson's story, and the other reason was to kill time until he arrived.

"What did he say?" She asked.

"He came to me in a worry, saying he had seen a woman."

"A woman?"

"Yes. He beliefed he had seen a lady they call Mary. I told him if she was bad spirit he would have known. He say she do only nice things. Why?"

"Well, I think, and this may sound silly, but I think I saw a man in my room trying to hang a painting I have. What did Michael look like?"

"Oh, he was skinny and not too tall and not too small. Kind of normal looking, you know?"

"Blond hair, blue eyes?" Lydia asked.

"No. Brown hair. Not too dark. I'm not sure about eyes. Could be blue. I don't look at men's eyes. I have wife."

"But his hair was definitely brown?"

"Yes. Definitely brown."

Lydia's telephone ringing in her pocket paused the conversation.

"Sorry," she told Mr K before fishing out the telephone and answering.

"Hi, It's Irving Stofferson. I've knocked on your door but you must not hear me." Stofferson told her.

"Oh, sorry, I'm just in the shop next door. I'm coming now." She turned to Mr K. "Thank you for your help. I have a visitor."

"My pleasure. If anything else you need, you know where I am," Mr K replied with a little bow of his huge head.

"Thank you," Lydia said again and trotted out of the shop to find Stofferson standing on her doorstep. "Sorry, I was just asking the shop owner if he remembered anything about Michael."

"He has lots to say, doesn't he? I've spoken to him myself. Fascinating man," Stofferson replied. "Have you seen any more of our young friend?"

"To be honest, after speaking to you, I went straight to Mr K." Lydia opened the main door and ushered Stofferson inside.

"Does anyone live on the bottom floor?" He asked as Lydia fumbled with the key to her flat door.

"No. According to the estate agent, it's only used for storage."

"Fascinating," Stofferson mused.

"Why?"

"Why, what?"

"Why, fascinating?" Lydia asked as she climbed the stairs much slower than usual.

"Was this estate agent called Daniel Greyson, by any chance?" Stofferson asked.

"I can't recall his surname, but his first name was Daniel. Does that make a difference?"

"Oh, huge, Miss Richardson. The background story will enlighten you fully. I promise."

"Okay," Lydia replied absentmindedly as they reached the landing. She waved Stofferson forward as the irrational fear that caused her to run once again took hold of her flight controls.

"What happened to your door?"

"I'm hoping Michael accidentally did it," she shrugged. "I came home to it the other day."

"He's evolving quicker than most."

"What do mean?"

"Well, from the spirits I've encountered, and there have been a few, they all say it takes years before they can move things. I sat and watched *Ghost* with one lovely lady called Agatha, a spirit trapped for some time due to unfinished business, and she scoffed at the rapid acceleration to dear old Patrick Swayze's character's ability. May his soul rest in peace." He leaned forward to examine the hole. "Did you happen to keep the panel?"

"Yes. It's in the living room. What else did Agatha say?"

"She went on to tell me that the intervention of the train spirit may have helped but it would still take much longer than days or weeks. And to rush around typing on so many computers at virtually the same time is nigh on impossible. She made it hard for me to watch the film ever again. A lovely lady but a complete pooper of the party. Do you mind if I enter and take a few pics of the hole and panel?" Stofferson asked.

"Not at all," Lydia replied with a shake of her head. "Would you like a coffee or tea?"

"Oh, tea, please. I've never been one for coffee."

"How do you take it?"

"Do you have honey?"

"Sorry, no. Just sugar."

"No worries," Stofferson produced a small jar of honey and a camera from his pocket. "One dessert spoon of honey, and milk please."

"Do you always carry your own honey?"

"Of course. It's from my friend's bees. Try some. It's good for you."

"I'm okay, thanks." Lydia turned and stepped into the kitchen. "The panel is by the side of the sofa," She called out.

"Thank you," Stofferson called back. He stood away from the door, faced the centre of the room and sniffed.

All this time, The Custodian sat perched on his windowsill, puzzled. He knew this man from somewhere but just could not place him.

"I can tell by the smell you are in here with me. I can also tell you have been trying to learn to pick things up and you have suffered one or two setbacks." The Custodian cast nervous eyes left and right before realising this strange man appeared to talk to him. He stood away from the sill. "You are a good soul. I know this because I know why you are here. I am here to help."

"What are you doing?" Lydia asked from the doorway. The sound of the kettle starting to warm up played in the background.

"I'm talking to Michael Parker," Stofferson said, turning to Lydia and then back to the centre of the room. "Although he may not remember his name." Stofferson pulled a ball made from wool from another pocket and rolled it into the centre. "Michael, can you please try and pick up this ball?"

Lydia and Stofferson held their breath, eyes on the ball. The kettle reached boiling point and clicked off. Yet, still the ball did not move. And why would it? The Custodian standing as still as the living, looking baffled, was a damned good reason for the ball's lack of movement.

"Was that the painting you saw the man holding?" Stofferson asked. He pointed, yet never took his eye off the ball of wool.

"Yes."

"Did you hang it back up?"

"Nope."

"Can you describe, with as much detail, what you saw, please?"

"I arrived home after speaking to you. I entered the room…"

"Was the door closed?"

"Yes. I pushed it open, entered the room and saw the man I described, brown hair, etc, holding the painting as if hanging or taking it down."

"You saw me?" The Custodian asked, aghast.

"Did the young man say anything?" Stofferson asked.

"No. I screamed and disturbed him. He dropped the painting and disappeared. I turned and ran out. I then called you from the car." Lydia said with an embarrassed shrug.

"You actually saw me?" The Custodian asked again, eyes almost popping out of his head.

"If the person Miss Richardson saw earlier is here, can you please pick up the ball? I promise you are safe and we mean you no harm."

In almost a trance, eyes still fixed on Lydia, jaw hanging loose, The Custodian stepped over to the ball, bent down and tried to pick up the wool. His hands, however, passed through the ball. Lydia and Stofferson did not blink as they willed it off the floor. Unbeknownst to them, The Custodian grew frustrated as he tried his hardest to grasp purchase on the ball.

For the briefest second the two air breathers saw the ball rock to the left but remain fixed to the floor.

"Hmmm," Stofferson mused. "Sadly, I have other business to attend to this afternoon and evening over in Haworth. Tomorrow, if it's okay with you, I can return with my equipment to perform a more in-depth study?"

"But, what happens now?" Lydia asked, a little nervy.

Unseen, The Custodian persisted, yet failed, to grab the ball.

"I wouldn't worry, my dear, it's completely safe. Although, if you are concerned, I'm pretty sure our friend cannot enter your bedroom. So, if it bothers you, spend most of your time in there."

"What? So, I'm supposed to barricade myself in my room like a hostage until tomorrow."

"Nothing so dramatic, Miss Richardson. I'm sorry, I really must go, but as I say, from research, I know the spirit is completely harmless, or it wouldn't be here." Stofferson placed a caring hand on her shoulder. "I know we have only just met but trust me on this."

"What is this research?" Lydia asked.

"I will enlighten you with the complete story tomorrow. I am sorry but I really must go. You have my number if anything happens. Though, I know you are safe. Until tomorrow." With a little bow, Stofferson left the flat.

Lydia heard his steps receding yet never took her eye off the wool ball Stofferson left in the centre of the room. Soon the silence grew to a heavy hum inside her head.

"So," she told the room, "it's just us then."

The Custodian, exasperated with his failed attempts to move the ball had sunk into a cross-legged sulk. "Seems so," he grumped.

"I don't suppose you'll want a cup of tea?" Lydia asked the empty room, shrugged and backed away to the kitchen. *I could always book a room at the hotel,* she thought as she filled her cup. *But then I'd be giving in, and I've never been scared of bloody ghosts, for God's sake.*

The words in her mind carried a little of her old resolve yet not much commitment. She threw the half-brewed cup into the sink and rushed out, locked her front door and sped off in her car. This wasn't a retreat. This was a regrouping. She drove around the outskirts of Burrstone and thought about the lost days when her strength drove back her fears. And as she left the bypass and headed back up Broughton Road towards the flat, she knew she no longer could afford to wallow in this new, brittle Lydia.

She pulled up outside the flat, took a deep, wilful breath and climbed out of the car before rushing inside and up the stairs in no time.

"Right," she called before her courage wavered, "I understand you're not harmful and are maybe here against your will, but this is my home too. So, boundaries need setting. No creeping up on me. No smashing of my house. Even if it is to learn how to lift things. No rattling of chains after I go to bed. And no appearing by my bed as I sleep. Do you understand?"

"Yes," The Custodian replied, a little scared.

Although all Lydia heard were the cars passing by outside and Mr K booming a "hello" to an unseen someone.

"Good," Lydia told the lounger and stormed off to her room.

The Custodian awoke inside the bath later that night to the sound of something rattling in the flat's lock. A faint noise, as if the intruder tried his or her best to remain undetected.

The Custodian, however, heard it. He climbed out of the bath and walked to the landing just as the front door crept open and two stooped silhouettes stepped in.

"Go steady on the fifth step," a male voice whispered. "Dan the Man said it squeaks."

"You told me that already," an obstinate female voice replied.

"I'm only saying," the man hissed back.

"Just shut up or someone will hear us."

The Custodian frowned as the two figures tiptoed towards him.

"Well, if they do, they won't for long," the man growled.

The Custodian cast a worried glance towards the lounge and thought of poor Lydia lying in bed. He knew what he must do. As the man reached the step below him, The Custodian swiped at his face. His hand, however, passed through the black scarf covering the lower part of the burglar's face, sending him off balance. With a cry only he heard, The Custodian fell through both the man and the woman, their horrific insides available for his viewing, and tumbled towards the bottom and the terrifying feeling he always felt if he strayed too close. An unseen barrier forced him back upstairs. Both burglars shivered for no apparent reason as they tip-toed into the lounge.

"NO," The Custodian yelled in a panic and bounded after them.

"I'll go check upstairs," the woman sneered. "You get what you can from down here."

The panic turned to anger as The Custodian imagined what the woman planned. A fearsome fury built inside him. He balled his fist. Blue sparks playing along his knuckles, He whacked the male burglar on the back of the head. The man crumpled to the ground with a groan.

"Who's there?" The woman asked, all bravado falling from her tone. "Show yourself."

The Custodian rushed towards her but something told him hitting a woman wasn't right. So, instead, anger still flowing through him, he grabbed the back of the thin black jacket she wore and dragged her towards the lounge door. The light streaming down from Lydia's room barely registered.

"GET OFF ME, YOU WANKER!" The woman screamed at the image of The Custodian and swung aimlessly with both arms but found herself hitting fresh air. "GET OFF ME!" On reaching the stairs, The Custodian pushed her down. He didn't want to face the unseen barrier, after all. "MALKY! WAKE UP!" The woman hollered from the door. She watched in horror as The Custodian's image faded before her.

Unseen to human eyes, he turned and rushed back to the lounge. Malky no longer lay sprawled on the floor.

"I've got the owner," Malky called out to the seemingly empty room. He saw the ghost of the man dragging his partner and then nothing. The woman creeping down the stairs seemed his only logical route. "You come anywhere near me and I'll slice her bastard throat." The glint of the steel pressing against Lydia's throat caught The Custodian's eye. "You tell him." The man demanded of Lydia.

"I don't know who it is," Lydia told him. She didn't seem as afraid as The Custodian thought she might under the circumstances.

"I don't give a shit," The man snapped with a slight quiver to his tone. "You tell him, if he so much as touches me, I cut your throat."

"I think whoever it is might hear you," Lydia replied, with a defiance that impressed The Custodian.

"You're going to let me walk this woman to the stairs," the man demanded, fearful eyes darting left and right. "Then she will live."

The Custodian sniggered as a strange, little plan formed inside his mind. He turned and left the room, only to wait on the middle step of the stairs leading to the front door. He looked up and saw Lydia, and the man the woman called Malky, shuffle towards the top of the stairs. Once there, Malky spun Lydia and pushed her into the bathroom before turning and rushing for the exit. He didn't see The Custodian's fist until it crashed into his nose. Malky crumpled to the floor and rolled down the steps, tumbling past the boundary of The Custodian's reach.

Chapter Fifteen

"So, to conclude," the tall, and to Lydia quite attractive, female police officer began, notebook open, "you awoke to noise in the living room, disturbing the intruders. They, a man and a woman, both wearing face-covering, both bolted. Is that all, Miss Richardson?"

"Yes, Constable," Lydia replied, lying. Thinking the truth would only paint her in the guise of a lunatic.

The Custodian sat on his perch staring at his hands. The still, inky night filled the window behind him, and, to human eyes, through him.

"As both wore gloves, we have little to go on. I can give you the number of a reputable security firm. They will fit better locks and security. Sorry, we can't help any more than that. You're just lucky they didn't attack you."

"I am," Lydia replied and rubbed her neck.

"Hello," an unseen Stofferson called from the bottom of the stairs. "Can I come in?"

"Anyone you know?" Another officer who waited by the stairs asked.

"Yes," Lydia told him, "He's a friend I called. Is he okay to come up?"

"Yep," the other officer said and waved Stofferson into the flat.

"Right, I'm leaving a crime number and my number if you remember anything else pertinent to the burglary," the first constable told Lydia and passed her a sheet of paper and a card. "Anything you need, just call, Miss Richardson."

Stofferson huffed and puffed into the lounge.

"Thank you," Lydia told the constable. "You've been a great help."

The constable said goodnight before both officers headed for the downstairs exit.

"Are you okay?" Stofferson asked.

"I'm fine," Lydia replied but placed her finger on her lips. Only after she heard the downstairs door click did she proceed. "Two burglars attempted to rob me but guess who stopped them?"

"Really? Did you see him stop them?" Stofferson asked, eyes wide.

"Yep, but I couldn't tell the police."

"A wise decision under the circumstances. Tell me all."

Lydia went on to recall the bizarre events of the evening.

"You sounded fearless," Stofferson said after she finished.

"I was scared witless but the way he dragged the woman out told me Michael had it covered. He was amazing! There was one odd thing about it though. I only saw him when he either hit them or when he held her as he dragged the bitch towards the stairs."

The Custodian, or Michael as we really know him, and the name I will use from now on, smiled a shy smile.

"That is amazing. Did you happen to see blue sparks on his hands when he did those things?"

"YES," Michael exclaimed to nobody. "I saw sparks."

"It all happened so fast, to be honest, I didn't notice," Lydia replied.

"That's fine," Stofferson told her. "I only wondered."

"So, what now?" Lydia asked.

"Well," Stofferson said and looked at his phone. It read, 02:16. "I'm absolutely shattered, but I'd really love to do a few tests tonight, if you don't mind?"

"I'm hyped up to hell after tonight and can't even imagine sleeping, so would welcome the company."

"Great. No time like the present. I'll bob downstairs and get my equipment."

"I'll put the kettle on."

"I'll just sit here then, shall I?" Michael shrugged.

A few moments later, Michael frowned as he watched Stofferson lug a rather large black case up the stairs and begin unloading the many odd gadgets into the centre of the lounge. Lydia soon appeared with a full pot of tea and all the trimmings.

"That's unusual to see, Miss Richardson," Stofferson remarked with a smile before checking the battery on something Lydia supposed fell off The Enterprise. "Not many use teapots in this age of one-cups and microwaves."

"More out of laziness than anything else," Lydia replied. "If I make a pot before I begin writing, I can just keep pouring and not have to get up every five minutes to brew another."

"Wise," Stofferson conceded and moved on to checking the battery power of what looked like an ordinary camera.

"I'm guessing you've brought your own honey?" Lydia asked.

"Oh, yes." Stofferson patted the pocket of his jacket.

Lydia filled her own cup with enough sugar to encourage a sloth to take up a sprint race and sipped before asking, "What is all that?"

"This is my equipment to find the rational evidence, Miss Richardson," Stofferson replied with a certain amount of pride.

"Please call me Lydia. You make me sound like a spinster. Why do you need all this?"

"My apologies, Lydia. I am a rare breed in the field of paranormal investigators, I don't just say a person is feeling a cold breeze from nowhere and declare an army of spirits. I like to make sure I clear away the things that may be creating the idea of a haunting before actually looking for the spirit."

"What kind of things?"

Michael, intrigued, strolled over to see for himself.

"Well, in here I have my night vision camera. This is handy if we are in a location with no light and need to identify the sounds of continual footsteps and other light anomalies." Stofferson lifted each object as he gave its name. "My digital voice recorder to capture and analyse any EVP's."

"EVP's?" Lydia asked, hoping Stofferson wasn't going to be one of those experts who continually throw abbreviations around the room just to sound important.

"My apologies. Electronic voice phenomena. It picks up spirit chatter, etc." Lydia nodded so he continued. "This is my little infrared thermometer for measuring if that eerie cold spot isn't just a natural draft. This is my binary response device."

This piece of equipment intrigued Lydia. It looked nothing more than a metal box with a red and a green light attached.

"How does that work?" Lydia asked, bending down to take a closer look.

"Well, depending on the question asked, the red light may represent no and the green; yes. Or they could represent left and right, up or down, etc."

"Okay," Lydia replied with a nod of her head.

"Sounds a bit basic," Michael said with a frown.

"This little monkey is my ghost box," Stofferson continued, showing Lydia what looked like a walky-talky had copulated with an old analogue radio. "I think this may come in very handy. And this is my EMF detector." Lydia thought the last piece of equipment looked like the stuff her father kept in his shed and only pulled out when he cleaned the shelves. "Although, I suspect we won't need all of this stuff as we already know we have something out of the ordinary in play. Less of course, you aren't telling me the truth and you are either actually a ninja who battered the two burglars or are making all this up. Please," Stofferson added with his hands up after seeing Lydia take a defensive stance, "If that were the case, you and many others are in on the little joke and have been so for hundreds of years."

"Okay, so, what happens first?" Lydia asked after relaxing.

"Well, from my research, we know Michael can only venture down here on this floor. We can sit here and hope he learns how to pick something up to show his presence, though for all we know, he's asleep. So, with my electromagnetic field detector I will sweep the room for any surges that may indicate his position. I will also turn on my ineloquently named ghost box in hope it may pick up his voice." Stofferson turned on the ghost box. White noise crackled from the speaker. He switched the box over to his right hand and turned the EMF detector on with his left. "Right, let's sweep the room."

"Why, when I'm right here?" Michael said, dropping his jaw as he heard the words also come from the ghost box a millisecond later. Each syllable appeared to swim a little but the voice was definitely his. Lydia snatched for Stofferson's arm. Stofferson merely grinned.

"Well, that worked faster than I thought. Good," Stofferson said with a wide grin. "No need to be alarmed, my dear." He patted her arm. She released her grip. Her eyes scanned left and right as if they followed a hyperactive fly in flight. "When you say you are right here, Michael, where is right here?"

"Erm… I'm standing in front of you and L-lydia," Michael told them slower than before. Having never conversed with another since appearing in the flat so many suns and moons ago, the exercise felt alien to him.

"Have you learned how to hold objects for more than a second yet?" Stofferson asked.

"Only when I'm…erm…feeling…" Michael stopped. He didn't know how to describe the feeling that helped him grasp other objects. "Erm…"

"Are you angry when you do it?" Lydia asked.

"No," Michael pondered. "Not angry but definitely feeling less… er… calm. Like when I threw those bad people out of the flat. I couldn't touch them at first. Then when I heard them say they were going to hurt you, I could."

"Interesting," Stofferson mused. "What about the door panel?"

"Ah, sorry, that was an accident," Michael replied, warming to the sound of his voice coming through the machine. "I was trying to push the door and I kept falling through it. I think I may have been a little angry then too. Though not with the painting or the pad I knocked on the floor when Lydia was upset."

"And my interest groweth," Stofferson said, scratching the stubble on his cheek. "So, *Ghost* had it right about the emotions helping. I wonder what spirit helped them with their research."

"Could it not just be a good guess?" Lydia said.

"Not from my experience. Even George Lucas had help with Yoda, or so I'm told. Though, I digress. I think you moving in has helped to focus Michael. What if I did THIS?" Stofferson's polite face morphed into a mask of dark evil as he lurched, hands claw-like, for Lydia's throat.

"NO," Michael hollered and dived in the way, knocking Stofferson down on to the sofa.

Lydia, shocked by the speed of the whole scene, stood frozen for a second before announcing, "I saw you again. Well, for a second."

"Good," Stofferson, lying on his back, grinned. "We have a baseline."

Chapter Sixteen

As the darkness of night gave way to the silver grey of dawn, the two living and one spirit gave up their experimenting. All hung heavy with exhaustion. This surprised Lydia, as she never considered spirits needing a rest. Therefore, around four thirty, Stofferson called a halt.

"I would really love to pursue our tests tomorrow if nobody has other plans," he told Lydia and the space Michael said he occupied.

"I'm guessing that's a cruel joke," a grumpy Michael growled from the windowsill and on through the ghost box.

"Oh, sorry," Stofferson replied, genuinely apologetic. "Exhausted oversight."

"Accepted," Michael said.

"What time tomorrow?" Lydia asked. "I only ask because I'm damned sure I won't be up for breakfast."

"Worry not," Stofferson said, shrugging into his coat. "My line of work has rendered me a night owl. I never see before lunch. So, how about around two-ish?"

"Ish?" Lydia asked.

"Well, I'm not a great observer of the time either. So, if I say two-ish, it will be anywhere between two and three. Is that okay?" Stofferson with a shrugged grin.

"Two-ish sounds fine with me," Lydia replied.

"I don't really follow a time schedule, so I'll see you when I see you," Michael said.

And that is how they left it.

Lydia slept well for the first time since arriving in Yorkshire, knowing that somewhere in the house there slept her own invisible rottweiler. Dropping off took Michael longer as he played over the greatest day he had experienced since occupying the flat. Eventually, his eyes closed and he dreamed of his angel.

The next morning, as expected, passed all three by. Michael yawned first and climbed out of the bath to check all lay well with the flat. He couldn't recall waking so late. Normally the world was just opening its eyes. He never woke to vehicles rushing past the front windows. It unnerved him somewhat. Lydia's appearance some thirty minutes later alleviated the concern. She stumbled down the short staircase leading to the second floor and turned on the ghost box Stofferson left her just in case she needed to speak to Michael.

"Morning," she yawned to the otherwise empty room.

"Good morning," Michael replied. "How did you sleep?"

"Too well. Where are you?"

"On the windowsill."

"Is that your favourite seat?"

"I suppose. I can watch the world pass by from here."

"Does that not depress you after a while?"

"Why? It's been my television before you brought yours into the flat."

"I suppose. But you're watching others live and not doing it yourself."

"I've never looked at it that way. It's all I've ever known. But now you mention it, I'm depressed now," Michael said, feigning upset.

"No, no, I'm sorry. I forgot you know nothing else," Lydia pleaded to the empty windowsill.

"In fact, I may just leap out of this window and end it all."

"You're messing with me?" Lydia grinned.

"Yep. Convincing, eh?"

"Too bloody convincing. I'm going to have to watch out for you, Michael."

"Why does hearing that name seem as alien as it is familiar?"

"I don't know. Maybe part of you, a buried part, remembers who you were. Do you mind if we continue in the kitchen? I'm dying for a cuppa."

"Sounds good. I'll have milk and one honey. Whatever that tastes like," Michael sniggered and followed Lydia as she picked up the ghost box and led him into the kitchen.

"Do you literally remember nothing from your past?"

"Nothing, nowt, sod all," Michael replied.

"Yet, you remember words. Especially as nowt is from the local dialect."

"I learned it from the workmen and women who visited. Same as I heard that fans of a football team called Leeds are not fond of another called Scumchester United."

"I've never heard of a team called Scumchester," Lydia frowned as she turned from the tap with a full kettle of water and plugged it in. "Though, I suppose they may have been referring to Manchester United."

"Who knows," Michael replied. He shrugged but Lydia never saw it.

"What else did you pick up from the workers? Did they mention anything about you? Surely, working in a flat where a young man… erm… ended his life must've bothered them enough to say something."

"I'm not sure they knew. Their vans said Ilkley on them. So, I'm guessing they weren't from around here."

"Makes sense," Lydia replied as the kettle finished boiling. She poured the steaming water into the pot just as a knock echoed from the front door. "Stofferson must just smell tea when it's brewing." She looked at the clock as she passed, ghost box in hand. It read quarter to two. "He's early." She frowned and decided to look down from the front window first. Stofferson wasn't early. The well styled hair and expensive suit belonged to the estate agent, Daniel. Lydia's frown deepened. "I'll just leave the box on the windowsill, Michael, and go see what he wants."

"Who is it?" Michael asked and then recognised the man as he too looked down. "Oh, him. No worries. I'll wait here."

"Be back in a mo." Lydia turned and wandered downstairs.

"Miss Richardson," Daniel smiled his practiced salesman smile after Lydia opened the door. "I hope I'm not disturbing you?"

"No. What can I do for you?"

"Well, word reached us that someone broke in last night and, as I'm in the area, I just wanted to make sure you're okay."

"That's very kind of you. How did you hear?"

"Oh, small town; good grapevine. One of our employees lives around the corner. Are you okay?" Daniel asked. His eyes flicked past Lydia as if looking for something.

"I'm fine. I chased them out. All's well. Not often an estate agency checks on houses after they've sold them," Lydia smiled. Something about his furtive glances over her shoulder unnerved Lydia.

"We like to go above and beyond at Greyson, Sutcliffe and Milner," Daniel said with a bow. "Well, if there's anything we can do, you know where we are."

"I certainly do. Thank you for your amazing concern," Lydia said, hoping her disingenuous words weren't noticed by the estate agent.

"Not a problem," Daniel said. He turned, yet spun back before Lydia closed the door. "Oh, word also reached us that a man has been seen hanging around here. Now, it's not for me to judge a person on their occupation but the man in question is a little eccentric and enjoys making up far-fetched stories about certain houses and the paranormal. They call him Irving Stofferson, I believe. He wrote a book on the flat. A complete fantasy. So, be careful."

"Why, careful? Is he dangerous?" Lydia asked, trying to sound shocked.

"No. No. Not dangerous per se. Like I say, a little eccentric and fanciful at most, He may fill you full of silly stories and add you into his book. You know what you writers are like?" He laughed.

"Oh, I know. Only worry if we kill you off," Lydia sniggered. "Thanks for the heads up, Daniel. And for your concern."

"No problem." Daniel turned and walked towards his shiny Aston Martin DB9 Sports.

Lydia, more suspicious than ever, closed the door with one last smile.

"You seemed bothered by what he said, Lydia. Are you okay?" Michael asked as Lydia entered the lounge.

"I'm not sure," Lydia replied, frowning. "That whole conversation seemed… I don't know… just false. Why would a guy who already sold me the flat check on me and mention Stofferson. What does it matter to him if he's only the agent?"

"To be honest, I've no idea what an agent does, Lydia. I'd say he might just be a kind person, but I do pick up something strange about him too."

"I know he's trying to appear kind, but something inside my gut says otherwise."

"You have something in your gut that talks to you?" Michael asked, flabbergasted. "Human or something else?"

"No," Lydia replied, trying to keep the amusement from her eyes, "It's an expression. When a person has a gut feeling, they suspect something is wrong. Does that make sense?"

"Ah, like me thinking I've seen him before and finding it odd that he bows slightly whenever he reaches the top step?"

"He bows?"

"Sort of. Like, a little bow."

"How odd."

"I think so. He didn't do it anywhere else in the flat. Just on the landing. And because of the colours around him, I feel he knows I'm here." A fast rapping on the main door echoed upstairs. Michael turned and looked down upon the upturned face. "Stofferson's here."

"I'll go let him in. Maybe he might have answers," Lydia said and headed back downstairs.

"That would be nice," Michael called after her.

While she finished brewing the tea, Lydia filled Stofferson in regarding Daniel's odd visit and did not spare his feelings.

"Eccentric and fanciful, eh?" Stofferson sniggered. "I like that. Better that than mysterious and underhanded."

"You think he's underhanded?" Lydia asked.

"Oh, very much so. And his company has been for centuries."

"What does underhanded mean, please?" Michael asked from his perch.

"Erm, devious," Lydia told the windowsill.

"And sly," Stofferson.

"And I'm guessing they are bad words?" Michael asked, more confused than ever.

"He's the sort of person to sell this flat knowing its history and what it will do to the owner, Michael," Stofferson said. "He certainly played his part in your entrapment within these walls."

"He trapped me here?" Michael asked. "Is that how I died? How did he trap me?"

"An excellent question," Stofferson conceded. "One with a long, historic and seedy past to explain it."

"What does that mean?" Michael asked.

"Have you heard of the Pendle witches?" Stofferson asked.

"As I didn't know my own name, I think you'll guess that answer," Michael replied.

"Fair point. I suppose I best start from the beginning…"

Part Two

Chapter One

The year was 1612 and the Lancashire villages surrounding the imposing Pendle Hill came to garner a reputation as a lawless, godless, wild area since Henry VIII stripped the local Whalley abbey of its power and wealth, and hung its Abbott, John Paslew. Without the influence of religion to guide the ill-educated, the locals are said to have resorted to witchcraft. Or at least, that's how the rumour mill in London reported the situation. Two rival families later accused of witchcraft, the Chattox and the Demdikes, may have spread word they practiced witchcraft in order to extort money from local farmers. Yet, some of the others to see trial, like Alice Nutter, merely practiced Catholicism in secret. However, such adherence to an outlawed branch of Christianity attracted the attention of the British Crown.

This did not sit at all well with a secret coven of magick practitioners known only as The Thirteen.

"Friends," a tall man in a cowled cloak began. The fire dancing in the grate to the left highlighted a prominent eagle-like nose poking out of the shadow of the cowl. "We have convened this eve not to worship but to discuss urgent matters whispered in the dark halls of Westminster." The man stood before the other cowled twelve in a converted barn. A chill wind whistled through the cracks in the large doors at the far end, lending a strange incidental music to the charade. "As thee all know, James still strides his warpath to eradicating the blood-thirsty Popists from England, and mine whisperers point to our area as his next target."

"But what hath it to do with us, William?" A middle-aged female voice asked.

"I tell thee what it hath to do with us, Bessie," William spat. "If they cometh a-hunting for Jesuits, they will find nought. But they will stumble across the petty twiddling and squabbling of your mother and the bloody Demdikes. And if they find the scent of witchery, they will send in Roger Nowell. An arsworm of the highest order."

"So, what do you proposeth, William?" Another male voice piped up.

"Within these walls, Master Holgate," William began, "where secrecy and discretion art the pillars, much the same as thyself with thine own cursed mother, we all have kin on either side of the Demdikes or the Chattox and some cumberworlders who slope off to rattle their beads, such as mine niece, Alice. Well, I say we let word fall into the willing ears of that fopdoodle and dorbel, Nowell, regarding such folk meeting up to practice witchcraft in Malkin Tower. It carries an air of foreboding the assizes will adore when pointing their foul fingers."

And so, it came about that William, or William Whitaker, jealous uncle to wealthy widow, Alice Nutter, paid nine-year-old granddaughter of Elizabeth Demdike, daughter of Elizabeth Device and niece to Christopher Holbeck, a shiny penny to say she had seen his own niece and many of the other twelve at Malkin Tower discussing their plan to murder

Thomas Lister of Westby Hall. Uncoincidentally, the older brother to another member of The Thirteen, James. While these plots swept along, William also laid plans to rid the world of a local peddler of magickal pins. Such paraphernalia were trumpet calls to the ill-educated witch-finders. William had spoken to the peddler, a man called John Law, a few weeks earlier about selling elsewhere. Law refused. So, The Thirteen sent a curse his way.

"The curse," William assured the other twelve with a sinister sneer, "will only bear fruit whence one born of Demdike or Chattox enquires of his wares. He will then refuse to sell them anything, even if he so wants, causing the dim-witted other to curse him. That is when the true curse will slither along his veins. Yet, he will only fall when witnesses can testify."

And that is precisely what happened.

"'Scuse me, friend," young, filthy Alizon Device asked Law as he hiked through Trawden Forest with his wares strapped to his rounded back, some four days later. "Might I buy some pins?"

"NO," Law scowled and then frowned at his gruff response. "I'm selling nowt today. Now, be off with thee, girl."

"But, I only wish pins, sir. Thou sold to me before."

"That as may be, young lady, but this time is a no. Now pester someone else."

"Please?"

"I SAID NON OTHER!"

"You rude wandought," Alizon snapped. "I curse thee to fall."

And so, he did. But only when he found himself at the nearest inn, where word soon spread like a virus. When news of his fall reached Alizon she did not rejoice. On the contrary, as William Whitaker predicted, she collapsed in distraught and sorrowful tears. And even apologised with all her broken heart to his son, Abraham.

"The dice are cast, brothers and sisters. Soon, we will have wealth and a hall in which to practice. Soon, the Hill will be rid of the stinking Catholics and the vicious pretenders. Soon, we shall rise." William told The Thirteen when news of Law's death reached his ears.

They did soon acquire a hall from Lister and land from Nutter. Although, only after the Witchfinder General, Roger Nowell, rode into the nearby villages with his party of crows and dragged away the matriarch of the Demdike clan, Elizabeth Southerns, her daughter Elizabeth Device, and her grandchildren, James and Alizon Device. They then arrested the octogenarian matriarch of the Chattox clan, Anne Whittle, alongside her daughter Anne Redfern. The others included poor, young Alice Nutter, Jane Bulcock and her son John, Katherine Hewitt, Alice Grey, and Jennet Preston.

The Hill soon cheered as the violence to the innocent and weak from the Demdikes and Chattox ceased. But their rise took much longer than any of The Thirteen hoped. William Whittaker and the 1612 coven of The Thirteen had neither the vision nor the lifespan to take the coven any further than keeping it afloat. Especially after his death and during the puritanical regime of Cromwell, who swept across northern England like a drab dark cloud, banning everything from alcohol to Christmas as we know it. The corresponding civil wars wrecked the country. New laws dictating religious beliefs swinging from Catholicism back to Protestantism pushed The Thirteen deeper underground. During this time, the coven spent most of their time learning their craft. They turned the coven into a school of esoteric and mystical thought.

However, then came the advent of the industrial revolution where the wealthiest landowners grew richer whilst their renters and employees slumped deeper into the mire of destitution. The Thirteen, most of them too tired from their long days in the filthy mills or in the fields, gave up the coven during the early parts of the eighteenth century. They grew disenchanted with what they saw as nothing more than parlour tricks.

Until, around 1740, then-leader Samuel Grayson and his wife Rebecca, for reasons unknown, took their large family and even larger stack of books they'd amassed over the centuries, including The Grand Grimoire, The Picatrix, the Liber Incantationum, Exorcismorum et Fascinationum Variorum, the Sepher Ha-Razim, and many more to a small town on the other side of Pendle Hill, called, oddly enough, Burrstone. They rented a small cottage near the centre and taught their nine children how to read the ancient languages, and thusly the wisdom, from the grimoires in their possession. A more practical approach to magick didn't occur until Samuel died of dysentery in 1744 when his destitute wife Rebecca took the reins. With no good money coming in, they moved to the poorer end of town to share a house with two other families on Broughton Road. Her family of one adult and nine children crammed into two ground floor rooms. In between her working long hours as a chamber maid for one of the local mill-owners, and the children slaving for pittance in the filth of the mills, they studied. Then, one night as the other children slept in a huddled pile in one corner of the musty room, and a single tiny candle flickered over his youngest sister, Sarah, as she coughed and wheezed with tuberculosis in the opposite one, her eldest son, Matthew spoke to Rebecca.

"Mama?" he asked. "I found myself reading the

Grimorium Verum and came across something that may aide our present dilemma."

"Pray tell me more, my son," his exhausted mother replied in a whisper, "But please keep your voice down."

"My apologies," Matthew said and lowered his head and voice. "The tome speaks of Clauneck, beloved of the morning star, who, when invoked, will bestow wealth on the magickal acolyte. Could he not be the answer to dear Sarah's problem?" He cast a sorrowful eye towards the silhouette of his sister.

"My sweet boy," his mother simpered, reaching forward to stroke his cheek. "What have we to offer in recompense? Remember, a demon always demands something in return. Look around, we have nothing."

"Could we not at least invoke him and enquire his price?"

"We would need more than just the two of us to invoke such a demon, my love, never mind the great risk if we are caught practicing the craft."

"Leave it with me, Mama. I am already assured the Milner's and the Sutcliffe's are no Jesuits or Puritans."

"How can you know this?" Rebecca hissed. "Please tell me you haven't spoken about the craft?"

"Of course, not, Mama. You raised no imbecile. I merely share the mule-room with Elizabeth Milner and Thomas Sutcliffe. Sometimes, when the machine pops a reel, we talk behind the mule. What could blind prying eyes and bung flapping ears more than joining families to practice in one house?" Matthew asked.

"Matthew, I know you think you are helping, but three teenagers prattling behind those damnable machines isn't the same as drawing the neighbours into an ostracized practice. Their parents may think differently to Elizabeth and Thomas."

"Mama, forgive me, but since this century's thirty-fifth year, is it not illegal to accuse others of witchcraft?"

"That is correct, but the Swansons may still release me from their employ if they were to find out."

"Then, what if I was to claim, for now, you know nought of my thoughts and I'm only involving myself in idle chatter?"

"Yet, if they were to lift our loose floorboards, they would find books with much more than nursery rhymes written across their pages. I demand you cease your talk."

Matthew, however, did quite the opposite. He didn't rush in, mind. With gentle hints that he may have found a way for the three families to claw out of their desperate situation, it took several weeks before Elizabeth Milner's mother, and also widow, Charlotte, knocked on Rebecca's door.

"Mrs Grayson, may I speak with you?" Charlotte began, wringing her jittery hands. "If the time is not inconvenient."

"Of course," Rebecca replied and stood back to allow her neighbour entry. "Is everything well with you?" She asked and closed the door.

"Yes. Well, no. Since the lord saw fit to take my John, as you more than anyone will understand, life has been trying, to say the least. And now that my youngest, William, suffers with his legs and can't work, life is only becoming harder."

"I do understand. What can I do to help?"

"Well, my Elizabeth talks of a way out of this dreadful life she has discussed with your Matthew. A way not used by most folk."

Rebecca cast a dark eye towards her eldest son. Matthew dropped his to the bare floorboards.

"I don't know what Elizabeth told you but..."

"She told me there are eldritch ways. My grandmother used such ways until the lords stamped upon them. Whatever is achieved will stay within these walls, Mrs Grayson. I guarantee that if nothing else."

"It is nice to know these things, Mrs Milner, but the invocation still needs more than me, you, Elizabeth and Matthew to complete it with care. And what if the Sutcliffes hear whispers and run to tell the Swansons?"

Mrs Milner left after an hour of trying but failing to persuade Rebecca. The Sutcliffes, Mary and David, knocked on her door four days later, saying they were willing to try anything to relieve themselves of such a dreadful life. Poverty and desperation can push the unassuming person to new and different horizons if they feel a puff of fresher air on their filthy, sallow cheeks.

For eight weeks, the three families met after supper to learn, study and prepare for the invocation. All the while, young Sarah, the shining light of the family, who, even when ill attempted a warm smile, grew worse.

Until, one late Saturday night, after a long day of labour, knowing they could all rest up on Sunday, The new Thirteen, including members of each family, sat cross-legged, in Rebecca's back room, in front of a stained looking-glass and two large candles stolen from the Swansons, and began their first invocation to Clauneck.

"Remember, above all else," Rebecca warned the others, "We must concentrate. And once we begin, nobody is to leave this room until we close the invocation. Because, doing so will leave a breach for all manner of unwelcome demons to enter this realm. Is this understood?" The Thirteen all murmured their agreement. "Then let us begin."

They all closed their eyes, took several deep inhalations and began chanting the words The Thirteen would pass down the generations, "Ahvalen esen Clauneck kiar."

The hours passed without sight nor sound of any demon, never mind the one they called. The younger members of The

Thirteen began to fidget and lose concentration, which was swiftly reprimanded. Yet, still Clauneck failed to show. Some members fought sleep as the litany began to whoosh with fatigue inside their ears. And just when Rebecca decided to call a halt to the invocation, the flickering flames of the two dribbling candles stood to attention and rose in intensity, brightening the room.

"AHVALEN ESEN CLAUNECK KIAR," Rebecca called louder, feeling giddy nerves fill her belly.

The others followed her lead. A mist filled the looking-glass and spilled out into the dank room. It swirled around their feet and knees. They repeated the invocation with nervous excitement. Within the swirl of grey mist, a tall, handsome man strode forth. He looked around the room. His nose wrinkled. "I don't need to ask why you've called me this day," he sniggered. "Who is this before me?"

"We are The Thirteen, Lord Clauneck," Rebecca replied and bowed her head.

"The Thirteen? Nice moniker. Now, I take it that you are the leader, my lady?" Clauneck asked Rebecca. His use of "my lady" surprised Rebecca. What she did not know is that by showing him respect and calling him "Lord Clauneck," a title that appealed to his pride, Rebecca had made an instant friend. Although, such a friendship would not change the following painful initiation.

"I am, my lord," she bowed.

"Then it is you who must stand on my auction block and find your needs assessed. Do you understand and comply?"

"Yes, my lord," Rebecca replied, trying to keep the fear from her tone. She knew, as head of the coven, she would have to undergo the test.

"Then pray stand, my lady," Clauneck told Rebecca. He

pointed to the right side of the mirror. A large wooden block appeared. The shapes of a brain, an eye, a heart, and a phallus were carved into the block. The sigil of Clauneck. Without a single glance to the rest of The Thirteen, lest her courage fail her, Rebecca walked, with as much dignity as she could muster, to the block. Only after stepping on to it, did she look their way. "Now, my lady Rebecca of The Thirteen, what can old Clauneck do for you and you me?"

Rebecca may as well have stood naked. She felt as much. "We wish your help to leave this hell of poverty, my lord."

"I can see why," Clauneck told her and rubbed his square chin. "Even the rats have abandoned this faecal hole. What can I expect to receive in return?"

"What can we offer you, my lord?"

"Oh, you may not like how I reply to such an expansive question, my lady." Clauneck turned away from Rebecca and circled The Thirteen, frowning in thought. He soon moved on to where little Sarah coughed and spluttered, and frowned even deeper. "How much are you willing to sacrifice in order to live a life less destitute, my lady?"

"What do you have in mind?"

The kind air and handsome face contorted into a twisted mask of hate and anger as Clauneck's eyes burned with fire, two horns sprouted from his head and two bat-like wings fanned from his back. "I ASK THE QUESTIONS!" He roared.

The younger members squealed in fear. The adults grabbed them and hugged them. One, a young male called William, peed his britches.

"Please forgive me, my lord," Rebecca whimpered.

The mask returned to human, and the wings and horns shrunk to nothing. "Apology accepted. Now, what are you willing to sacrifice, my lady?"

"Anything, my lord."

"Interesting. You see, I have recently made a little deal with a certain white-lighter, upstairs. An angel who, shall we say, is a little less tedious than the other do-gooders. He isn't, in his words, up to scratch with his quota of good souls and, over dinner, suggested a way for upstairs, downstairs and in the lady's chamber to feel satisfied. I can offer you, and your descendants to come, steady wealth if you gift me one small thing."

"Anything, my lord," Rebecca urged, her fear giving way to excitement.

"Oh, you silly kitten. You don't walk into a deal saying such wet words," Clauneck chuckled. "I want a good soul. A pristine, angelic soul. That is all. A willing party ready to sacrifice themselves."

"A human soul, my lord?" Rebecca asked, confused.

"Of course. Why on the many earths would I want a pig or a stoat? Silly kitten."

"But, erm, how do we find such a soul, my lord?"

"Oh, we already have one to start the show, my dear." Clauneck pointed to Sarah.

The world turned cold.

Chapter Two

"But, my lord, please, there must be another way. Sarah is my daughter," Rebecca pleaded. She stepped off the auction block and fell to her knees before Clauneck. The other Thirteen sat in a stunned and fearful silence.

"Oh, there are other ways, my dear. Although I know without doubt that dearest Sarah won't last another fortnight."

"But how could you know such things?" Rebecca asked as tears flowed down her cheeks.

A cold and sinister look filled the demon's eyes before he said, "Trust this if you trust nothing else. I know."

"I cannot do it to her," Rebecca cried. She looked to the thirteen. Her eldest son, Matthew, ran to her, dropped to his knees and embraced his stricken mother.

"There is one saving grace if your daughter ends her own life for your well-being," Clauneck began with a shrug. "You will see her again fit and healthy before she traverses the veil to the white-lighters. She may even stay for several years before another soul is found to replace her."

"I just can't, my lord."

"Very well, I'll tell you what, as I'm in a convivial mood, I will gift you one whole week to decide or find another soul.

We shall convene here on the eve of next Saturday. If you can't decide, the deal is off and you can enjoy your bleak existence," Clauneck told Rebecca with no malice.

Without another word, he turned and re-entered the mirror. The grey, foreboding mist followed and the flames died down. The wracking coughs and wheezes from Sarah soon became the only choir.

"What do you suggest, Mama?" Matthew asked, when the silence grew too heavy for his heart and head.

"We need to find another soul." Rebecca muttered, wiping the tears and snot from her face with a rather grubby kerchief.

"But, how?" David Sutcliffe asked. "You heard him, Mrs Grayson. The soul must be willing to commit to their own death. Else, I understood wrong. How do we ask that of someone? Do not get me wrong, I am not saying the soul should be your beautiful daughter. I just don't see how we can fulfill his terms. I say we abandon the whole notion."

Soon enough the room filled with opinions. Yet, not one of them came up with a solution. So, they decided to repair to bed and speak after church the next day.

Later, Rebecca stared into the darkness until the sun rose to offer new light. Her head swam with the quandary and fatigue.

However, they found no resolution to their problem Sunday afternoon, and neither did they for the five days afterward. And still Sarah grew worse. Rebecca called for the doctor.

"I am sorry to say this, Mrs Grayson," the kindly, old doctor told her, "but the fluid sitting heavy upon her lungs is grave."

"How grave, sir?" Rebecca asked, trying to stay strong.

"Grave enough for me to predict no more than a week to ten days at best. I am so sorry to impart such dreadful news."

The usually forthright and ironclad Rebecca broke down for the second time in a week. When composed, she spent as much time as life permitted by her daughter's bedside, if you could call several rolls of dishevelled cloth a bed. Sarah's coughing grew even worse.

Until the sixth day, when she appeared to feel a little better. Enough to croak, "Mama, I heard your meeting with Lord Clauneck some days past."

"Worry not, my love, I would never do that to you," Rebecca told her daughter and rushed over to hug her.

"I want to."

Rebecca pulled away from her daughter in shock. "Why would you want such a thing, my princess?"

"Lord Clauneck said we will still see one another. If I must die, such a thought makes me happy. And you will be able to eat food and buy new material for dresses. I would like to see you wearing a new dress, Mama. You would look so beautiful in new cloth."

"I cannot, my petal. I just cannot." Rebecca began to wail anew. Although, whether it was because the sun shone through the window and lit up Sarah's face as if she were an angel, or due to the warm smile she had missed since Sarah, the beacon of her family, fell ill, a part of her felt in awe of this wise little girl with the courage of a warrior.

"Did you not once tell me Great Grandma Bess used dwale?" Sarah asked in between a fresh bout of coughing. "Maybe I can drink some of that and I will go to sleep and wake up healthy enough to see you again."

"How do you recall such things, my sweet?" An astounded Rebecca asked.

"I always loved your stories, Mama."

After Sarah fell into a fitful sleep, Rebecca hushed her children squabbling in the other room, closed the door with a soft click and moved to sit with Matthew who had just arrived home, filthy, from the mill. She told him of her conversation with his sister.

"Is that not just Sarah through and through, Mama?" He replied after his mother finished recounting her tale. "I must confess to not remembering you talking of Great Granny Bess and this dwale. What be it?"

"It is a potion many of the craft used to put to sleep the injured or infirm before cutting them. It worked upon my father when a bore mauled his leg. Granny Bess was all but hobbling with old age herself. Yet, she made the potion, father drank it, and then she repaired his wounds, good as new."

"But how will that help Sarah?" Matthew whispered, so not to wake his sister with such talk.

"Drink a little and it puts a person to slumber, drink too much and they will ne'er wake again," Rebecca sighed and cast a tearful eye back towards her brave daughter.

After more begging from young Sarah whenever she found consciousness, Rebecca taught Matthew the recipe for dwale. She could not bring herself to make the potion but would allow, with a new stoic silence, her son to make it. Rebecca spent the remainder of Friday and all of Saturday wrapped around her wheezing daughter. She only moved as the sun faded and The Thirteen arrived to begin the ceremony.

This time Clauneck took less time to step through the grey mist dancing seductively around the looking glass.

"And how are we all, this balmy eve?" he asked with a jovial smile.

The Thirteen, as if rehearsed, all replied, "We are well, my lord."

"And what of our proposed deal?" He asked this question looking directly at Rebecca.

"I will do it," Sarah croaked, knowing her mother did not have the will to say the words herself.

"Good. You will find yourself much the better for doing so, my dear. And might I commend you on your bravery." He stopped for a moment in thought. His eyes swept the room before he frowned. "From this day forth, this room will be used only for sealing all future guests inside these four walls. In between an arrival settling in and preparation for a new one, no one other than The Thirteen will enter. Do you understand?"

"But, sire, what if the landlord requests entry?" David Sutcliffe asked.

"Landlord?" Clauneck scoffed "You will soon have enough riches that buying this sorry excuse for a home will hardly dent your purses, my good man. Fear not. So, to conclude, you will buy this house and no other person, other than The Thirteen, will enter these lower rooms. You will say these rooms are for storage. If anyone attempts to enter, the charms will dissuade them. Understand?"

"Yes, my lord," The Thirteen replied in unison.

"The other floors will be rented out as one for new guests," Clauneck continued, scratching his chin and cheeks as he thought up the plan. "For now, it may be best if you form a company to rent the property to Rebecca and her brood. That way she can be there for Sarah until her time arrives to cross the veil. I can point you to accountants and solicitors in my employ who will help you divert the funds I will pay you."

"Divert, sire?" Charlotte Milner asked.

"Yes," Clauneck told her. "If you all just suddenly walk the muddy cobbles outside dripping in gold and finery, do you think the law will just look the other way, my good lady? No, they will want to know where you received such quick wealth. The solicitors will set up accounts from far off places such as the Americas and the Indies. There, one of you will have a rich uncle who just died and left you a fortune. Did you not ply your trade in building before times grew too difficult, David?"

"I did, my lord," Sutcliffe replied.

"Good. Rebecca here will make you rich through the designing of her nice, big manor house she will need to house her many treasures and large fatherless family. Lady Charlotte will receive patronage from Rebecca because they are friends who have both suffered the loss of a beloved."

"But, my lord, I can only build from another's specifications," Sutcliffe pleaded. "I wouldn't know how to design such a grand house."

"You silly, tiresome man, you will hire another with an eye for blueprints. I will ensure he keeps quiet and you will take the glory. It is cover for the wealth you will find inside your vaults. Do you understand?"

"Yes, my lord," Sutcliffe replied with a sheepish bow of the head.

"Good. Now enough finance talk for the evening. We must commence setting charms and carry our dearest Sarah up to the top floor. And before anyone asks, we are moving to the uppermost room because we need a distinct lack of prying eyes as we prepare for Sarah's departure and return. For she will be the first of many to ascend from that room. A room she will never enter again after this night."

With the demon, Clauneck, leading them like a conductor, The Thirteen set up many charms that evening. Four around the ground floor, and one in the back room where Charlotte kept a steel bath, as paupers did not have complete bathrooms in those days. Clauneck told them that room was as good as any for the spirit-soul to arrive in after leaving the host body. Later, as the clock in the Milners' lounge rang three times, Matthew and his brother, Simon, carried the ashen-grey Sarah up to the attic rooms usually occupied by the Sutcliffes' small family. There, they rested the stricken girl, already clutching a stoppered bottle of her great grandma's dwale recipe, on to the couple's rickety double bed.

"After we have set up the charms to keep the spirit-soul from entering, you can leave Sarah with me if it pains you less, Rebecca?" Clauneck said, feigning compassion quite well.

"If it pleases you, my lord, I would rather stay," Rebecca replied.

"As will I, please, my lord," Matthew added and clutched his mother's hand.

"As the man of the house, I would expect no less," Clauneck conceded.

The other Thirteen gathered around Clauneck and began the final charms before ushering out. Charlotte, Elizabeth and Mary hugged Rebecca and Matthew, David and the others patted them on the shoulder as they passed.

"I will ask thee one last time, brave child," Clauneck began after the others left. "Do you commit the following willingly?"

Sarah smiled from her mother to the demon and nodded in between racking coughs, "I… do," she added. "I no longer want the pain." Despite her smile, a single tear appeared in her left eye and tumbled down her cheek.

"Then take the drink and be gone with the torment," Clauneck bowed.

Sarah reached for her mother and brother. "I will see you soon?" she asked, as if uncertain. Before either could answer, little Sarah pulled out the cork stopper and downed the mixture of hemlock, opium, henbane, bile, bryony, lettuce and vinegar. The vile concoction made her retch. Her eyes grew wide. A look of fear crossed her face. Her racking grew ever worse.

"SARAH," her mother screamed and reached for her. Matthew stood looking lost.

With slow blinks, Sarah, still coughing, closed her eyes. The hacking became softer for the first time in so long that the silence added to the horror. Her body grew limp in her mother's arms and her breathing became laboured until it ceased altogether.

"It is done," Clauneck said in almost a whisper.

Chapter Three

The mill owners, The Swansons, ever gracious to their downtrodden employees, gave the Graysons one day to mourn the loss of Sarah. Hope of seeing her daughter once again carried Rebecca through the cheap ceremony. By the third day of her passing, the members of The Thirteen began to suspect the demon, Clauneck, had reneged on the terrible deal. Rebecca soon felt she had died, too.

"Sarah?" Her children heard her whisper over and over in the dead of the night. Sometimes she would add, "Come to Mama."

"Mama," Matthew began, hugging his mother, "You need your sleep."

"But, he promised. He promised she would reappear, and I swear her scent grew in my nostrils earlier."

"Maybe it did and it takes her a little while to appear in spirit."

"I did smell her, Matthew. I did."

"I believe you, Mama, but missing out on your rest will not help you or her. If you smelled her once, she will come back." Matthew reassured her. The smile he offered over the flickering candle flame hid the doubts bubbling inside him.

He persuaded his mother to at least lie down. Soon, she fell asleep. After checking on his younger siblings, he followed minutes after.

The next day, as the pale sun pushed away the tar black of night, they readied themselves for another long day of labour. The tiny loaf of stale bread and mug of cloudy water hardly filled their bellies. The abominable bells calling them to the mill made them all groan as they headed towards the front door. The Milners and the Sutcliffes met them there.

"Morning all," Mr Sutcliffe said with as much cheeriness as his positive side could muster. "Fair thee all well and may…" A stiff rapping on the front door stopped his flow. "Who might this be?" he mumbled, puzzled, as he pushed past the children and pulled open the heavy, wooden door.

A bespectacled homunculus man, wearing finer clothes than any in the house smiled up at the many faces. In his left hand, he carried a brown leather case. Almost like a doctor's medical bag. In his right hand he clasped a gold-topped walking cane.

"A fine morning to you all," he declared in a cultured, yet squeaky voice. "Am I correct in finding myself at the abode of…" he stopped to study a sheet of the finest bohemian paper. "The Graysons, the Milners and the Sutcliffes?"

"Yes, sir. That'll be true," Sutcliffe replied, a little dumbstruck.

"Splendid. My name is Abraham Goldman from London. May I speak with you all away from other eyes and ears?" He cocked his head at the passing, staring crowd. "You have Thirteen good reasons to listen to my propositions." He emphasised the "Thirteen."

Sutcliffe flicked a quizzical expression towards the three matriarchs, received the same from them and then turned back to Goldman. "Please, come in, sir," he said and beckoned the curious gentleman inside. "Move back everyone," he told the brood crammed behind him. Excited, they shuffled down the short hall and into Rebecca's rooms.

"I'm sorry, I've nothing in the way of refreshment to offer you other than water, Mr Goldsmith," Rebecca said with a sad bow.

"Worry ye not, my lovely," Abraham replied, "I have no plans to stay long. My carriage awaits for another appointment in Shipley. May I ask your names?"

"Sorry," Rebecca said, "I'm being rude. I'm Rebecca Grayson."

"Ah, the head of The Thirteen," Goldman replied.

"How could you know such things?" Rebecca asked.

"Lord Clauneck informed me thusly of all your names."

"You know Lord Clauneck?" David Sutcliffe asked, aghast.

"Of course. My family was not always so affluent, you know. We lived in conditions much worse than this. It was my grandmother who called his lordship forth and we have served each other's needs ever since."

"In the same way?" Matthew asked.

"As I do not know the intricate particulars of your deal with his lordship, I cannot compare, young sir. Needless to say, he contacted me, in my position as an astute solicitor, to deliver your first remuneration."

"I'm sorry, I don't know what that means," Matthew conceded.

"My apologies. I am here to fulfill Lord Clauneck's side of the bargain and pay you for your services." He dropped the bag on the floor by his feet and flipped the brass catch. "Now, I have a reasonable amount to allow you the freedom to at least eat a glorious meal and to purchase new garments." With a quick smile, he pulled three stringed suede purses from the bag and held them out for David Sutcliffe to take. "If you open these, you will find five thousand in various coins to share out between the thirteen." The room gasped as David opened the purses to reveal more gleaming gold and silver than any of them had ever seen. "Now, unless I am thoroughly mistaken, Lord Clauneck's plan is that Mrs Grayson, as head of The Thirteen, had a wealthy uncle she never knew existed in the East Indies. He died and left you with everything from his estate. Here are the papers that declare such details. Please sign." Goldman produced several documents and placed them on the table next to the purses spilling out their treasures. He then produced a quill and ink from a side pocket of the bag. "I mean no disrespect when I ask the following, but can you sign your name, Mrs Grayson?"

"Yes," Rebecca said without offence. She took the quill, and after dipping the end in the ink, she signed wherever Goldman pointed.

"Thank you," Goldman said after she finished. "Now for the important document all the members of The Thirteen will sign for Lord Clauneck."

"For Lord Clauneck?" Matthew asked.

"Oh, yes, young man," Goldman smiled. "He has proven he stands equal to his side of the bargain you struck, has he not?"

"Well, my daughter still has not returned?" Rebecca said in almost a whisper.

Goldman patted her arm. "Trust me, if Lord Clauneck promised the return of your beloved daughter, Mrs Grayson, she will return. I have worked with him all of my life and as long as I continue to fulfill my side of the bargain, he has never failed me."

Rebecca looked deep into the tiny man's eyes and felt a wave of reassurance flood over her. "Thank you," she told him.

"My pleasure. Now, the deal you have struck with his lordship is not only for life, but also for your descendants' lives. As long as they, as I have already mentioned, do not veer from the bargain. That said, his lordship demands reassurances of his own in nothing more than a signature from each member of The Thirteen."

"Will our descendants have to sign too in the future?" Elizabeth asked.

"Of course. Whenever one passes and another takes their place, I, or one of my descendants, will appear with this document and amend the signatures. So, you see, we will all be one big family from here on in." After each member signed the document, some with only a cross, Goldman informed them about bank accounts he had set up and ways to contact him if they needed advice or more money moved. He finished with a warning that at first amused The Thirteen and then chilled them all to the core. "Before I leave you to enjoy your new standing, I advise you all to do one more thing. I can complete things for you now or gift you time to ruminate on the issue and come back to it at a later time." Everyone frowned. "But I do advise you to prepare a document to ensure each receives equal share."

"But we trust each other, sir," David told the solicitor, chest out.

"Admirable, my good man. And looking around this room, I see no reason to believe such strong feelings of trust will sway anytime soon. Yet, you forget your descendants to come. And I speak from experience. Wealth is wonderful to those who had none. However, the next generation, the ones who are used to the finer things in life, and define such grandeur as their right, will grow spiteful with greed. I once saw a loving family, not three separate families, mind you, tear each other apart when the second and third generations demanded more. A document such as the one I have in my bag sealing equal rights forever will make such horrific actions impossible. Trust me." He looked around the small, cramped room and watched their expressions change as understanding dawned on them all. They all signed the document without further thought.

"Right, my new friends," Goldman began after completing all formalities, "I must depart. I leave my address if you have any queries or worries. I will travel back up in two weeks to see how you are all getting along." He smiled and turned to leave before stopping. "Oh, before I forget, his lordship asked me to find an architect to work with Mr Sutcliffe on the plans for a new abode. Is that correct?"

"Yes," David replied.

"Good. I will find a suitable candidate, one in the service of our lord, and have him accompany me when I return. Until then, fair thee all well."

They all said their goodbyes to the funny but amiable little man and closed the door. Nobody appeared to breathe for several minutes. They merely returned to the room with the money winking up at them from the table and stared in disbelief.

"I cannot believe it," Charlotte Milner eventually gasped. "I just cannot believe it true." She then laughed hysterically. The others joined in.

Chapter Four

Over the next week, many aspects of life for the three families involved in The Thirteen changed dramatically. No longer did they follow the bedraggled and starving throng of filthy families who filled the mills of Burrstone. No longer did they live on gruel. The willingness of the Swansons to allow them to buy 67 Broughton Road did come as a huge surprise to them all, though. They expected much more resistance. Yet, for reasons beyond some, Bartholomew Swanson agreed on a reasonable price on his visit to the house. Although his face predicted much more of a fight on arrival.

He arrived on the afternoon of their third day of reasonable riches, sitting, regal and austere, in the back of his carriage. He rapped on the front door with the brass end of his walking stick. Despite their new standing each head of the three families passed worried gestures until David straightened his new britches and waistcoat before striding with many nerves to the front door.

"Sutcliffe," Swanson growled on facing David, "May I enter?"

"Of course, sir," David replied, unable to see himself as any way equal to his former master. He shuffled aside and allowed Swanson entry. And on stepping inside the house, Swanson's demeanour altered somewhat from prickly to as edgy as a peach.

"I… erm… came to enquire about… your…" Swanson stuttered as his thick brows danced under his hat. "I'll be damned if I know now."

"Something tells me you are wondering why we have not attended work, sir," Rebecca simpered. She knew exactly why a change had flowed over Swanson. "And maybe to discuss our purchasing of this house?"

"I must confess I am not entirely sure, good woman. Yet, the notion does sound correct."

"Please, enter our parlour and we will offer a good price," Rebecca cooed, much to the surprise and confusion of the other Thirteen. Although, they knew enough to stay silent and allow her room to work.

An hour later, with Swanson's signatures on the paperwork Goldman had left Rebecca, the former owner of everything including their breath left the house with a purse of one thousand pounds. As time wore on, he came to wonder where the money came from and how his signature sat on the deeds for a property he, with no memory, signed away.

"The charms," Rebecca shrugged. "No other person, whether a magick user or basic housebreaker can harm a single one of us within these walls. Furthermore, although I have never put the charm to use, they can, if weak-minded enough, be bent to our will. And, as I always suspected our dearest Barty to be nothing more than a bully not fit to wear his astute father's shoes, I gave the charm a chance to work."

"His whole demeanour altered as soon as his toe passed our threshold," David said with much surprise.

"As would anyone else's, my friend," Rebecca said. "That said, I must warn you all that we cannot abuse such a charm. And in some cases, it is best we forget its will-bending capabilities."

"But, why, Mama?" Matthew asked, excited by the prospect of such power. "We could run the town from this one house."

"We could do no such thing, my boy. You are better than that, surely?" Matthew lowered his head in shame. "The more we use the charm to influence others for gain, the more we are open to speculation from the law, gossip and those who will be jealous of our success. We may be safe within these walls and the coming walls David will build but we would be nothing more than prisoners unable to function in the world without fear of dagger or musket. Do you see?"

"Yes, Mama," Matthew said. "That is why Lord Clauneck will give time between each new soul, is it not? As not to arouse suspicion?"

"Correct. Now, if you all do not mind, I need to meditate on the first floor in hope to see our darling Sarah."

However, Rebecca did not see Sarah once that week. Nor the next week. Even after Goldman returned and, seeing the state of the woman's mind in threads, pleading with her to have hope that their lord would be true to his word, Sarah's smile remained absent from her sight. Rebecca hardly slept and ate very little. The nice, new dress she had purchased soon after receiving their new riches hung limp and lifeless form her bony shoulders. The others, worried for her mental well-being, persuaded her to help them set up a ritual to see Lord Clauneck and at least hear from him why her daughter had not appeared. This they did. They picked the wrong day to summon him.

"WHAT?" He screamed as soon as he appeared from the misty mirror, horrific horns and tattered wings visible. "I

DO HAVE ANOTHER LIFE AND OTHER BASTARD FOLLOWERS TO ATTEND TO, YOU KNOW."

"Please, my lord," Matthew said, eyes lowered. "We only summon you out of concern for my Mama and Sarah. She mourns her daughter so. She does not eat nor drink, nor even sleep more than three winks a night. Please, could you advise her when she may see Sarah again?"

Clauneck's wings and horns shrunk, and his eyes shifted from fiery red to brown before he said, "Your daughter is and has been within these walls since her last earthly breath, dear lady."

"But, I have not seen her once, my lord. And I so miss her it tears me apart."

"Oh, you mortals and your love and loss. Okay," he began, scratching his square chin. "Once and only once will I perform the following. Special circumstances and all that. The reason your dearest has not appeared is because she has not learned to pick up objects. When attempted, the energy she uses spreads forth and allows her form visibility. I can aide her to learn faster, but it comes at a price." As all things do when dealing with a demon.

"Anything, my lord," Rebecca cried. Tears streaming down her sallow cheeks. "Anything."

"So, you wish me to speed up the process?" Clauneck asked with a cold menace in his voice all but Rebecca shrunk from.

"Yes, my lord. I beg of you."

"Be careful what you beg for, my dear. Remember I warned you of a price." Clauneck turned to the altar and lifted The Grand Grimoire. He closed the book and kissed the front cover before tossing it lightly towards the corner of the room. The astounded Thirteen's eyes followed the tome and gasped as it stopped in mid-air. Sarah appeared, shocked and frowning, as if confused, holding it.

"I take my leave," Clauneck bowed and entered the mirror. The smoke followed and the candles grew dim.

"SARAH," Rebecca hollered and dashed towards the form of her radiant-skinned daughter. She fell to her knees in front of her. "Never have I seen you look so well."

Sarah opened her mouth, yet only silence fell into the ears of the living.

"My lovely child, I cannot hear you," Rebecca told Sarah. "Can you hear me?"

Sarah jabbered in silence, but her head nodding suggested she heard her mother. Rebecca turned to The Thirteen for some guidance, anxiety filling her already sore eyes.

"What about offering her a quill, Mrs Grayson?" Elizabeth suggested and rushed into the next room to acquire said quill and a sheet of paper. She rushed back in and offered them to Rebecca. Not daring to lock eyes with Sarah in case she turned out possessed by evil.

Rebecca thanked Elizabeth and offered the writing materials to her daughter. Sarah dropped the grimoire, disappeared for a split second and reappeared after taking the paper and quill. The rest of the room, all twelve, watched on, silent and fascinated. Sarah nodded and squiggled a message before showing it to Rebecca. It read, **Where am I?**

"You're home, my sweetheart," Rebecca told the spirit. "Do you not recognise your home?"

I apologise, Sarah then wrote, **yet**, **I recall nothing before catching that book the strange man threw. Why can you not hear me?**

The shock of reconciling with her daughter only to find the poor girl had no memory of her life nearly sent Rebecca into a new, dark spiral. Until David Sutcliffe duly pointed out to her, "the memory loss may just be temporary as part of the payment due Lord Clauneck for the deal struck to get Sarah to appear."

His logic made as much sense as anything else going on of late to Rebecca. So, she decided to devote as much time as possible trying to get her daughter to remember who she was. Alas, after nearly a decade of trying, Sarah's memories failed to return. Rebecca spent most of those fast years floating between her new home of Clifford Manor and visiting Broughton Road where she spent her days chatting to the dead and not actually living herself. During this time, the house changed from a three-storey house to a two-storey flat with a disused ground floor.

Then, in 1754 as Thomas Pelham-Holles took over as Prime Minister after the death of his brother, Henry Pelham, and corruption ran free in politics, Lord Clauneck appeared to The Thirteen in their dreams.

"The time approaches for a meeting. Prepare to summon me on the evening of the equinox. I have news."

The next day, the nervous Thirteen began their rituals. All abstaining from sex and red meat until the day of the ceremony.

During this time, Sarah surprised Rebecca by recalling certain events.

"Mama, I have enjoyed many strange visions of late," Sarah told her days before Lord Clauneck's visit.

"Visions, my sweet?" Rebecca asked as the rains splattered against the lounge window.

"Yes, they were too vivid to be mere dreams. They almost felt like memories."

Rebecca laid down her sewing needles. "Do tell, beautiful child."

"I remember a chilly night. We were all dressed in our thickest wools and sat out in a frosty field to watch the magic of the falling stars. You were there, Mama. Papa too, surrounded by Matthew and Kate and Jonathon and we sat in awe."

"YES," Rebecca cried. "Yes. It is a memory, my sweet child. We watched the meteor shower every year. You adored the event, my love. What else can you recall?"

"I remember a tiny lady with a limp who wore a tight bun upon her grey head and always smiled the kindest smile. She took me foraging for flowers and fungi."

"That will be Great Granny Bess," Rebecca sobbed.

"Why do you cry, Mama. Have I upset you?"

"No. No. Not at all, my sweet, Sarah. These are tears of happiness. I have cherished every extra minute with you and now my heart bursts that you may truly be coming home. This could be why his lordship wishes a meeting."

That night Rebecca returned to Clifford Manor and gathered all around her to express her fantastic news. Seeing their leader and matriarch's easy smile and glistening eyes sparkle for the first time in a decade fed the souls of everyone. They celebrated long into the night.

From that evening until the 20th of March, Rebecca and The Thirteen floated on air as every day Sarah recalled a new memory of picnics and warm summers, of snowball fights in the freezing winter to swimming in the steam as the flowers bloomed. So confident were they that his lordship would bring good news, they carried no nerves as they prepared for his arrival. His wide, confident smile as he strode out of the misty mirror only added to their calm state.

"Good evening, fine friends," Clauneck announced, arms out wide. "I trust you fare well?"

"We do, my lord," they replied in unison.

"Good. Good. I expect a fresh supply of gold and silver

will not go amiss, eh?" Clauneck sniggered. The Thirteen smiled back. "Loving the new abode, by the way. Most swish. Better than those horrific rooms in which I first found you, eh?"

"Yes, my lord?" The Thirteen replied. "We give thanks."

"So, I expect you may wonder why I asked you to summon me this night of equals. Well," he strode back and forth as he spoke, his arms now clasped behind his back. "It turns out the dear, old white-lighter upstairs is ready for another soul to show his boss how much of a good boy he is." He stopped talking but continued to stride as if waiting for the crux of his visit to strike home. It soon did.

"My lord?" Rebecca asked, fear filling the space between the words. "Another soul?"

"Yes, that is what I said, my dear."

"But does that soul mean my Sarah, my lord?" The happy red that once filled her cheeks was now replaced with the white of anaemia as the blood drained into her feet.

"I'm afraid it is exactly what it means, my dear. I am sorry. But you have had an extra ten years more than any other fool would. So, cherish that, if nothing else."

Chapter Five

Rebecca lay in her super king-sized four-poster bed, the finery of a bought life surrounding her. The silent tears flowed down her cheeks to well in the space between neck and clavicle. She wanted more time with her daughter.

"I will gift you three weeks to find the next soul, as you all should have prepared for this moment the second after the last ceremony," Clauneck had told The Thirteen the night before when he dropped the terrible dark cloud over Rebecca's joy.

"What if we are unable to find a willing soul, my lord?" David Sutcliffe asked, fearing the answer.

"Then, I'm afraid you will have received your last penny from my coffers, my good sir, and will have to pay a hefty forfeit for breaking your contracts."

An audible gasp swept twelve of The Thirteen.

Despite the finery around her, Rebecca already cared little for the riches. She wished for more time with Sarah and no amount of shiny currency replaced such joy.

As the grey, wet morning arrived and Emily, the maid, entered to prepare the fire, Rebecca cleansed her face and created a mask of serenity to hide the pain inside. Hoping, if she fooled the staff and the members of The Thirteen living in the manor, Sarah wouldn't detect her misery either. The last thing Rebecca wanted was to mar her final weeks with her daughter.

Her attempt failed.

Mama, why do I sense pain emanating from your soul this day? Sarah wrote as soon as Rebecca entered 67A's first floor lounge.

"I'm sure you are mistaken, my child," Rebecca replied, feigning a wide smile that only added to the grief.

But, I can see it? Something ails you.

"The only thing that ails me, sweet child, is that I cannot wrap my arms around you as a mother loves to do." They had tried to hug several times over the last few weeks since Sarah's memories had returned. It never ended well. "Let us veer away from such longing and talk of new memories you might have remembered."

And that is what they did. For two and a half weeks, each day Rebecca arrived with new masks; Sarah, however, saw through each, so Rebecca steered her daughter to chatter of her past life. Each day passed like a minute, each week an hour. Every night, Rebecca lay in her golden bed and cried. Those times dragged like an old man pulling a cart across a bog.

Until, three nights before the ceremony for the new soul, as the clock in the hall rang four in the morning, a wild idea struck Rebecca. A plan so solid, his lordship would surely bow with pleasure. A proposal that would allow Rebecca to have Sarah in her arms and satisfy the deal. Her mind swam with such a stupendous strategy, she could not understand how she missed it before that hour. To succeed, she would need to visit familiar fields for supplies long since dry from lack of use. The hours between her joyous notion and the light of day again dragged with her eagerness to begin.

At eight, with the sun brightening the fields around the house and the clouds fleeing to the north to leave a clear sky, Rebecca ate a quick breakfast of kedgeree and left for Burrstone with a packed lunch, a flask of water, a small garden fork and several glass phials. At nine-thirty she hopped out of the carriage and bolted up the stairs to the first floor of 67A Broughton Road. There she found Sarah.

You seem happier today, Mama. This pleases me, Sarah scribbled.

"I am, my sweet. I believe I have developed a way for you and me to hug. But first I have to spend the day collecting the correct herbs and powders. Sadly, because I need to travel many miles there and back, I will not be able to spend much of the day with you today. Yet, I wished to see you to explain. If I am back in time, I will pop back in. Else, I will visit tomorrow. I love you with all my heart," Rebecca said and shed one tear. This time borne from joy.

She soon left and began the seventeen-mile ride to old haunts.

"It's such a pity," she mumbled to herself as she inhaled in the sweet smells of spring. "Sarah would love to see the places from her growing memories."

"Sorry, milady?" Parsons, the kindly, ginger-haired driver asked.

"Nothing. You caught me thinking aloud." Rebecca turned her attention to the fauna and flora. Whether hare or daisy, all appeared to smile as if moved by a new positive conductor. Ahead, she saw the imposing feature of Pendle Hill, sitting like an upended keel of a large war vessel. It almost sang of her lost home. She sighed and cast her eyes back to the verge of the potholed track, searching for one of the ingredients to the dwale she would take to join her beloved Sarah. "Stop, please, Parsons," she called after a few minutes.

"Woah," Parsons called out to the two chestnut horses as he reined them in.

Rebecca slipped out of her seat and began inspecting the flora. Satisfied she had found the amount of hemlock she needed, she rushed back to the trap for her gardening gloves, a knife and a large leather pouch and returned to the hemlock standing like a terrible imposter to the bushier, yet similar, elderflower bush next to it. She sniggered as she heard Granny Bess' croaky voice telling the story of Witless Winnie.

"The clodpate of a child decided one summer day to make Elderflower wine to impress a boy called William. A boy of good looks but similarly challenged in the mind. She trumped out one sunny morn' with a sack and a knife to collect the flowers. However, in either her ignorance or eagerness, the nincompoop plucked the flowers from the hemlock, took them home, brewed them and killed the asshat of a boy and most of her kin."

"Is it so hard to tell the difference, Granny?" A young Rebecca asked.

"Not at all, sweet child. One, the elder, grows in bushes and does not flower the umber shaped leaves. The hemlock grows much higher stalks. Sometimes higher than most men. Its hairless stalks are stained with droplets of the blood of those fat-kidneyed enough to pluck and swallow the devil's parsley."

With another smile at the memory, Rebecca returned with a full pouch to Parsons. Her mind already fixed on the next ingredient: henbane.

"Good lady?" A cultured male voice behind her asked.

Rebecca turned to face a filthy vagabond who in no way suited his voice. "Yes?" She asked.

"Might I trouble you for a cup of water and a conversation? It's been some time since I have conversed with someone of such radiance in these dark times." The man asked.

"I can offer you the water, but I have little time for chitchat, I'm afraid." Rebecca replied. "Parsons, could you prepare a cup of water for this gentleman, please."

"Yes, milady," Parsons replied, finding it difficult to hide his distaste. He looked down and rummaged inside a pack between his legs

"It may be in your best interest to take two minutes, my lady," the vagabond said with a slight nod. Parsons hopped down from the trap with a full mug and handed it to the vagabond. "My eternal thanks, young man." Parsons frowned as if confused before returning in a fog to his seat. "Now it is just we two," the vagabond smiled, sipped the cup, grimaced, handed it to Rebecca, and stretched his arms with a cunning smile. Seconds later, stunned, she understood why. As the vagabond stretched, his mask fell away to reveal Lord Clauneck grinning underneath. "Worry not; dear old, conceited Parsons will remember nothing except arriving home in a few hours with you by his side."

"But, I have things to…"

"Do?" Clauneck cut in. "Do you think I would not see your bent plan before you even set it in motion like a broken cartwheel? Tut-tut."

"But I must be with my Sarah, your lordship," Rebecca wailed, her eyes welling with tears. "I must."

"As any mother worth her soul would want, my dear. However, you signed a contract and sweet, little Sarah's time on this plane is almost over. If another soul is not there to replace her by the time the Seraph calls, you and the whole of The Thirteen will lose more than just shiny things in your life, my lovely magpie. You will all lose everything." His voice turned colder than a winter's night without timber to burn.

"Could I not be the one to replace Sarah and then one day be by her side, my lord?" Rebecca pleaded.

Clauneck sniggered before asking, "Are you a good soul, child? Would the do-gooder welcome you with wide arms into the halls of the deluded and weak?"

"I would like to think so, my lord?"

"We all would rather like to think so, my child. Yet, you bow to me. Not a tick in their spotless, pathetic books, I'm afraid."

"But Sire…"

"But, Sire, nothing. And you can save your tears. They are as pointless as the holy sacrament to me."

"But…"

"Now stop it." Clauneck said with a cold firmness that clamped her tongue. "Be warned, I never give second chances. That said, I see something in your Thirteen. A fortuitous longevity that will benefit all. Although, only if we all follow the plan and do not allow base sentimentality to guide us down the wrong path. And believe me, for the sake of the rest of your kin, you do not want to step on the wrong path. Do you understand me, mortal?" He asked with unambiguous menace.

Rebecca nodded and lowered her head. For the first time since Sarah's passing, Rebecca saw how the lives of the others sat in her hand. "How long before another soul is needed, my lord?" She asked, resigned to her fate.

"Worry not. I have the ideal soul. However, you will have to say your goodbyes to Sarah as the young lady will move into the house on Broughton Road in three days." Clauneck told Rebecca, softening his voice.

"How does this lady know about the house, my lord?" Rebecca asked, aghast.

"I have acolytes in many areas across the world, my child. I ordered the house advertised for rent some time ago. Others then vet the prospective renter's past and present."

"Is she from Burrstone, my lord?"

"Now that would be the definition of ridiculous, child. No. She is not even from Yorkshire. As you will come to learn, utilise and understand, each soul should come from far afield and have no other to miss them when they pass."

"Please, excuse my ignorance, my lord, but why does the soul need to occupy the house for a time before the Angel takes them onwards?"

"Angel?" Clauneck scoffed. "What an infantile term, as the soul will come to see." He cackled for a moment before saying, "This *angel* needs time to arrange things at their end. The despot the seraph serves must not find out or the whole deal between me, them, and The Thirteen would surely collapse. That is why you must never place a person inside the house who others will miss and avoid locals as much as possible. Also, and remember this, the time in between the person taking residence and its soul taking custodianship needs to pass a while or the locals will grow suspicious. Let them make up their myths and stories. However, if too short a time passes those stories will turn into questions. Do you understand?"

"Yes, my lord."

Part Three

Chapter One

"And so, the never-ending cycle began," Stofferson concluded.

"So, you're telling me for hundreds of years, the estate agency, founded by Daniel's ancestors, have enticed people here to replace a ghost who shuffles off, guided by a dodgy angel who wants to keep his quota of good souls up to impress the almighty, who is also in partnership with the demon of wealth?" Lydia asked with a cynical smile that hid her worry.

"Don't forget the wealth the estate agency and countless others on Clauneck's payroll receive."

"But it doesn't make sense," Lydia dismissed. "To what end?"

"There isn't an end where eternity lies." Stofferson shrugged. "I know it sounds ridiculous, but I've followed every clue given me, and now I'm here, inside this flat, with the latest Custodian attempting to twirl a pen."

"What first pushed you to look into this place?" Michael asked. Not noticing he now held the pen in steady hands.

"I'd heard rumours on the paranormal grapevine that this place was haunted and did a little piece for my show. Sometime later, I received an email from a man called Lord Markham asking me to visit him in a folly his great-grandfather built. The strangest building I've ever visited. Anyway, I met him a few weeks before you died…

"Nice place you have here?" Stofferson called down the long dining table.

"Please, come closer. My eyes and ears aren't what they once were," Markham croaked back. His old, milky eyes seemed to dance within the flickering candlelight. Stofferson did as the Lord bade, resisting the urge to touch the skins hanging like trophies on the wall. "Please take a seat. And before you ask, I don't think they're real. Although, where they came from, or who made them, I haven't the faintest idea. Would you like a drink or something to eat?"

"I'm fine, thanks." Stofferson replied and pulled a metal flask from his coat. "I have trouble with my stomach and can only handle filtered water. What is the purpose of this castle?" He tried not to stare at the bloodstains flowering the elderly gentleman's cream suit, indicating a man riddled with cancerous sores.

"It's a folly. Unlike many follies, though, a person can live inside it. However, it's not really fit for anything but a macabre museum. There's no running water or electricity, you see. Now, to the reason I asked to see you. Because we must be quick as great danger will surely await me for telling you the following. What do you know of Broughton Road?"

"There are rumours of paranormal phenomena," Stofferson shrugged. "Just rumours, I'm afraid. As I, nor any other investigator, has entered the place."

"Have you petitioned the owners?"

"At present, the estate agents involved with the sale won't give the name of the owner."

"Greyson, Sutcliffe and Milner?"

"The same. Have you dealt with them?"

"You might say that," Markham said with a sardonic smile. "What do you know of The Thirteen?"

"Again, only rumours," Stofferson replied. "Some say they are one of many who have made a deal with Clauneck, though nobody knows who they are or where they are based."

"And what deal does the rumour mill say The Thirteen struck with the demon of wealth?" Markham asked before taken with a wracking cough so intense it took him a moment and a good full glass of water to still.

"Going back to your earlier question," Stofferson began, "Rumours have ranged from souls to blood pacts."

"One is correct. There are other groups who deal in blood but not The Thirteen. They have set up charms around Broughton Road to not only trap a soul but also to make the new owner suffer suicidal thoughts whenever The Thirteen decide a new soul is needed for their despicable Lord."

"I'm not buying that," Lydia scoffed. "I can go with the whole trapped soul business, Michael is almost a testament to that, but suicidal thoughts whenever they want? Nobody can do that. And believe me, if anyone would feel suicidal, especially after the shit I've gone through, then it wouldn't take much. But, I've been fine."

"They may have decided to not invoke the spell yet." Stofferson shrugged.

"So, I'm supposed to wait, biting my nails, before they do it, am I?" Lydia asked. "And saying the estate agents are this Thirteen is ridiculous. Surely there's been some sort of investigation into all those suicides. Come on. Maybe this Markham is just some eccentric who's messing with you or has some complaint against the estate agency and wants trouble for them."

"Oh, he definitely has some complaint against them." Stofferson told Lydia.

"And what's that? Did he buy his weird house and they said it had running water?" Lydia scowled.

"No. His great-great grandparents were none other than the Milners."

"But that makes even less sense," Lydia insisted. "Why would a member of The Thirteen run the risk of pissing off a demon by telling you?"

"Because he never joined them."

"Then…" Lydia began before Stofferson cut her off.

"Allow me to finish, please, Lydia," Stofferson said. Lydia shrugged. "Markham's father, a prominent member of the coven, sent his son to the best prep and finishing schools, earning him an envious education…"

"If you ignore the buggery and loneliness," Lydia said with a contemptuous sneer.

"Yes, if you ignore all that, he received an excellent education in which he shined. Then, at the age of eighteen, just before he entered Oxford, his father summoned him and explained the reason for their success and wealth in the hope of standing him in line for the next place in The Thirteen's coven. Markham, wise enough to know he needed his father's wealth to help him through university life, said he would graduate first, so as to have a solid background, and then enter the coven afterwards."

"Sorry," Michael said, "But what is an Oxford and a university?"

"Oxford University is one of the oldest and most respectable higher education schools," Stofferson told Michael. "Where men and women go to learn."

"Thanks," Michael replied.

"So, after university, did Markham join them?" Lydia asked.

"No. He joined an even worse coven," Stofferson told her.

"An even worse one?" Michael asked. "What could be worse?"

"The government," Stofferson smiled. "And before you ask, Michael, the government is the ruling house of the country. Full of liars and thieves."

"Oh, I know that one," Michael told him. "One of the builders, Figgy, hated the government. He called them a lot worse names than thieves and liars, believe me."

"So, Markham went into politics. What did his father do?" Lydia asked.

"Well, at first, his father thought it a great opportunity for The Thirteen. Having someone within the walls of parliament gave them all sorts of new avenues. However, Markham, showing surprisingly more soul than most politicians, didn't want his future endeavours tainted by demon worship. In his words, he found the whole sordid business despicable. So, he turned his back on the family wealth and set out, with his new contacts, on his own."

"Why didn't he expose The Thirteen, if he was so good?" Lydia asked.

"Because, as a child, he had snuck from his bed to watch The Thirteen and saw Clauneck with his own fearful eyes and heard what The Thirteen did to the innocent. He knew, if he told the world what he learned, his life would mean nothing."

"Then, why now?" Michael asked.

"Because he's dying, Michael," Stofferson replied. "Riddled with cancers. And now, though he knows the danger, he doesn't fear death quite so much. He figures the pain he may receive from the demon lord cannot be any worse than the horrors he already suffers. He decided he wanted to assuage his guilt by passing on the information before the cancer finally took him."

"Do you believe he has cancer?" Lydia asked. "I mean, what if he's just a fraud with a grievance."

"Oh, sadly, he is, as I said, riddled. I saw the bloodstains from the many sores staining his clothes. And he carries a certain smell not to have wrinkled my nose since my dearest grandma passed from the horrific disease."

"I'm sorry to hear that, Stofferson," Lydia said.

"So am I," Michael added.

"You would've liked her," Stofferson told Lydia with a wistful smile. "She had the same grit as you."

"Do you want a cup of tea?" Lydia asked, following a longstanding British convention whenever sorrow enters a room.

"That would be lovely. Plus, we could do with a break," Stofferson replied.

"Just the one sugar for me please," Michael said with a grin.

"So, where do we go from here?" Michael asked as the two with flesh sipped their hot teas.

Stofferson simply offered Lydia a glance as if to say the answer lay with her.

"I'm sorry. Stofferson, but this all seems tenuous at best. You don't know what medication this Markham is on for his cancer. If he's as riddled as you say he is, he could be high as a kite. I mean, why would a little town's estate agency use this inconspicuous flat to store souls for a deal done between the demon of wealth and some dodgy angel."

"It's probably only one deal they've done with the demon. And if Markham is speaking the truth, there's a huge conspiracy of deals between the demon and his worshippers spread across the globe," Stofferson said.

"You see," Lydia began, "It's all probables and ifs. Nothing concrete. I mean what do you plan to do with this information? Do you want me to sell the flat and then watch as someone else, who may be suicidal, comes in so you can then say you were right all along? It's just all a bit silly. Sorry."

"I agree, I have some more digging to do to turn those doubts into certainties, but you can't tell me you don't suspect something surreal going on here?" Stofferson asked.

"Look, get me an interview with Markham, I'll do some digging on my side, and we'll see. But for now, the only surreal thing, and please don't take this the wrong way, Michael, is that I share a flat with a ghost."

"None taken," Michael shrugged. "Though I do prefer to be called a person unburdened by flesh."

"A little bit of a mouthful," Lydia sniggered.

"Yes. The only flaw," Michael laughed back.

"Okay," Stofferson said, downing his tea as if it was cold, "I will correspond with Markham and do some more digging. I'll also leave you the ghost box so you can talk to our friend unburdened by flesh. But, please call me straight away if you feel changes in mood or anything strange occurs. Yes?"

"Yes." Lydia replied.

"Don't worry," Michael added, "I'll keep an eye out."

Stofferson left minutes later after packing up his equipment and reiterating his warning to Lydia. Exhausted, Lydia waved him off from the doorstep. As she turned to re-enter the house, though, something strange caught her eye. A plump, elderly lady in a flowery dress stood further up the road armed with an open pad and biro. She appeared to scribble a note as Stofferson drove away. Lydia frowned towards the woman. The woman, catching the look, skittered away up a side street of terraced houses.

"I've seen a woman looking how you describe once or twice. I remember seeing her on the night those burglars came. She had a pad and pen then too," Michael told Lydia after she ran upstairs and told him about the woman.

"Damn," Lydia scowled, "She must be the employee Daniel spoke about."

"But why keep an eye on you? Maybe Stofferson's right."

"Oh, don't you bloody well start with all that."

"I'm not starting, but it does make me wonder."

"Well, maybe I'll go see the estate agent and ask him face to face."

"Maybe you should."

So, she did. An hour later she entered the luxuriance of the agency's office, determined to clear the whole thing up.

"Miss Richardson, how are we?" Daniel called from the back before striding with confidence towards her. She noted how perfectly fitted his Savoy blue suit was and how much such a garment would cost.

"A little bit pissed off, if I am honest," Lydia snapped, cursing herself silently. Because all the way to town she had practiced calm.

"I'm sorry to hear that. Is the flat not what you expected?" Daniel asked, his voice remaining syrup-serene.

"There's nothing wrong with the flat. It's the old woman you're using as a spy. And for having a bloody spy in the first place."

"Woah, we don't employ spies, Miss Richardson, never mind elderly women."

"You said yourself a work colleague reported the burglary."

"And I didn't lie," Daniel admitted and turned about face before calling, "Jenny, can I have a word?"

A tall bottle-blond with legs Lydia imagined kissing forever stepped forward. "Yes, Daniel?" Jenny asked in a silky voice that matched her legs and made Lydia's stomach flutter.

"Is this the lady you saw spying on you, Miss Richardson?" Daniel asked.

"Well, no. The other lady was frumpy and wore a flowery dress," Lydia replied.

"Did she have a large, shabby Harrod's bag?" Jenny simpered.

"Now you come to mention it, she may have had one dangling from her hidden arm."

"Mrs Trumpton," Jenny giggled. "I live up the road from you, four doors. She lives around the corner on Sarson Drive. She's harmless but a bit strange. Did she have her pad and pen handy?"

"Well, yes," Lydia said, feeling her cheeks heat up out of embarrassment.

"Biiiiig trainspotter is Mrs Trumpton, and not quite right in the head, bless her. If anyone looks at her, she scuttles off. I wouldn't worry about her," Jenny told Lydia with the kind of smile that could undo a bra from forty metres. Lydia's cheeks felt even hotter. Now more out of lust than embarrassment.

"So, have we cleared that up for you?" Daniel asked without any apparent condescension.

"I feel so stupid," Lydia told them. "Someone told me a ridiculous story and I put six and twelve together and arrived at three hundred. I'm sorry to you both."

"Hey," Daniel hushed and stroked her arm. "No harm done. I like the fact that you don't beat around the bush, Miss Richardson. If you have a problem or something to say, you say it. The world needs more people like you."

"Please call me Lydia."

"Lydia it is," Daniel smiled. "Out of interest, who's been filling your head?"

"It doesn't matter now. All silliness. Anyway, sorry for barging in. Thank you. Goodbye," Lydia said. Nerves jangling, she almost stumbled out of the office in her rush to leave.

Back in the estate agency, Daniel watched Lydia pass the large front window and stroked his chin in thought. "I get the impression you won her over, J. You wouldn't mind reassuring her with an impromptu bottle of wine one night, would you?"

"Why not?" Jenny smiled. "Might be fun. What about the storyteller? He must be getting his information from somewhere other than books."

"Leave that with me." Daniel said in almost a whisper.

Chapter Two

Meanwhile, inside the castle of skulls, Lord Markham shuffled to the back of the dining room to a long oak bookcase. He groaned with the pain throbbing through his old, bent frame as he reached to pull a large leatherbound book entitled, *120 Days of Sodom* by Marquis de Sade. The book tipped and a latch clicked before the section of books Markham faced slid open to reveal a small room. His great-great grandfather once used the space, circular in shape, as a summoning room. Now it housed a cot bed; a desk with a pill caddy sitting on top; full to the brim with tablets of all shapes and sizes; a diary; an old Dictaphone; an alarm clock; several bottles of fresh water; tea brewing equipment; and several chocolate mousses. A stained mirror with a gold edge reflected the room from above the bed. Markham picked up the Dictaphone and clicked it to record.

"I must prepare some defences for tomorrow's guest. I fear the last ones have run their course." Markham said and checked his watch. Time for more pills. He pocketed the Dictaphone and grunted as the clock clanged into life as he dragged himself to the desk. "I beat you to it," he growled and turned off the alarm. He opened one of the caddy's compartments and emptied ten tablets into his quivering palm. "Is this what my life meant?" he croaked before shovelling the pills into his mouth. A mouthful of cool water followed. He always hoped he would choke, yet never did. Although this time, with news of another visit from Irving Stofferson in the morning, he only wished it with half a heart. Markham had suffered another day of slipping in and out of sleep when his housekeeper, Mrs Williams, woke him to inform him of Stofferson's visit, giving him a purpose.

"You had a purpose, you stinking offal," A voice he had not heard since childhood growled into his ears. Markham turned his head and body as fast as possible. The room contained only him.

"The pills," he told himself. "It's only the pills."

"You wish, you ungrateful, little weasel," The voice cackled. "You had the world in your hand and preferred to trade with the dead on the waves of the eternal sea. But, we know your secret."

"It's just the pills," Markham insisted, his voice whining. He rushed over to the mirror, as if facing himself would stop the voice. What he found made him regret the decision. The ghoul in the glass stared back at him with frightened eyes. Patches of skin hung loose where his sallow cheeks should sit. Mucus dribbled from his partially-severed left ear. He screamed and touched his cheeks. His rotting fingers passed through the fetid flesh so that they felt his warm, wet tongue beyond. "Aaarggh!" he hollered again. He gagged, turned from the nightmare image, and rushed as fast as his unstable legs could carry him towards the exit.

"You can't leave, old boy," the voice sneered as Markham crashed into the corner of the dining table. "We have your room ready down here."

"Please, this isn't real," Markham pleaded as he dragged himself down the table towards the entrance. The candles, once dancing, now shot up to the ceiling with soaring, ferocious flames.

"Oh, Jonny, it's real. As real as the naughty vice we know you loved when once you could get a reaction from the little lord. And now it hangs as useless as its owner."

"I don't…know what you're…talking about," Markham said through gasps of air.

"Of course, you do, you filthy child," The voice cackled. "You know very well what I mean. I bet you acted all innocent and wise to the writer, didn't you?"

"I don't know…what you mean."

"Liar, liar, their bums were on fire," the voice cackled.

Markham reached the end of the table and looked towards the entrance. He groaned in anticipation as the door crept open. A heavy buzzing played beyond. Markham screwed up his eyes as the sound grew louder…and louder. His own internal voice became lost over the rising cacophony. And then its creators arrived. A thousand locusts shot through the entrance and swarmed upon him. He cowered and raised his arms across his face. The locusts gnawed at any available cell of his skin. Markham screamed in pain and fury. He knew if he stood still, they would bring him to his bony knees, so he pushed through the furious cloud of insects and reached for a candle before waving left and right. Most of them retreated from the light. Yet, many continued to nip his skin. Markham pushed on towards the entrance. As he stumbled into the hall, the sound and sight of the locusts disappeared as if never having arrived.

"Still kept your keen mind, Jonathon, eh?" The voice sneered. "Grabbing a candle was a smart move for a drug-addled pervert."

"I'm…not a…" the words of protest stuck in Markham's throat as a gold and black Egyptian sarcophagus stored in a glass cabinet by the main entrance fell open with a boom, and then a smash as the glass case shattered, covering the floor.

"Pity you weren't closer, Jonny. This portion of the nightmare may have ended if that landed on you. Ah well, still more to come. You better run before your mummy comes." Markham groaned as a searing pain shot from his chest and down his arm. "Don't you die now. That would be sooooo naughty. We have some sightseeing to do first. Now…RUN!"

The evil intent enveloped in one three letter word pushed Markham forward, just as the sarcophagus' owner's rotting carcass fell towards him. Its right arm grabbed his upper arm. Markham yanked with all his worth. The grip was surprisingly strong. Markham pulled again. The arm came away from the corpse and just hung, still gripping his upper arm. Screeching, the old lord staggered, chest on fire, away from the corpse's left hand as it snaked forward and fell towards the main entrance. He didn't know how much more he could take. The stench of the corpse receded. But only for a moment. As Markham struggled to unlock the front door, the aroma of death grew closer once again.

"For the love of God…" Markham pleaded, "Please… open."

"He's coming to get you," The voice cackled in a sing-song way.

Markham felt the smell filling his nose and gag his mouth as the mummy dragged itself ever closer. It's amputated right arm appeared to grip Markham tighter as if warning him of worse to come. Markham held his breath and opened the door before falling out onto the front step and the rainstorm beyond. The arm fell away, twitching. The howling wind and needle-like rain refreshed him for only a moment. The violence of both soon made him shiver like a like a rice-paper building in a high wind.

"I wouldn't stay there, pervert," the voice sneered over the weather. "You might want to keep moving. Hypothermia is a real danger to the dead."

"Why are you doing this?" Markham sobbed.

"Because, we left you to go your own way, against my better judgment, and look how that turned out."

"But, I didn't do anything," Markham pleaded.

"You told the writer everything about The Thirteen. And that's rather discourteous, Jonny. Not acceptable at all."

"I didn't say anything," Markham cried and stumbled around the corner of the building to the east side where he face-planted the grass. His consciousness soon faded, leaving him floating in a fear and pain free void as the songs of the skulls sang their dreadful song into his ears…until…

"Hello?" a sweet, young, concerned voice asked. "Are you okay?"

Markham wished the voice would walk on by. He did not want to leave his comfort bubble when reality carried so much pain.

"Can you hear me?" The young lady's voice asked above the thrashing rain, howling wind and song of death. "Here, sip this."

Markham felt warm arms lift him to a seated position before soon placing a flask cup of steaming tea to his quivering lips. With the warmth came the terrible pain. "Please don't," Markham pleaded, desperately wanting the void to take him once more.

"You need to drink," the girl insisted. Markham looked into her eyes, her warm blue eyes and sipped, despite his defeatist judgement. "That's better. Isn't it?" the girl simpered. Markham, lost in her gaze nodded and sipped more hot goodness.

As the tea warmed his insides, he noticed the girl had wrapped a blanket around his shoulders. "Thank you," he whispered.

"No need," she replied. "It's just lucky I was passing on my way to the campsite. You shouldn't be out in this without a coat. Do you live here?" Markham nodded. "It's a strange place. Did you build it?"

"No, It's my family's."

"Right. Now you've warmed up a little, let's get you inside, eh?"

"No!" Markham cried, fearful of what waited inside. "I can't. Someone's trying to hurt me."

"Seriously? Well, let's get you somewhere safe." The girl took the cup from Markham, packed it as fast as she could, lifted a pack onto her back and helped Markham on to his feet. "Phew, you're heavier than you look," she whispered as Markham stood quivering. "Come on, we'll follow the cliffside. It's not far to the site. What's your name? I'm Jess."

"J-Jonathan Markham," he stammered as they staggered north. He cast a fearful look behind but whatever chased him seemed to have given up.

"Not *the* Jonathon Markham, as in Lord Markham, MP?" the girl asked, excited.

The song of the skulls began to fade as they moved on into the darkness and followed the trail of the girl's torch.

"Yes," Markham simply stated.

"Oh my God," the girl exclaimed, "I love you. I'm studying politics at uni'."

"Really? I studied it too."

"I know. You're the reason why I'm doing it. You should've been Prime Minister in my opinion."

Markham felt his chest swell at such kind words. "I'm not sure I would have..."

"Are you kidding? The way you fought against those child prostitution rings was amazing."

"But, I can't take all the credit and there was so much more we should have done," Markham told her, the guilt of a shadow life weighing heavy on his shoulders alongside the dripping blanket.

"What? You're a legend. An absolute legend. I can't believe I'm even talking to you." The girl's infectious manner lifted Markham. He felt taller and stronger. Her words almost made him drop thirty years and the flesh-eating cancers. "If I'd known you lived here, I would have visited before now. You are a god to me."

"Well, I wouldn't say that, my dear," Markham replied, his chin now pointing to the sky. He hadn't felt as good since...well...too damned long.

"I would. I bet you could reshape this world if you still wanted. I bet you could shake up the whole shitty system."

"Well, in fact I am trying to help a chap shake up the world, as you say," Markham told her, his pride now running his tongue. "Just the other day, the chap visited and I told him exactly what needs doing."

"Really?" Jess asked, wide-eyed.

It struck Markham for a split-second that her eyes glowed even when the torch pointed away from her face, but his old hubris now ran his logic, so he let it pass and said, "Why, yes. The corrupt will rue the day."

"I bet they will," another voice, the voice who chased him earlier, said with a cold sneer. Lord Clauneck, towering and frightening with his true guise visible, stepped out of the darkness. “Allow me to introduce my old friend and colleague, Ose. He’s a cheeky minx, is he not?”

“Ose?” Markham whispered, his bowels and bladder ready to empty. He turned from Clauneck to see him usher the girl forward. Her blue eyes turned to flame red. “You are like a god to me,” Ose mocked before pushing Markham over the edge of the cliff to fall to his death on the rocks below. It all happened so fast; he did not even have time to scream.

Chapter Three

Lydia and Michael sat in the front room of the flat watching history documentaries. The idea crossed Lydia's mind soon after Stofferson had left the previous day.

"It may help you dredge up some of those lost memories," she told her roommate.

"Do you think it will work?" Michael asked, excited to find out.

"We're not losing anything by trying," Lydia shrugged.

So, they sat through an array of documentaries from World War Two, Music Through the Ages, and even one regarding UFO sightings. If truth be told, Lydia enjoyed such documentaries whether or not they manifested a past life for Michael. They, however, sparked nothing in his memory. If they weren't watching television, she showed him how to use the various gadgets around the house. She even bought a second telephone for him to call her if he needed her while out.

And even though she knew he floated in a divide between her world and the next, it still unnerved Lydia when Michael dropped the ball of tape he had grown attached to and disappeared.

"Sorry," he said after each occasion. "I get a little tired."

"It's funny, I still don't expect you to become tired. Though, I suppose like any form, fleshy or not, it must take energy to keep you going."

"I've never thought of it like that," Michael admitted.

A series of knocks on the main door stopped him thinking any more about it. Noting the look of concern on Lydia's face, Michael rushed over to the window, dropping the ball as not to be seen, and peered down to the street.

"It's a pretty lady with a bottle of something," his voice informed her from the ghost box.

"What does she look like?" Lydia asked, hoping to God that Julia hadn't found her.

"From what I can see, she's blond and looks quite tall."

"Is her hair tied up or loose?"

"Loose and wavy, I think they call it?"

Too intrigued to stop herself, and knowing a woman with wavy hair could not be her worst nightmare, Lydia rushed to the window and looked down just as the lady looked up and waved.

"It's okay," she sighed, "It's a lady from the estate agency."

"Why would she come here?"

"Only one way to find out?" Lydia shrugged and jogged out of the room and downstairs.

"Hi," Jenny said with a huge, gorgeous smile that made Lydia a little giddy inside. "Sorry to drop by unannounced, but I should have done this days ago when I saw the police car. Welcome to the road." She offered the wine.

"That's really kind of you. Thank you," Lydia said and took the bottle. "Do you want to come in?"

"Are you sure I'm not bothering you?"

"No, please." Lydia stepped aside to allow Jenny entry

before stealing a quick look at her behind. Shapely in the tight jeans. *Stop it,* she told herself, closing the door. "Go on up," Lydia told Jenny and followed her up.

"So, what do you think of our little town?" Jenny asked with a quick glance over her shoulder.

"So far, it seems lovely. Attacks and attempted burglaries aside."

"That's very rare. I'm sorry you had to go through that."

"It could've been worse."

"Have the police found them yet?" Jenny asked as they entered the lounge.

"They haven't said. Do you want a glass now?"

"Why not?"

"You go make yourself comfortable and I'll grab us two glasses," Lydia looked at the bottle. "And a corkscrew. A classy girl, eh?"

"As long as I don't drink too much," Jenny grinned and turned to enter the lounge.

"Are you from Burrstone, Jenny?" Lydia asked from the kitchen.

"Born and bred."

Lydia plucked two glasses and the corkscrew from a cupboard. As she entered the lounge, she found Jenny hunkered down, inspecting the ghost box. Lydia noted it turned off and wondered if Michael had taken it upon himself to do so.

"What is this?" she asked when she saw Lydia. "Looks like it fell out of a UFO."

"Something a friend left with me. So, what's to do here?" Lydia asked to change the subject.

"We have a few pubs, restaurants and a nightclub," Jenny said as Lydia poured wine in her glass.

"Any good?"

"If you like cheesy pop and drunken teenagers."

"That good, eh?"

"Hmmmm. So, what brought you here?"

"Now that's a question," Lydia replied, unsure whether she wanted to go into something so painful on a first meeting. "Do you mind if we save that for another time?"

"So, there might be another time?" Jenny asked with a coy, well-rehearsed smile.

"There just might be, but I have to warn you, it will be slow. My last relationship wasn't nice."

"That's fine, Lydia," Jenny and patted Lydia's leg. "I understand. I've had some shits too. There's no rush."

"Thank you."

The conversation took a lighter tone before Jenny said, "There was another reason I wanted to come 'round…" she then paused as if trying to find the right words. "I didn't want you to think I was sent to spy on you because I told Daniel about that night with the police or the ghost fella."

"Why did you tell him?"

"I just mentioned the police thing when I got in the next day. You know, out of concern."

"What about Irving Stofferson?"

"Daniel asked me to keep an eye because we tried to sell this place a while ago and his stupid stories lost us a quick sale," Jenny explained. "Has he told you his strange ideas?"

"One or two," Lydia shrugged. "Some lord or other told him some horror stories that made no sense, so he's gone to try and get some sort of proof. All a bit weird, really."

"What sort of proof?" Jenny shuffled closer as she asked. This unnerved Lydia for reasons she couldn't highlight.

"Oh, a fantasy about this place. Don't worry about it."

Jenny didn't hang around for long after that. Although, she did linger at the door for a little while as if waiting for a kiss but did not push it. Following waving Jenny off, Lydia returned to the lounge and switched on the ghost machine.

"Michael?" She asked, looking towards the windowsill.

"Damn," his voice crackled, "you know exactly where to find me."

"You have your spot," Lydia smiled.

"That I do," Michael admitted.

"What do you think of Jenny?"

"I'm a little confused."

"Why?"

"Well, I can usually tell a person's mood by the colours surrounding them like a cloak, but her colours were a little contradictory."

"Really? What were her colours?"

"Well, she had plenty of bright, warm, reds, greens, blues and oranges, but now and again some or all would turn a little muddy looking. Normally, folk are either one or the other depending on whether they're happy, angry, ill, healthy and so on. But hers were one minute one and then another. I can't really work her out. Sorry."

"Not your fault. If you had to guess from seeing lots of people's colours', what would you say?"

"I'd say she sort of likes you but is covering something up. But, I could be wrong. I really haven't seen enough people to compare. Maybe she was nervous."

"What were mine?"

"You liked her but were nervous to let her in. Which is understandable after all you've been through with Julia."

"How do you know about Julia? Can you tell people's names from colours?"

"Noooo," Michael sniggered. "You spoke about her to your loud friend on the telephone."

"Sneaky," Lydia laughed.

"Well, it was before the ghost box and Stofferson. Why do you think he hasn't called, by the way?" Michael asked.

"I don't know," Lydia replied. "Maybe he's still busy trying to persuade the mad, old lord to talk to me."

Chapter Four

The sun shone and the sky smiled down upon Stofferson as he drove east for his meeting with Markham. Not a single cloud marred the sky. Mozart's Sonata No. 16 in C Major played sedately from the stereo as he pushed his Audi A3 along the narrow, winding hedge-lined road to Markham's folly. He thought about the time spent with Lydia and Michael, already plotting the first chapters of the next book. He knew with a name like Lord Markham attached, the publishers would take his hand off to get the book.

The piece of music changed from calm to jolly as the pianist's fingers jumped along the unseen keys, however, his mood changed in the opposite direction as he took a right turn and slowed down. The police cars and cordon ahead of him can do that to a calm mind. He slowed to a stop as a police constable waved her hands.

"I'm sorry, sir, nobody's allowed into the folly," she told Stofferson. Her eyes scanned his car as she spoke the words. Stofferson wondered if they practiced such behaviour in the police academy.

"I understand, Constable, but I have an appointment with his Lordship," Stofferson told her with a smile.

"Ah," the constable said as if finding the words with care, "Well, Lord Markham won't be accepting visitors today. Can I get your name?"

"Yes, certainly. My name is Irving Stofferson." Something in the way she spoke told Stofferson Lord Markham wasn't just too busy to see him.

"Give me a moment please, Mr Stofferson." The constable turned and walked away as she spoke into the mike on her shoulder. After a moment, she returned. "Sorry about that. I just needed to confirm you had an appointment. My inspector asked if you could wait for him to come down. He has one or two quick questions for you."

"No problem," Stofferson said. He watched her stroll back to her car as Pachelbel's Canon in D replaced Mozart and somehow the sombre first notes seemed appropriate to the circumstances. The next gentle strings calmed him of the many questions queuing up to poke and prod his mind. He closed his eyes and allowed the elegance to float through and over him.

"Mr Stofferson?" A gruff male voice, however, eventually cut through the calm. "Mr Irving Stofferson? I'm Inspector Carlisle."

Stofferson opened his eyes and said, "Nice to meet you, Inspector."

"You the writer fella?"

"The very same. Is Lord Markham okay?"

"Can I ask, before I reply to that, what your business with his Lordship was today?"

"We've been collaborating on an idea for a new book."

"Lord Markham was collaborating with a ghost hunter..."

"We prefer paranormal investigator, Inspector." Stofferson cut in with his best, winning smile.

"Either way, you're telling me a respected former politician and yourself were collaborating on a book about ghosts and ghouls?"

"You make it seem childish, Inspector. It's how I make my living," Stofferson explained, trying his best to remain civil.

"Even so," the inspector sneered. "Can you tell me your whereabouts last night?"

"Yes. I was presenting a slide show to the Wakefield branch of the W.I. until ten and then I stayed in a small B and B in the town centre."

"And this can be verified?" The inspector asked, not looking up from the notes he made.

"Absolutely. The B and B, Sleepy Hollow, has CCTV. So, they would corroborate that I arrived around ten thirty and stayed until about the same time this morning. Can I ask why you need to know that, Inspector?"

"You can, but I can't answer why at this time." The inspector struck Stofferson as the officious type who loved saying those words. "Well, that's all the questions I have for you at this time. If we have any more, myself or one of my colleagues will be in touch."

"That's it, is it?" Stofferson asked, knowing full well the inspector had ended the conversation. But, some part of him that had never grown up, and still despised overbearing authority, just couldn't help himself.

"Yep," Inspector Carlisle said before turning and walking away.

Frustrated, Stofferson fought the temptation to stop on the way back up the road and walk back to the folly over the fields. Instead, he rang an old friend.

"Superintendent Fisher," a female voice soon answered.

"Jan, you old stinker," Stofferson replied, "How ist?"

"Bloody hell, Stoffa," Fisher said cheerfully. "Are you ringing to say some ghostie's going to prevent you from coming to the reunion?"

"Definitely not. Couldn't pass up on a piss up with the crazy gang. Has Jeffers persuaded his wife to let him come yet?"

"Who bloody knows? And less of the crazy gang. I'm a respected officer of the law, you know?"

"Sorry, but this is the main reason for my call, Jan."

"Oh, shit. What have you done?"

Stofferson chuckled. "Not me this time, Occifer. No, I've just had an odd encounter."

"I'm guessing with your line of work, that happens a lot, Stoffa?"

"Depends on one's tolerance for the supernatural, old girl. No, I had a meeting with a former politician who wanted to collab' with me. Well, the second meeting, actually. But, when I got there, your lot had cordoned it off. I just hoped, because the guy, a Lord Markham, said speaking to me may put him in danger, that he's okay. The inspector, a Carlisle, wouldn't say a dickie bird."

"I should think he wouldn't," Fisher said. "He doesn't know you from Eve's bloke."

"Ah, but you do."

"More fool me, eh?" she sniggered. "Look, where is the constabulary? I'll look into it."

Stofferson gave her the details, thanked her and ended the call.

Less than ten minutes later, as Stofferson pulled his car on to the A64, Fisher called back.

"Well, you won't be meeting Lord Markham again, Stoffa," Fisher began as soon as Stofferson answered. "Unless you summon his ghost, I suppose."

"He's dead?" Stofferson asked in almost a whisper as the news hit his stomach with thump. "Shit. How?"

"Apparent suicide, I'm afraid. His housekeeper arrived with his breakfast and found the main door unlocked. She then entered his bedroom and found his bed hadn't been slept in. She thought it odd, so rang the police. They searched the grounds and found no sign until one sergeant looked over the edge of the cliff surrounding his property and there he lay. Sorry, old bean."

"But, how can they know it's suicide? Maybe someone pushed him. He had a story that put him in danger."

"No signs of a break in or a struggle. They did find a Dictaphone in his pocket that beyond luck didn't smash on impact. They found him speaking of a meeting with you and then rambling to himself like a madman before he apparently jumped. No screams. No pleading for his life before he fell. Nothing Stoffa. Sorry."

"Oh, now you say sorry," Stofferson said as a joke. "You need to work on your bedside manner, old love."

"Has that, in all the years you've known me, been my strong suit?"

"Not in the slightest. Is there any chance I could get a transcript of the Dictaphone? It might be a big help."

"With what?" Fisher asked, aghast.

"If I find anything you will be the first to know."

"Seeing as though it's you, I'll see what I can do."

"Cheers, my lovely," Stofferson said, "I owe you one."

"One?" Fisher laughed. "One of many. If your Lord Markham was in danger, does that mean you are too?" She asked in a serious tone.

"Nah," Stofferson scoffed. "I'm wearing my amulet." He touched the ornate amulet hanging from a chain around his neck as he said the words.

Further down the road and heading towards Stofferson, Jack Pickles yawned as he drove his haulage truck. He'd had a busy few days. With pick-ups and drops from Southampton to Harrogate, back down to Loughborough and then back to the base in Scarborough, he felt shattered. The skinful of beer and the argument with his long-time girlfriend the prior evening helped little. He yawned again and rubbed his heavy eyes.

Not long now, he thought. The truck stop in which he would rest lay only a mile or so up ahead.

"Sleeeeep," a calming voice whispered into his ears. "Sleeeeeep, Jack. You deserve the rest."

"In a bit," Jack mumbled, already feeling a dislocation between his mind and body. He shook his head to clear his thoughts.

"Sleeeeep," the voice insisted.

Jack felt his eyes droop.

Meanwhile, Stofferson ended the call with Fisher after promises to join the reunion. Erik Satie's Trois Gymnopedies began as soon as the line broke. Although one of Stofferson's favourite pieces to write to, he needed something more upbeat after the news about Markham. He looked down at the stereo screen in order to pick another piece. It took him no more than a split second to shoot a glance back and forth. On looking back to the road, his eyes widened with fear as Jack Pickles haulage truck, in slow motion, veered onto his side of the road and smashed his car beyond repair, sending many of its blood-covered pieces scattering into the summer air like confetti at a wedding.

Chapter Five

Days passed without a single call or message from Stofferson. As the sun hid behind heavy clouds and the rain arrived to wash the poor wincies away, Lydia came to believe the whole saga was just that. A tale devised by a senile politician and a fanciful man willing to believe them.

Due to the change in the weather, she spent more time inside the flat with Michael. He asked his many questions about life out in the world, and she got down to her own work. In between the researching and chapter planning, Jenny popped by every odd day to flirt and giggle. The trouble was, Lydia no longer fancied the other woman. She had everything a person could want, the looks, the banter, the body, but Lydia failed to move past the uneasiness Michael felt. He was the only one she felt didn't have an agenda, so she trusted him.

A week after the last time she saw Stofferson, Lydia remembered her promise to Harriet and rang her, clicking speaker so that she could carry on researching as she talked. Which suited Michael.

"Jesus, my old cotton bud," Harriet began in her usual bluster, "I've been so worried, I've had to change my undergrots at least three times a bloody day. Where've you been?"

"Sorry, Harry, I've had a few things on," Lydia replied, feeling a little guilty for not calling earlier.

"A few things on? Not Barrister Bitchface?"

"No. Thankfully. She hasn't been in touch with you, has she?"

"Sadly not. I'd give the dangerous dyke a piece of my grey matter, I can tell you. So, what's happened now, my little love pump?"

Lydia went on to recall everything that happened between the last call. She even blurted out the appearance of Michael.

"Is this the outline for the story you were telling me about, you crazy love-muscle?" Harry eventually asked, sniggering.

"Seriously. As mental as it sounds, it's true. Although, I don't know how true Stofferson's side of the story is as he's disappeared after I challenged him to get me a meeting with some lord called Markham."

"Lord Markham? As in the politician, Lord Jonathon Markham?" Harry asked, aghast.

"That's who he said his source was and left here to meet with him. Why? Do you know him?"

"Know him? My old chicken pinkle-pot, do you not watch the news?"

"No. I haven't watched the news since leaving Julia. The last thing I need is to see her damned face. Why?"

"Markham committed suicide about a week ago."

"He did what?"

"He supposedly went up to stay in his weird bloody castle somewhere near Scarborough and dived off the cliff. So, he won't be sharing anything with you now, old love. Well, unless you plug him into your ghost thingy."

"I'm not plugged into it," Michael said indignantly.

"Who in the all the blue blazes was that? You got company there, my chocolate munchkin?"

"That's Michael," Lydia simply stated. "Say hello."

"You're pulling my pisser," Harry replied. "Have you got FaceTime on your phone? I want to see for myself."

"What's that?" Lydia asked.

"Honest to God, you're turning into a trog since moving up to the sticks. It's part of Facebook. You do know what that is?"

"Up yours," Lydia laughed. "I know, but I'm just not part of it. Julia didn't like me on it, and to be honest, I'm glad she didn't. It would be just another way for her to track me. I'll make a video and send it via message. Give me a few minutes and I'll call you back."

"As long as it is a few minutes, you cheeky monkfish."

So, Lydia went about videoing a conversation with a ghost holding an object, in this case his favoured ball of tape, and then filmed him dropping the ball and still talking. She then sent the video to her agent.

"You are fucking kidding me? Is that for real?" Harry screeched down the phone on answering.

"As real as you and I," Lydia replied.

"You've got a best seller right there, my candy queen. A best bloody seller."

"I'm not sure about that, Harry," Lydia said. "But you can speak to him yourself. I've put the speaker on."

"Erm…" Harry stuttered.

"Oh my God, is the great and wise, motormouth Harry Breeden-Soames lost for words?"

"Well, what does one say to a person from the other side?" Harry said.

"Just say hello and take it from there," Lydia suggested.

"Hello," Harry said slowly as if talking to a mute.

"Hi," Michael replied. "How are you?"

"A little dumbfounded. How often does one chat to a member of the spirit world?"

"As I've never met anyone else like me, I couldn't say."

"Do you have some desperate task to perform before you move on?"

"Not that I know of," Michael replied.

Lydia went on to tell Harry Stofferson's theories, as wild as they sounded now that time had passed.

"Have you checked out if any other owner committed suicide?" Harry asked.

"Don't tell me you believe it now?" Lydia asked, having rarely heard Harry speak with such seriousness.

"Well, he was right about Michael. There's no harm in seeing if anything else he said checks out. I've just talked to my first, hot spirit man. This girlie wants to know more, my flowery-patterned-panty."

"Now, that's the Harry I know and love. Right, I'll do you a deal, I'll see if his story rings true if you do me a big one and find out if he's still in the land of the living. I want to know why he never came back and ask him straight."

"Done," Harry told her.

It took Harry no more than half an hour to ring back and her voice carried no joy.

"You're not gonna believe this, my lovely, but your young man was involved in one hell of a crash on the way back from trying to visit Markham. My gal in the Met says a lorry hit him head on."

"Is he dead?" A shocked Lydia asked in almost a whisper.

"Not quite, Lyd. He's been in a coma since."

"Which hospital?"

"York General."

"Jesus," Lydia said. "I should go visit."

"And do what? They probably only allow family, my old fruitcat."

"Well, I need to do something, Harry. I was the one who sent him. If I hadn't, he wouldn't be in a coma..."

"You can't think like that, chicken leg. That kind of thinking will drive you insane."

"But, it's true," Lydia sobbed. "I pushed him to a meeting where one man is dead, and the other is in a coma. How is that not my fault?"

"Because," Harry soothed, "you aren't some jinx or Jonah. Yes, you wanted proof. That's only reasonable. Any more than that comes down to coincidence and circumstance. Yes?"

"Yes, but…" Lydia began to plead.

"No buts, gorgeous lady. You've been through the ringer in many ways recently, your mind looks for more to pile on your plate. Did this Stofferson have your number?"

"Yes."

"Then wouldn't he have called you as soon as he felt danger at his shoulder if he thought Markham's death was suspicious?"

"I still need to speak to him."

"I'll find out what ward he's on. Just promise me you won't carry this on your shoulders."

"I'll try." Lydia never liked to promise things she couldn't deliver. "Also, I need you to find out one more thing…"

Chapter Six

Within the strange echo of his coma bubble, Stofferson floated in near darkness with no concept of time. Now and then, he dreamt of his childhood and his earlier fascination with the occult. Of images containing himself and a boy called Rygel attempting astral projection and candle magick as teenagers. In between flashbacks of soaring candle flame and gasps of fright, voices from the darkness of the present filtered into his consciousness.

"He doesn't look his age, does he?" One female voice asked a male.

"No. He's actually quite cute," the male replied, sighing. "Have they found any family yet? I do hope he's not married."

"Yes. They found his mum and sister yesterday. She rang this morning. Says she's coming at visiting time."

"Aww, that's nice."

"What do you think that pendant on his necklace means?" One asked.

"No idea. Looks foreign to me."

"Everything looks foreign to you."

Listening to the intermittent interactions around him fascinated Stofferson. He'd read much on the subject, though never expected to utilise the information, and there he lay, wondering when his peace would end. Because that is how the bubble felt, peace. No worries, no ambitions, no pain, and no heartache. Sometimes he experienced pangs of hunger or the odd itch, but Stofferson had practiced meditation for years and could cut out the irritation with some ease.

"Good afternoon, Irving, I'm Claire," a new voice said during a particularly annoying itch on his left eyebrow. "I'm going to take your obs and then give you a bed bath before your visitors arrive." He felt her attaching equipment to his arm and his thumb. "I bet you're excited for your mum, sister and girlfriend coming."

If Stofferson carried the capacity to frown, then he would, due to not having a girlfriend. He often told people he was married to his work but finding his ex in bed with a so-called friend slouched closer to the truth.

Stofferson spent the rest of the day wondering what the hell was happening. Even when the nurse cleaned his unmentionables, he found it difficult to stop thinking of this mystery girl. An hour later, ten minutes after his tear-toned mother and sister awkwardly said hello and told him about his cousin's dodgy hysterectomy following her eighth unexpected arrival, a new player entered his room.

"Sorry," he heard Lydia say in almost a whisper. "I'll come back in a bit."

"It's okay," his mother cooed. A chair scraped. Stofferson presumed his mother stood to greet this new guest. A typical act for his matriarch. "Do you know my son?"

"Yes. We've sort of been seeing each other," Lydia lied. Stofferson laughed. The outburst appeared to echo around his bubble. "It's all very new," he heard Lydia add. Stofferson wanted to open his eyes more than ever just to see her face.

“Awww. Come here, love. I’m Brenda and this is Louise, his sister,” His mother said. He knew she would cuddle Lydia.

After a round of, “Nice to meet you,” from all concerned, Stofferson heard nothing but silence for at least a minute, meaning the hug, before his mother squeaked, “They say he’s lucky to be alive.”

“What are his injuries?” Lydia asked. A question that seemed odd when Stofferson lay listening and no one really acknowledged his presence.

“A fractured skull, a broken pelvis and cuts to his chest and face. They say he lost a nipple. Can you get a transplant for that, do you think?” his mother asked. A typical question from her that caused more echoing laughter inside the bubble of Stofferson’s mind.

“Why would he want someone else’s nipple, Mum?” his sister asked in a humourless tone. “It’s not like men need them.”

“He might not want folk staring at his one nipple,” his mother protested. “You don’t know.”

A new silence rested over the room before Lydia asked, “What about the other driver? Is he okay?” The silence grew pervasive. Stofferson suspected something strange lay in wait.

“He came out without a scratch,” his sister said. “Then he…he…he topped himself.”

“Louise,” his mother scolded. “Don’t say it like that. The man obviously regretted putting your brother in hospital and it troubled his mind.”

“How do you know he was troubled?” Lydia asked. Stofferson sensed a little fear in the spaces between the words.

“His wife heard him muttering to himself. Though, she said it sounded like he was talking to someone else. Like proper mental,” Louise said.

"Did she say what he said?" Lydia asked.

"Well, his wife told the police, he muttered things like, please, my lord, no. I'm a good person. I won't do it. You can't make me do it to them. I'll do it to myself first. Weird, eh?" Louise asked.

"That does sound like guilt though," Lydia conceded. As Stofferson knew she would. "I'm surprised the police told you that, to be honest."

"He has an old friend in the police from university. She used to stay with us a lot. A lovely girl. I hoped they would… you know…before you, of course."

Inside his bubble, Stofferson rolled his eyes. His mum always dredged up that same murky lake whenever the moment presented itself. As if Jan and he ever stood a chance. Any minute now and Lydia would hear more of his past, and he could not have that. He stood inside his bubble and balled his fist in preparation of his crashing exit.

"Mum," Louise hissed, "look."

"Mum, could you please stop with the biggest love he lost routine," Stofferson croaked without opening his eyes. He felt the wave of pain hit him after such a peaceful time, and he did not need piercing sunlight to add to his discomfort.

After the doctors and nurses rushed in to check on the patient, and the awkward chats and silences between the three women in the waiting room, the cries of relief and hugs back in the room made Lydia feel no less comfortable. She had not banked on Stofferson waking during her visit and hoped he missed her conversation with his mother and sister about their fallacious relationship.

"Come on, Lydia," Brenda cooed. "Give him a hug."

"You get yours in first," Lydia replied with a strained smile.

"There's room for everyone," Brenda said. "She's been worried sick about you, love," she added, turning to her son.

"I'm sure she has, Mum. Don't push her. We'll have our hugs when you've gone," Stofferson said.

"Oh, I know what that means," his mum sniggered.

"Mother," Louise hissed. "That's your son and my brother you're talking about. Any more and I'll be sick."

"It's great to see you awake, Stofferson, but I'm gonna have to go. I've got to get back soon." Lydia said.

"Yes, you'll have Michael to see to," Stofferson said. "Mum, Lydia cares for a young man who can't look after himself."

"Awww, my neighbour has a special child she looks after. I was thinking of doing the same," Brenda said.

"Don't you think one special child in the family's enough, Mum?" Louise said with a grin towards her brother.

"I agree," Stofferson grinned back. "Maybe ask for a boy this time. If you get another special girl, Louise will turn green."

"Up yours," Louise threw back. "At least I would've grown out of that stupid amulet you've been wearing since you were a kid. Didn't do much for you, did it?"

"It doesn't make me Superman. It's just saves me from death by demon."

"And you think I'm special," Louise sniggered.

"Now, now, you two," Brenda scolded. "Lydia doesn't need to see you two acting up."

"If she joins the family," Stofferson said with a mischievous glint now pointing towards Lydia, "she'll have to get used to it."

"A bit early for that," Lydia smiled.

"Anyway, Lou, let's give these two a chance to say goodbye. We've got all day," Brenda said with a smile towards Lydia.

"If you think we're staying long with this lunatic, you've got another thing coming," Louise scoffed. "Lydia, run. Run like the wind." she added with a grin before giving Lydia a hug. "Nice to meet you."

"Thank you," Lydia replied. "Nice to meet you too."

Before Lydia took a breath after Louise had released her, Brenda squeezed more life out of her.

"Hope to meet you again, love," Brenda cooed into her ear. "We'll go get a coffee and be back soon, love," she told her son before leaving the two faux lovers to their goodbyes.

And then there were two.

"Well, this is awkward," Stofferson smiled.

"Sorry, I pretended to be your girlfriend," Lydia began. "I just needed to see you, and you know what hospitals are like with family and that. You okay?"

"I've been better."

"Do you remember anything?"

"More than I care to and some that fascinates me."

"What would fascinate you?"

"I remember," Stofferson began, absent-mindedly stroking his little pendant, "driving away from Markham's place after finding out he'd supposedly killed himself. I'd just finished talking to an old friend of mine in the Met. After asking her if she could get the transcript to the Dictaphone recording he made just prior to his death, that's when the lorry hit me. I remember seeing huge red eyes as it hit. Then nothing until snippets as I lay here."

"Might you have imagined the red eyes?" Lydia asked as she rested on the end of his bed.

"Possible. I'll know as time goes by. How did you know I was here?"

"A good friend of mine with lots of connections."

"Do you trust this person?"

"With my life."

"Good. But do me a favour. From now on don't tell anyone, not even your friend, I'm awake."

"Okay."

"And while we're hovering over the subject, did you tell anyone about me visiting Markham?"

"Why would I?" Lydia asked and then stopped. "I did tell Jenny when she mentioned she hadn't seen you for a while. But you can't think they had anything to do with it?"

"Hmmmm," Stofferson mulled.

"What? You think she went straight back to The Thirteen and they managed to possess some randomer? If that's the case, why aren't I in danger?"

"Oh, you're the safest person on the planet. Believe me on that."

"Because they want me to do the deed myself?" Lydia said and shook her head.

"Yes, in the flat," Stofferson added.

"Oh, not this again. You know, I've had some peace since you drove away," Lydia hissed.

"So have I, as it stands."

"Now you're just being flippant."

"Not at all. When they say coma victims hear all, they're right."

"Really?"

"Yep. It's a little like floating in a sensory deprivation tank, but you can hear folk outside. I just floated without any worries. I'd recommend it," he said with a tired grin before yawning.

"Listen, you look like you need some rest. I'll leave you to it and come back tomorrow."

"And if anyone asks?"
"You're still floating around in your nosy tank."

Chapter Seven

Lydia drove home along the picturesque A59 that divided a flatland of bright yellow rapeseed fields, no wiser than when she left home earlier. She felt relieved that Stofferson had come out of his coma, but the guy left her with more questions than answers. It was true, Michael felt no trust for Jenny, yet Lydia just could not grasp the idea of them trying to murder Stofferson via a disturbed lorry driver.

"It makes no sense," she said aloud.

A confused screech hung at the back of her throat. She needed someone else to talk to. So, she called Michael. The dial tone sprung from the speakers of the car and began its monotony. Cold worry soon played its godawful tune inside her stomach as the seconds rolled on and still Michael didn't answer.

Until, "Sorry," Michael said at last, a little exasperated, "I got so excited by the sound that I went to pick the phone up and sort of flipped it under the couch. You okay?"

"Well, I'm glad you're okay. Was worried for a moment."

"No need, I'm just clumsy. I wonder if I was like this when I had flesh," Michael said and sniggered. "How's Stofferson?"

"Well, he's awake at least. But, Jesus, is he still a head wrecker."

"What do you mean?"

"Well, he seems to think Jenny may have told The Thirteen about his trip to Markham's and they made a demon take over the driver that hit him," Lydia explained.

"Really?" Michael asked.

"Mad, eh?"

"In all honesty, Lydia, I have no frame of reference," Michael laughed. "I mean, for one you're talking to a trapped spirit on a telephone."

"Fair enough. But, surely the chances of picking the right lorry driver driving towards him at the exact time to hit him seems a bit much?"

"Did he say if you're in danger of the same thing happening?"

"He seems to think I'm safe because they want my death by my own hands."

"Then, as much as I love living with you, why don't you move out? You've gone through enough already."

"If I did that, I'd just be admitting that this madness Stofferson talks is real. I don't know, Michael," Lydia groaned. "It just can't be true."

"Is there anyone else you can talk to about it?"

"That's the thing. I could talk to Harriet, but Stofferson doesn't want anyone to know he's out of the coma, just in case they try something else."

"That's understandable. Did he say anything about Lord Markham?"

"We didn't really have chance to discuss it. He was tired, so I left. I'm gonna go back tomorrow."

"Well, I'll get the kettle on for when you come home. Just drive safely."

So, she did just that. She arrived home around an hour

and a half later and felt a kind of relief to find Michael waiting at the top of the stairs, holding a steaming cup of tea.

"We're like an old married couple," she smiled after thanking him for the tea. "And just like an old married couple we don't have sex."

She traipsed into the lounge and plonked herself down on the sofa.

"Another thing I wouldn't know anything about," Michael shrugged. Unbeknownst to him, he hadn't known much about sex in life, either.

"I'd say you're not missing out but I'd be lying." As if on cue, there came a knock at the main door. "That's probably bloody Jenny. You wouldn't go invisible to check, would you, please? I don't want to see her right now."

The knocking came again. A little louder.

"No problem," Michael replied and dropped his favoured ball. A few seconds later, he said in almost a whisper, "Yes, it's Jenny."

"Are you picking up anything from her?" Lydia whispered back.

"Mixed as always. A little nerves, excitement, deceit." The knocking came even harder. "She's looking up at the window. Now she looks frustrated. Now she's going."

"Thank God for that. As much as she is hot, I don't need to see her today."

Nor did she need to see Jenny the next afternoon but what we need and what we get sometimes are two separate things. Lydia had said goodbye to Michael, left the flat and reached her car without incident until, "Hi!"

Lydia turned to face Jenny, almost skipping towards her from her own house.

"Were you waiting for me to leave the house?" Lydia asked, trying to sound as if she joked but not exactly pulling it off.

"Of course, not. That would make me a stalker," Jenny simpered back.

"Shouldn't you be at work?"

"I was. I just nipped back because I'd shown a client a house last night and forgot to take the keys back to the office." She pulled out a set of keys with a blue tag on, as if to cement her case. "How are you? I popped by last night but you didn't answer."

"Sorry, I wasn't feeling well, so I went to bed early."

"Oh, you feeling better now?"

"A little. I'm just gonna go for a drive to take my mind off things."

"Pity I have to work. I'd come with you."

"Maybe next time," Lydia lied.

"Sounds good."

"I'll see you later," Lydia said, hoping to end the conversation. She turned to open the car door.

"Cool," Jenny said, before asking, "Hey, have you seen that ghost man lately? Daniel told me he'd seen on the news that he'd been in some kind of accident."

"I heard the same. They say he's in a coma."

"Oh, that's better than what I heard. I heard he'd died. What hospital is he in? We should mend bridges and send him flowers."

"I heard Harrogate General," Lydia lied with photon speed. She had seen a sign for the hospital on the way to visit him and wished Stofferson was in that one as it was at least an hour closer than York.

"I'll speak to Daniel about flowers. Poor man," Jenny sounding about as genuine as muzak. "See you later, chick," she added and left before Lydia could add more.

Chapter Eight

Jenny skipped into the office, less than ten minutes later, pleased with her little reconnaissance mission. Daniel strode out of the back as if on cue.

"I have news," Jenny grinned in triumph.

"Back here," Daniel said, returning the smile.

Jenny followed him into a large back office, again lined with oak. Daniel rounded his ancestors' large, ornate desk and seated himself in his luxuriant, red leather chair. "Well?" He demanded.

"I managed to catch her leaving."

"Good. Did you fix a date to gather info?"

"Better than that, I said you'd heard about his accident. She told me he's in Harrogate General, in a coma. We can catch him defenceless. No more ghost loon," Jenny announced, pleased with herself.

"Hmmm," Daniel mused behind arched fingers. After a couple of seconds, he stood and rounded the desk as if deep in thought. On reaching a smiling Jenny, he pulled back his hand and whacked her across her cheek, sending her reeling. "You stupid, brainless bitch," he hissed. "I gave you one simple job, to get into her bed, and you couldn't even do that."

"But, I got information," Jenny sobbed, holding her burning cheek.

"So, you think getting him in hospital is easy? Do you think Lord Clauneck will be happy with that?" Daniel growled. "Don't you think he would know exactly where he is? And for that matter, that I know where he is?"

"He's in Harrogate General," Jenny cried.

"What you've done is play your card too early and Lydia lied to you. She won't be opening up to you now, you idiot."

"But…"

"But, nothing. No, we will have to resort to Plan B and you will leave her alone. Do you hear me?"

"Yes," Jenny whimpered.

"I said, do you hear me?"

Jenny wiped the tears from her already swollen face and looked her boss in his furious eyes. "Yes," she said. "I'm sorry, Daniel."

Chapter Nine

Lydia headed over the flat, desolate tops of Blubberhouses as she drove back along the A59 and sighed. She'd called Michael earlier, as she left Burrstone to confirm her suspicions about Jenny.

"Yes, she was lying. Although her aura did show signs of attraction."

"Well, she can think again about that one," Lydia spat. "Julia was a horrible bitch but at least she never lied to me."

She cut the call as the signal began to crackle, not wanting to leave him worrying.

So, on she went, as the heavy sky promised rain, and arrived at the hospital just in time for visiting. She found Stofferson's mother and sister already waiting to gain entry with a small crowd of whispering strangers.

"Hello, Lydia, love," his mother said in hushed tones before giving her one of her bear hugs. "It's lovely to see you again." Louise offered a smile and a small wave.

"Thank you," Lydia said, waving back to Louise, "It's lovely to see you both again too. I didn't get chance to ask before, do you live far?"

"Not too far," Brenda said. "A little village called Wighill. How far did you come?"

"A town called Burrstone. Do you know it?"

"Oh, yes. Lovely market."

"I didn't know whether to bring some treats," Lydia said, showing her empty hands. "Hospitals frown on flowers and fruit these days, don't they?"

"I hope not," Brenda frowned, "I brought grapes and mandarins. He likes mandarins, does our Chris."

"Chris?" Lydia asked. "I've only ever known him as Stofferson."

"He never really liked Chris, and especially not Christopher. His Grandad Irving used to call him Stofferson after Kris Kristofferson, and when he died, our Chris changed his surname to Stofferson in remembrance and used his surname as his Christian name. I just can't get used to it, though." His mother sighed with a smile.

"It's better than the actual name you wanted to call him," Louise grinned.

"What? You don't like your name either?" Brenda asked.

"On me? Yes. Though to be fair, it would've been funnier if you kept it for him."

"We thought," Brenda began, "Chris was going to be a girl. Back then, we didn't have the greatest scans. The midwife told us he would be a girl," she shrugged.

"So, what did you and Dad do?" Louise asked, her grin widening.

"We bought all girl's clothes."

"And he had to wear them for the first few months," Louise sniggered.

"He was a baby. He didn't know. Until you told him."

"With absolute pleasure," Louise added.

A red-headed staff nurse opened the door to the ward and the three followed the other visitors inside. They soon branched off upon reaching Stofferson's room, only to find the bed stripped and his room empty.

"Oh, no," Brenda gasped, putting her hands to her mouth.

"It's okay, Mum. He's probably been moved. That's all," Louise said and hugged her fretful mother.

"I'll go find out," Lydia said, turned and almost sprinted to the nurses' station, where two nurses stood reading charts.

"Excuse me," she began, trying to keep her voice even, "I'm here to see my boyfriend, Irving Stofferson in room six, but his bed's stripped. Is he on a different ward?"

"No, my love," the smaller of the two nurses began with a frown, "I came on to hear he discharged himself yesterday."

"He did what? But what about his injuries?" Lydia asked.

"His notes said he said he would manage the pain himself, against the doctor's orders, and left."

"Did he say where, or leave a note for his mum?"

"No, lovey. Sorry."

Lydia thanked the nurse and ran back to Stofferson's former room.

"This is so like him," Louise growled after Lydia shared the information. "He's done this before."

"Before?" Lydia asked.

"Louise," Brenda said with a stern look towards her daughter. "If he hasn't told Lydia anything about those times, then it's not our place."

"Those times?" Lydia persisted.

A look passed between the Irvings. "She asked," Louise shrugged.

"Well," Brenda began. "If we must tell, at least let's go for a cup of tea. We'll not get anything by standing here."

The three left the ward and made their way, in an awkward silence, via a busy lift, to the ground floor. After entering the small café, Brenda, on her insistence, bought three teas and three millionaires shortbreads.

"Stofferson is a complicated person," Brenda began after they all seated. "He's always tried to do things on his own. When he was a teenager, he left home to go to university and fell in with the wrong crowd. Well, not wrong crowd, just a bit too experimental."

"I'd say wrong crowd," Louise muttered.

"Well, whatever," Brenda sighed.

"What happened?" Lydia asked.

"Let's just say, he experimented," Brenda said.

"A lot," Louise added.

"We don't know quite the extent, but he came back malnourished, underweight, and a little broken. What he didn't tell us, until the police visited, was he'd been arrested and bailed to appear at the police station where he lived. He forgot the date and came home for his cousin's birthday. Two days later the police arrived and took him away."

"My god. That must have been devastating?" Lydia asked.

"To be fair, the police where we live are all decent. They didn't embarrass him by cuffing him and dragging him out. They walked him out as if he was helping them. We were quite lucky really."

"Do you mind me asking what he was arrested for?" Lydia asked.

"Drugs. It was only cannabis. But in those days, people didn't wander around the streets smoking it like tobacco," Brenda explained.

"How did he get caught?"

"One of his so-called friends had been caught with one

of those joint things and said he got it off Chris. They tried to do him with dealing but had no proof. The silly thing is, he could've told us, but he wanted to deal with it on his own. As he said, he got into the trouble, he would get himself out. Anyway, they shipped him off to the station he was bailed to and kept him there all weekend until his court case on Tuesday."

"How was he through it all?" Lydia asked.

"He was Chris. His dad was furious. Not with Chris, mind. But with the police for keeping him in for something so stupid. He was in France at the time, driving a busload of tourists. I told him about Chris when he rang home to say he'd arrived in Dover. His dad de-toured the bus past the police station and demanded to see his son."

"Aww, that's quite sweet," Lydia said.

"Not for the coppers," Louise giggled. "They wouldn't let him see Chris at first. They changed their minds, though, when he said if he didn't see Chris, he would park the bus through the front door of the police station."

"Did he really say that?" Lydia asked, astounded.

"Yep," Louise said. "Our Chris told me later that he heard him from the cells."

They sipped in silence for a moment before Lydia asked, "So, where do you think he will've gone now?"

Brenda merely shrugged. Louise replied with, "Your guess is as good as ours. He's spoken of sacred places he can go if ever the demons attack, but I just thought he was being, you know, dramatic."

"Did he say where they were?" Lydia asked.

"No. He said he didn't want us to know just in case a demon tried to read our minds. Honest to God, I think he took too much acid for his own good," Louise sighed.

"I thought you said he was done for cannabis?" Lydia asked.

"He was, but that wasn't all he experimented with. He never did the really stupid drugs like heroin and that. But he did play with mushrooms, acid, cannabis, speed. That one was the worst for him," Louise added.

"Why?" Lydia asked.

"It allowed him to stay awake for days," Louise said.

"Days?" Lydia asked, astounded.

"Oh, yes. His longest was a full week without sleep. Experimenting with astral something or other. He said he could actually feel his skin cells falling off and his hair growing. Idiot."

"Jesus. That's some heavy shit," Lydia said and added, "Sorry," as Brenda winced at her acidic choice of words.

"That's okay," Brenda told Lydia. "I've just never been good with swear words. You're right though. It took him quite some time to find his feet again."

"What do you mean?" Lydia asked.

"His head spun all over the place for a number of years afterwards. I don't think the pills they put him on at first helped. It certainly didn't help his dad's shed," Brenda said, rolling her eyes.

Louise sniggered at the memory.

"What do you mean?" Lydia asked.

"Well, his dad was building a stone shed in the back garden at the time but every morning he woke up to find the wall he worked on knocked down. Years later, Chris told me, after his dad died, the pills made him hear voices and they said to knock it down. After the third time, he flushed the pills down the loo and the shed got built. His dad would laugh now but at the time he went around to all the neighbours asking if they knew anything."

"He was fur-ious," Louise added with a grin.

"Can I ask you a question?" Lydia asked them both. After they both said yes, she said, "all this demon stuff and their worshippers, do you think it's all in his head?"

"He's a nutjob," Louise said, "But not that much of a nutjob."

"What Louise means to say is he has always had a weird knack with the other side, even as a kid," Brenda said. "We both saw a spirit together once."

"Really?"

"Yep," Brenda began. "We used to live in this tiny village called Wimple. Built in the early fourteenth century. All kinds of weird things happened. One time…"

Thirteen-year-old Stofferson lay in bed reading *Magick by Aleister Crowley*. The moon shone through the lead-lined window. A soft knocking pulled him away from the bizarre poetry.

"Yes?" he called.

The door opened. Soon followed by his mum's face. "Fifteen minutes more and then sleep. School in the morning," she told him with a smile.

"Okay," Stofferson lied. As soon as she closed her door, he would lay a towel behind it to block out the light and read until he fell asleep. "Night."

"Night, love." His mum closed the door and moved on to his sister's room. He heard a similar speech play out before his mum entered her own bedroom, turned off the landing light, and closed the door. His dad was away in Germany with a party of skiers, so Stofferson knew there would be no more movement.

Sometime later, and just as he readied himself to lay down the towel, his attention once again turned to the door.

Because, where once darkness bordered the door, now a bright white light shone. So bright it seemed the bulb that produced it would soon shatter. Stofferson frowned and placed his book on the table to the right. Still frowning, he shuffled out of bed and stepped slowly towards the light. The closer he stepped, the more it looked nothing like electric light. It shone so much whiter and brighter as it stabbed through the cracks in the door. Stofferson, hardly breathing, raised his hand to turn the handle, counted to three, and pulled. The light disappeared as mysteriously as it had appeared.

The voice of his mum saying, "what in blue blazes was that, Chris?" startled him.

"I've no idea but I can see it coming from the living room door now," he told her without turning away from the light in case he lost it.

"Seriously?" His mother asked as she shuffled towards him and joined him to look down the steep staircase. Just as her son told her, the light now illuminated from under the door in piercing beams. "What do you think it could be?"

"I'm guessing a former resident of the house." He stepped slowly down the staircase, one step at a time. His mum followed. On arriving at the door, he again reached out with tentative fingers for the handle. Again, after pushing the door open, the light vanished, only to reappear under the closed kitchen door. This went on until they pulled the larder door. The light then abruptly disappeared, leaving two astounded faces hidden by the dark.

"It happened a few times after that. Usually when my husband was away. But we never did find out what it was," Brenda sighed. "It never did anything bad, though."

"So, his interest grew from there?" Lydia asked.

"Goodness, no," Brenda told her. "He was about eight the first time he said he saw something strange. I was in my bedroom, reading, and he came running in…"

"Mum," the young Stofferson said, almost out of breath. "Mum. A man was in my room."

"A man?" Brenda asked, eyes wide behind the Mills and Boon in which she sat engrossed. "Is he still there?"

"No," Stofferson told her as he climbed on to her bed. "I was reading Treasure Island when I felt someone there. I looked up and a man with yellow hair stood at the bottom of the bed, holding out a black book. He didn't seem scary. He seemed kind. But, when I reached out to take the book he sort of disappeared."

"Could it be a dream, sweetheart?" Brenda asked as she laid down her book and took her bewildered son in her arms.

"No, Mum. I wasn't asleep. I was reading."

"What did he look like?"

"Tall, not old, really short hair around the side but yellow on top. He had on a black tank top, white shirt and black trousers. I didn't see his shoes."

"Would you recognise him if you saw a photo?" Brenda asked, now intrigued.

"I think so."

"Wait here." Brenda pulled away from her son, slid out of bed and began rummaging in her photo cupboard. His mum kept thousands of photos. Especially of the one man of whom she could never be prouder. After a few moments and a good scouring of her many albums, she returned to the bed with an old, grey, dog-eared album, open at one particular page. "Does this man look like him?" She turned the book around to face her son.

The proud, young man staring back, wearing his

regimental sergeant-major's uniform was the same man Stofferson had seen standing before him. "Yes, that's him, Mum. Who is it?"

"That was his grandad," Brenda told Lydia. "Now, I know what you might think, he'd seen that picture and dreamt he appeared. But, I'd only just got those albums from my mum. You hadn't even seen Grandad so young either, had you, Lou?"

"Not until after you showed Chris," Louise replied. "But all of his little adventures don't give us much clue to where the nutter's gone now. Don't you tell him, Mum, but I'm a little worried he might not have food and that."

"We should swap numbers," Lydia suggested. "That way we can keep each other in the loop.

And that is what they did. Soon afterwards, they all hugged, with promises to keep in touch, and went on their way.

Chapter Ten

A dense cloud of fear hung over the heads of The Thirteen as they summoned their lord. One voice in particular, Jenny's, quivered as she spoke the invocation. Daniel promised he would tell Clauneck he had already punished her, but some in the group knew it did not guarantee anything. Daniel felt the ice in his stomach because he led the coven. An honour but also a curse. Only one woman did not fear. On the contrary she, Diana Pennington, bottle blonde and daubed with makeup struggling to hide the cracks of age, hoped Daniel received the full extent of her lord's wrath so she could finally take his place. A part of her, though, suspected he would worm his way out of any punishment.

And still the invocation continued.

When Clauneck eventually sauntered through the smoke and mirror, in the guise of a handsome man, Jenny's sobbing began to irritate Diana. She, however much she wanted, could not tell her to shut up.

"Evening all," the demon said with a casual bow. "You wouldn't believe the fun I've been having." He sighed as the memory played inside his mind. "Well, what news?"

"My Lord," Daniel said and bowed low. "I'm afraid it's not all good but we are rectifying it."

"Do tell," Clauneck replied and picked his teeth.

"Well, it turns out Stofferson may have come out of his coma and has disappeared. We can find sight nor sound of the imbecile. I beg your forgiveness, but we are looking into other avenues."

"Did you scry?" Clauneck asked, showing a distinct lack of fury that did not please Diana one bit.

"Yes, My Lord. We found nothing," Daniel said.

"Hmmm," Clauneck mused. "He's obviously found himself a hole in which to hide. If he stays hidden before the next soul takes up residence, all the better. When he raises his head, we lop it off. How did this come about?"

"A misunderstanding, My Lord."

"Not much of an explanation, Daniel. I'm guessing this pathetic, cowering wench had something to do with it. Weren't you sent to seduce the next soul?"

"I-I-I…" Jenny sobbed.

"Stop your stuttering or I will stop your heart," Clauneck growled, his eyes turning blood red. Jenny clamped her mouth with her hands. "I see by the pretty bruises; you have received a level of punishment. Daniel?"

"Yes, My Lord. Your servant Jenny repents. She saw the next soul leaving the flat and took it upon herself to ask if she had seen Stofferson, thinking it may help. However, it only alerted both parties."

"It's a good thing you're pretty, my dear," Clauneck simpered, his eyes turning back to blue. "Come to me, I will soothe you." Jenny appeared frozen. "Come, come. I only mean to ease your pitiful mind." His words floated around the room as soft as down. As if hypnotised, Jenny stood and floated towards her master. When midway between the group and the demon, he raised his arms as if to welcome her before a ball of red flame soared from his palms and engulfed the screaming girl. Within seconds, a pile of blackened ash remained where once a beautiful girl stood. "That should ease her pitiful mind. Because, as sure as heaven is dull, it eases mine. Worry not, children, I will play with her later. Daniel, consider yourself lucky I am only demoting you for your incompetence. You have some use to me. She did not. Diana, welcome to the top table. Come, let us shake on it." Diana, fighting to hide a satisfied smile, stood, bowed, and walked towards her lord. "Can I trust you will not let me down, my dear?"

"You can, my lord. Although, because of the damage done and the new avenue we must travel, it may take longer than expected."

"I gift you three months. Any longer and you will see my patience begin to evaporate. I'm already getting an earache from the Seraph."

"Yes, My Lord."

"Can you guarantee this new plan will push her over the edge?"

"Definitely, My Lord. She is weak."

"It best had. For all your sakes."

Chapter Eleven

In the centre of a wild wood, somewhere in North Yorkshire, there sits what most people regard as a folly designed to look exactly like Stonehenge, only much smaller. The same people say the owner, Lord Tillotson, built it to attract tourists. Of course, they only said such things after his death in the early twentieth century. A select few lucky enough to find his obscure books in tiny, dusty bookshops know differently. Irving Stofferson is one of the latter.

He came across a natty, tatty copy of Tillotson's book, Ley Lines and their Key To Hidden Realms, at the age of fourteen during a school trip to York. After visiting the Jorvik Viking Centre, most of his fellow pupils and the teachers who supervised them sat on the grass outside the Minster to eat their packed lunches and enjoy the sun. Stofferson always wanted to explore the narrow, ancient Shambles, with its line of rickety shops, so he snuck off while the teachers had their back to him. He felt a little disappointed to only find stores catering to the tourist trade. Until he made his way down an even narrower alley between a sweet shop and an apothecary. Something drew him into the cool darkness, and he did not resist. What he found cemented his trust in his gut's intuition.

The tiny shop with a dusty window full of books he had never heard of bore a rectangle sign above the door which read, "THere's nOwt heRe iF youR eYes arE Shut." This intrigued Stofferson all the more. So, he tried the latch and pushed the door. It creaked in such a way that pleased his imagination. The heavy, musty air wrinkled his nose as he entered a tiny tunnel he soon recognised to be made entirely from books. This intrigued him further.

"Hello," he called down the little tunnel.

"Proceed," a squeaky male voice called out. Stofferson did as the voice told him and exited the tunnel into an entire room of books shaped like the inside of an igloo. A tiny-bodied man with extraordinarily long, thin legs sat in a red leather chair with a book open across his pin-like thighs. He wore a gold-rimmed monocle over his left eye and a red spotted neckerchief around his neck. "Master Irving, I presume," he said and offered a kind smile.

"Yes," Stofferson said, shocked. A novel emotion for him. "How can you possibly know my name?"

"Oh, I know a great deal about you, young man. Both your past and your future. Would you like to know your future?"

"No, thank you." Stofferson had pondered such a question many times in his life. Especially when he watched his sister get excited whenever she read a horoscope prediction in his dad's newspaper that only vaguely mirrored her life.

"Why not?" the man asked, leaning forward.

"If you tell me my life, will it only happen that way because you told me or because of fate? I think I would drive myself mad trying to not think about every minute of the day instead of just enjoying them."

"Wise for someone of such tender years."

"My mum says I think too much."

"She may have a point," the little man sniggered.

"Sorry, but what's your name?"

"Oh, come now. For a thinker, you're a stinker if you haven't fathomed out my name before you even entered the door, Master Irving."

Stofferson thought about the words the tiny man used and soon realised the clue lay in the bizarre sign on the door. "Thor Fryes?" Stofferson said struggling with pronunciation.

"Very good," Fryes said and clapped his hands. "A little wonky with my surname but not the first, I'm afraid. Think Fry and add Es. Now, what can I offer you?" The question struck Stofferson as one more for the owner than for himself. "I think I have just the thing." Fryes heaved the book on his lap to the side and dropped from the chair to the floor. "Follow me, please, young man, as you are the only who can be retrieving the book you need." He pushed himself to his tiny feet and strode across the floor with one stride. He reminded Stofferson of a Daddy-Long-Legs. Fryes humphed as if he had heard Stofferson's thoughts before pointing to a tattered book crammed into the igloo wall. "With care, please, take the one written by a man called Tillotson."

Stofferson did as the long man bade, careful not to pull the whole wall down upon them both. The book slid out with ease and the wall remained intact.

"Good. Now go with care, Master Irving, and read the book with equal vigour." The little man ushered him through the tunnel and out of the door before he could offer any money or even thank him.

Years later, at around twenty years old, Stofferson visited the shop. Only to find the alley mysteriously no longer there. This did not surprise him in the slightest.

Now, back to Tillotson's book. It begins with a warning. "To whomever finds this book, check your heart. If it be pure, then read on. If darkness resides within even one ventricle, atrium, or septum of the heart then I advise you to find the golden path before reading on. Otherwise, not only your flesh but your eternal soul is in peril."

The younger Stofferson did not dare read on until certain of his virtues. He spent three years studying the great philosophers, from S.E. Paces, Descartes, Kant, Hume, Russel, Sartre and on. He meditated, which caused much amusement at school. He volunteered for anything to help the community. He stripped his soul bare and re-evaluated his opinions in order to establish a solid foundation in which to see the world through kinder eyes. Obviously, some days he struggled. Though, eventually, four years after his drug conviction, he felt ready to open the book with tentative fingers. The bizarre poetry inside surprised him. He expected some kind of Dante-esque nightmare. Yet, the challenging couplets within the pages led him to find the sacred places, such as the one Tillotson built.

The dangerous part came when, armed with nothing more than an open mind and candles, he followed the lessons to open the gateways. A feat not attempted since Tillotson. Before attempting, Tillotson told him to abstain from sex for forty days. An easy challenge for Stofferson as most girls thought him too weird to sleep with anyway. The next called for him to eat only the root of vegetation growing nearest to the sacred place. This, Tillotson said, gave a better connection to the gateway. The last warned of the fight for his soul he would surely face from any demons nearby. With an added warning that, "There are always demons nearby. Yet, when one opens the gateways, you are safer than any king inside his keep, if you best the demons. Good luck goes with you, my friend."

Stofferson decided, because Tillotson's gate stood closer, he would hike from Granby, the nearest train station, hoping it contained a spring or river in which to draw water. For the most part, he enjoyed the trek from town to thick forestland and arrived just before dusk. He need not have worried about candles as a strange, green glow lightly illuminated the stones of the circle the more the darkness fell. After foraging for mushrooms and other roots such as Meadowsweet, Elder, Pignut and Common Beech, Stofferson pitched his tent, built a fire and sighed as the crackle lulled him. His tired body sank into the earth around him.

"You look like a good soul," a beautiful red head simpered across the fire. Stofferson shot to a sitting position, his eyes darting left and right for other players. He saw none. "Would you keep me warm this night?" As she spoke, she unbuttoned the top two buttons of her white blouse to show her ample breasts. "I could make you happy." She licked her lips in a slow, deliberate show of her promise.

"Away with you, foul demon," Stofferson growled. "I may look green but I am no cabbage."

"You are mistaken, my love," the woman simpered. "I am just in need of warmth for the night."

"Then, why undo your buttons? Surely you would feel warmer buttoning them all."

"That's true. But, don't they say two naked bodies stay warmer when pressed against one another?"

"There's no need. It's not winter."

"You miss the point. My skin will sustain your body and soul no matter the temperature. Allow me to show you the wonder of my flesh." She smiled a smile that could make the phallus of a statue twitch as she undid another button.

"Demon!" Stofferson spat. "You have nothing for me."

The lady's face contorted into a twisted mask before she shrieked in rage and flew straight across the fire towards Stofferson. He ducked just in time and turned to see her swoop away into the darkness.

The second night, after a long warm day of contemplation, and with a pot of nettle soup bubbling before him, two sobbing children arrived on the other side of the fire.

"Please, mister," the dishevelled boy pleaded. "Could we warm ourselves against your fire? My sister and I have lost our parents somewhere in the forest." Their wide eyes looked across at Stofferson with an expression that could coax the last drops from a dry well.

"Of course," Stofferson told them. "What are your names?"

"I'm James and this is my sister, Amelia," the boy said.

"Have you eaten? I can spare some food."

The boy looked at the girl as if communicating before saying, "No thank you, our parents taught us not to accept food from strangers."

"And yet, you are willing to sleep opposite a stranger to keep warm?" Stofferson replied, keeping his tone calm and impassive. "Surely you must be hungry?"

"We are," James replied with little certainty. "But…"

"But nothing," Stofferson cut in and stood to lift the little pan of soup from the frame he made over the fire. "Come. Eat." He poured a bowl full and passed it to the girl, because, in his mind, girls should always receive first.

The girl looked from her brother to the proffered bowl, screamed, returned to her own warped form, alongside her brother, threw the bowl at Stofferson and flew off into the dark night.

The third night, a tall, regal man appeared and asked to take a place by the fire, his well-styled black beard hung near his chest and his shimmering attire looked cut from the finest cloth.

"May I sit?" he asked, his voice rich and deep.

"Please," Stofferson replied, wondering what trick this one would pull.

"No tricks," the man said with a knowing nod. "Yes, I can read your thoughts. And a fine mind it is too, Irving Stofferson. Save your worry. Not all of my kind are uncouth tricksters. I merely want to know your purpose."

"My purpose," Stofferson mused. "A fine question."

"Thank you," the man bowed. "I pride myself on such things."

"What's your name?"

"I go by many names. None are important. And you only ask to deflect and buy yourself time. Yes?"

"I suppose," Stofferson conceded.

"I do not suppose," the demon smiled.

"Surely, if you can read my mind, you can answer the initial question for yourself?"

"I can read your thoughts, Master Stofferson," the demon simpered, "not your mind. A large difference. And even if I had the skills to delve deeper, I would still want to hear you translate such thoughts. You see, I meet so many who are black and white with their philosophies. I hope you are a different animal."

"Are those who think in black and white the demons that you meet?" Stofferson asked.

"Not only some of the fallen, as we prefer, have such monochromatic ideals, Stofferson. The Seraphim and their kin can also act wildly black and white. They are sooooo tiresome, I can tell you."

"Where do you lie?"

"I suppose I'm a relativist," the demon shrugged.

"Ah, like Protagoras."

"I met with the old sophist once or twice in Athens. Interesting fellow for a mortal."

"Really? Who else have you met?"

"Deflecting," the demon grinned, wagging his finger. "Quid pro quo. I've answered your question. You must answer mine. What is your purpose?"

"To be fair, it's quite an expansive question. Do you mean my purpose here or my life's purpose?"

"I know very well why you're here, Stofferson. You are here to open what you know as a demon gate. A silly name if you ask me. Such nomenclature makes it sound like a gate fit for a demon and not one to keep the fallen out. But, hey—oh, just my opinion. Now to your life's purpose."

"I suppose I just want to use the knowledge I've acquired to help others who can't help themselves."

"There are other ways to help your fellow mortals, Stofferson. Why this route? Is it atonement?"

"There are other ways to help, I agree, but I have some knowledge of this subject and most don't."

"Most think demons and angels are mere fantasy these days. Aren't you concerned others may ridicule you?"

"A great trick your kind conjured to keep under the radar, no doubt," Stofferson said, looking the demon straight into his smiling eyes. "And if any of your kind lift their head into view, I will do my best to expose them. As far as ridicule, that's been part of my life since I started wearing my amulet. It doesn't bother me."

"Ah, yes, the amulet. You do realise that trinket only protects you against death by demon. But it won't save you from pain by demon." The demon told Stofferson with no sign of threat. "You see, a fallen, and not me, of course, may beat you to the brink of death over and over, and there is no other soul for miles who can help you."

"They can try, but there's a protection spell set up round this whole area."

"Prudent," the demon conceded. They both sat in contemplation for a few minutes, the crackle of the fire the only noise. "Tell me, wouldn't you just want a normal life, Stofferson? One with at least a girlfriend? Or is your lack of bedroom action due to you conforming to Plato's idealised form of beauty?"

"Goodness, no," Stofferson sniggered. "I'd love to have a girlfriend. But, I accept I'm just not made for such intimacy."

"Of course, you are. Just let them in, lad. You can have any life you want. What your choosing is hermitage." The demon's tone seemed to soften and become almost patriarchal.

"Probably," Stofferson conceded.

"Well, on that note, I must go. I have other issues in which to attend," he stood and held his hand out. Stofferson stood and shook his hand. Manners, after all, cost nothing. "I'll see you again," the demon said and disappeared without a sound.

Stofferson sat and stared at the flames until the dark sky turned that peculiar shade of aubergine as dusk arrived, daring not to sleep in case another demon dropped by. None did, so he settled down to sleep.

He dreamt of all the girls he ever carried a torch for. From pre-school to university. The Janets, the Ambers, the Kirstens and the Elizabeths. Each girl flitted and danced inside his slumber, smiling and laughing as they beckoned him forth to join their ballet and kiss. He awoke feeling wretched and alone for at least three hours until he analysed the reason for such torture: the demon with many names.

"It's a test," he grumbled after a lunch of mushrooms and wild garlic, and a cup of nettle soup. "He's planted those thoughts to steer me away from my goal. Tonight, I'll be ready."

Night soon arrived with the familiar hoot of the unseen wood pigeons. Stofferson built a fire and prepared for the next test, his stomach bubbling in apprehension. The demon did not come. Nor did it show up for the next four nights. Each morning Stofferson awoke confused and lonely, with visions of flesh and lost human connections playing behind his eyes, and by each night his resolve returned. On the fifth day since the demon with many names had visited, Stofferson almost persuaded himself the demon would never return. Until, "I'm surprised and happy to find you re still here," the dapper demon announced as he appeared on the other side of the crackling fire.

"Where else would I be?" Stofferson asked, curling his legs into the lotus pose.

"Who knows?" the demon shrugged. "Many of my kind wagered I would find you gone on my arrival. I'm owed quite a jolly sum. Thanks."

"I'd say you're welcome, but you know…"

"I know. What have you meditated on since last we spoke?"

"Oh, you know, your attempt to get inside my head."

"I hardly needed to try, Stofferson. I'm glad to see you're stronger than that."

"Are you glad?"

"Of course. One enjoys a challenge. Now, let us examine your present atonement for such a hedonistic approach as a teenager."

"I'm not trying to atone for that as it wasn't out of a hedonistic need."

"Really? Are you telling me your previous drug abuse wasn't an example of your corrupt soul?"

"Absolutely not. To quote Epicurus," Stofferson began, "Where pleasure concerns the body, perfect health is the way forward. Where it concerns the mind, freedom from pain and anxiety is the way forward. Although, all pleasure is good, some pleasure will inevitably bring with it pain, and this is where wisdom comes into play."

"Forgive my language, young man, but poppycock," the demon replied. "You abused cannabis. You abused amphetamines. And you sure as upstairs is mind-numbingly dull, abused LSD and psilocybin."

"I disagree. I do admit to taking it too far, but I wanted to see if I could widen my doors of perception."

"Don't tell me you're going to quote Huxley to me next," the demon laughed.

"No," Stofferson simply stated.

"Good. I've spent the last five days looking forward to your original thinking and would suffer much disappointment to find you spewing out other people's thoughts the entire night."

"Isn't any original thought just an expansion of another's contemplations?"

"That's better. I suppose it is to some degree. However, just willy-nilly quoting every other great mind without adding to their thoughts is no better than living like a human encyclopaedia. No?"

"I suppose."

"So, rowing back along this calm river to my original question, are you sure your previous drug abuse, or experimentation as you perceive it, wasn't due to your corrupt soul? I mean, you say were pushing the boundaries, yet it involved hurting the innocents around you. Surely if you did those things out of a higher reasoning, you would consider the impact on others?"

"Innocents around me?"

"Yes. Your family for one," said the demon.

"They never knew about my experiments," Stofferson said. "I would never worry them by dropping a tab and popping around for lunch."

"True. However, they just had to endure the upset and humiliation of the local constabulary turning up during breakfast and dragging you off to a cell," the demon explained. "Your father was even forced to detour a bus load of passengers to visit you in said cell, confusing said passengers and endangering his job. A little selfish, do you not think?"

"It's unfortunate they had to find out that way, sure, but never my intention. I merely confused the bail date. If I had not, they would never have found out."

"And worried?"

"Yes. And worried. A genuine mistake and nothing more."

"Would you really risk the final ceremony of opening this demon door when it may tear your soul apart because you failed to see the corruption that lies within you?"

"If that is truly the case, why are you trying to talk me out of doing it? Surely you can see my corrupt soul?"

"Because, despite your lofty, yet ridiculous ideals of right and wrong, I enjoy your company and would hate to see you die for nought."

"Why do I struggle to believe you?"

"I don't know," the demon shrugged. "Trust issues? Something to think about. See you again, young man. Take care." The demon once again shook his hand and left him to more questions.

Every four to five days of the thirty-three days left to serve, the demon appeared to torture Stofferson with doubt, and every torturous day in between, the young man fought his way back.

The last time the demon visited was on the eve of the final ceremony.

"Good evening, my friend," the demon said jovially. "Are you well-rested for tomorrow? Because, if you think my visits are tiring, wait until your soul is ripped into a thousand screaming pieces."

"That's a pleasant thought," Stofferson growled.

"Isn't it? How are you feeling?"

"I'm okay."

"You look tired. I can end all this for you, you know? I could make you anything you want to be."

"I want to be here, so you can't offer me anything."

"That's a little myopic, Stofferson." The demon shuffled around to Stofferson's side of the fire for the first time. "Don't worry, I mean you no harm."

"I'm not worried," Stofferson said, sitting as straight as his inner resolve.

"Good. Allow me to show you something." The demon touched Stofferson's hand and the scene changed from the centre of the stones in a forest to that of a lavish restaurant. Opulent people sat at tables surrounding him, chatting or dining. The aroma of finely cooked food enticed Stofferson's hunger. "Come. Sit."

"Where are we?" A wide-eyed Stofferson asked.

"One future you could live in if you choose wisely. Come." The demon ushered him into an empty seat at a table set for three. It took the seat opposite.

"Why three chairs?" Stofferson asked.

"All good things to those who wait," the demon said with a knowing smile. "Are you hungry?"

"No thank you."

"A lofty reply for someone who has sustained himself on the roots of the forest. I'm sure if I only ate roots for weeks and was human, my chin would be sopping wet with drool. But have it your way. Pride before a fall and all that."

Stofferson kept his eyes firmly on the demon. As much as he knew the whole scenario was a game to drag him from his purpose, the smell and the sight of plates containing the finest fodder would tempt a man with no stomach. "Why have you brought me here?" he asked.

"To show you what you are missing playing the martyr. Oh, look. Here comes our esteemed guest." Stofferson, against his better judgment, turned slowly to see a stunning lady in an elegant dress float towards them wearing a warm smile. Something about her eyes seemed familiar. "You can't tell me you don't recognise your biggest crush."

"My god, it's Amber," Stofferson said in an awed whisper.

"Hello, gorgeous," Amber said and kissed him on the lips. "Hi, Luca," she said, looking at the demon. "Sorry, I'm late." Stofferson stood to pull her seat. "No need, sweetie. I've just got to pop to the little girl's room first." She cupped his cheek and kissed him again. The fire whizzing around his nether regions threatened to blow the top of his skull into the cut-glass chandelier above him.

"She kept her looks, eh?" The demon hissed salaciously into Stofferson's ear as Amber flounced away.

"This isn't real," Stofferson hissed back.

"Of course, it is. Well, real if you choose it so," the demon replied.

"If I turn my back on opening the doors?"

"A life of peace and luxury with the girl of your dreams, Stofferson. Or a life of struggle, pain, and loneliness."

"If it was going to happen, it would've in uni."

"Not necessarily. There are numerous occasions of former lovers rekindling lost love."

"Yes, but we didn't even have that. She fancied my roommate and never me."

"And then you meet up at a gala function for orphan children, of which you are one of the directors, by the way, and boom, she's in your arms and in your life. Nice, eh?"

"I don't believe you."

"That's hurtful. Is it not Amber?"

"Yes, but some kind of illusion."

"I can show you your future, Master Stofferson. I can't create something from nothing. Not even the ineffable one can do that. Despite what some believe."

"Why did she call you Luca?"

"Because that is the name by which you introduce me when I first meet Amber. In this future, we become good friends, you and I."

"Even more unlikely," Stofferson muttered as he looked towards the ladies' toilets in thought.

"And there's me thinking you pertained to goodness, Master Stofferson," the demon grinned.

"I try but my path and yours are so far from one another. You've got to admit that."

"I disagree. We are parallel, for certain, but if this is another future you may or may not choose…"

"Will not choose," Stofferson cut in.

"May not. The evening is not quite over. And as I was saying, if this is one future, and I help you get everything you need and want, then, of course, we will be friends."

"What are you two rogues talking about?" Amber asked with a smile that reached into Stofferson's chest and gently rubbed his heart until it glowed. "Or is this another one of your philosophical debates that could baffle a boffin?"

"The latter," the demon said. "I must admit your other half is in top bafflement form tonight." Stofferson helped Amber into her seat as the demon stood. "Please order without me. There's a chap over there I haven't seen since the big flood. Won't be a moment." He bowed a little from the hip, smiled a little too salaciously for Stofferson and strode over to the bar where a rather worried man with very little hair shook his hand and tried his best to smile.

"I still can't believe you swung tickets for this place," Amber said. "I swear I saw that footballer for Leeds. Are you okay?" She leaned across the table and took Stofferson's hands in hers.

"I just find it hard to believe you are sitting opposite me."

"I swear you say that every time we have dinner with Luca. Well, we eat, he never seems to. What's with that?" Amber asked.

"He's a picky eater," Stofferson lied and cursed himself inwardly for such indiscretion. "What if I told you he isn't what he seems?"

"I'd say, you're stating the obvious. He's charming but I would be blind and stupid if I said I fully trusted him. Why?"

"Then why are we friends with such a person?"

"Because, he's fun. And to be fair, if it wasn't for him dragging you to that charity gig, we wouldn't be sitting here. So, in a way we owe him for our happiness."

"And that's what worries me."

"You overthink things, my love," Amber said and squeezed his hand.

"Maybe. Although, what if I knew there was another path, one where I truly help people, but we never meet?"

"Then, I'm glad you're not on that path. I want you right where I can find you." Amber smiled and ran her foot slowly and seductively up the inside of his legs. "Why don't we blow this meal off, pick up a takeaway and go eat it in bed… naked?"

The feel of her foot reaching his groin made Stofferson gasp. "Amber, you can't do that here."

"Why? Will walking out be too difficult for you?" She asked in a way that he never remembered her acting in university.

Stofferson looked around the busy restaurant in hope to rid his mind of the image of his beloved beckoning, naked, from the bed. In the far-off corner of the huge room the face of a gangling man with a gold-rimmed monocle caught his eye for a split-second. However, a waiter blocked his view. After the waiter passed, the man, Stofferson recognised from somewhere, had vanished.

"What do you say, Stoff?" Amber asked, bringing him back to the present. "I might even let you do what I only allow on your birthday."

He looked deep into her eyes and saw her lust burning. He had no idea what she allowed him to do only on his birthday but a huge part of him, well a throbbing average part of him, yearned to find out. Another part of him screamed, "RUN!" The latter voice grew more insistent, like a trapped prisoner in a dark cell at the back of his mind. He cast his eyes around the room again, almost hoping to see a sign. Instead, his eyes connected with the demon's. He leered back, his arms around the shoulders of the fearful man. Everything now seemed to slow down, yet, the voices and sounds of diners eating grew louder as they soon boomed inside his head. He turned back to Amber in a panic. She grinned. She had acquired a fig from somewhere. Stofferson watched with equal levels of horror and arousal as she squeezed the fruit into her open mouth. The juices ran down her chin to stain her dress. She cackled and wiped her face with the back of her hand. Beyond their table, a couple, previously quietly eating, began tearing at each other's clothes. Soon, Stofferson watched with disgust as the whole room, young and old, waiter and customer, men and women, men and men, women and women fornicated with one another.

"NOOOOO!" Stofferson hollered and stood away from the table.

The scene dissolved and the light faded to reveal the stone circle hiding behind it. He shook his head to clear the restaurant from his mind and saw Thor Fryes sitting cross-legged on a horizontal lintel stone, smiling down at him.

"Are you real or another trick by that demon?" Stofferson asked.

"Real, I hope, Master Stofferson. You've got to give him his due. He tried, did he not?"

"Yes. Where is he now?"

"I banished him."

"Were you in the illusion?"

"No. Why? Did you see me?" Fryes asked, leaning forward.

"I think I did. Just before the scene turned into an orgy."

"Ah. Interesting. All your meditations have served you well."

"How?"

"You must have sensed me close, even as the demon battered your senses with his false reality."

"No offense, but could you not have come earlier? Like maybe several weeks earlier?"

"No. And I shall not apologise. You needed to go through these tribulations to grow. Imagine if I popped up to help you rid the demon much earlier. Would you now understand why you do what you do?"

"No," Stofferson conceded.

"Take all of the last forty day's experience, the highs and lows, the fight and the conversation and learn from them. Most mortals miss that point," Fryes said.

"Why don't you open the demon doors if you are strong enough to rid such powerful demons?"

"For two reasons. I cannot. I can only show those I deem worthy."

"Are there others you have shown?"

"Many. Including the author of the book you acquired from me."

"Why can't you open it? Has it something to do with why you don't?"

"Very much so. Any thoughts of your own?"

"I'd say you are what the demon called Seraphim, but you don't seem monochromatic in thought."

"Although the demons, or the fallen as they regard themselves as different from the seraphim, both are from the same seed. The fallen fell for a reason. I am neither nor. I first walked as seraphim, then I rejected their absolute adherence to rules I did not get. I then fell and found no kinship with the demons. So, very much like yourself, Master Stofferson, I followed my own path and now assuage my guilt by helping mortals. Simple."

"If you say so," Stofferson said with a tired, cynical smile.

"I do," Fryes added and offered a little bow. "Now, I suggest we sleep. Tomorrow is a spectacularly huge day for both of us."

"Why? I thought you said you couldn't open the doors?"

"I can't. But, I can fend off the assault you will receive as you open it. As you wouldn't manage to force a crack in the door to widen if you had to perform both. Now, sleep."

Without another word, Stofferson felt his body grow heavy and the earth rise up as he fell into his first dreamless sleep for many years.

Chapter Twelve

Stofferson sat back in the brown-leather Coleridge chair and sighed as he remembered the day he opened the devil doors. He recalled little of the battle Fryes endured. He needed all of his focus to concentrate on the spell he chanted repeatedly…

When, eventually, a rip appeared in the fabric of reality, revealing a room beyond, Fryes grabbed him by the scruff and all but tossed him through the hole. For a slightly built being, the bookshop owner carried the strength of a man several times his size.

"Yes, I'm like an ant," Fryes said in almost a dismissive tone, "Now close the bloody hole."

Stofferson said the words to the next incantation without even a glance towards his companion. Flashes of light and flames flew back and forth around him as Fryes fought his battles. Soon enough, the rip closed and both collapsed in a heap, breathing heavily. It took them some minutes to recover. Both sat covered in jets of sweat.

"It didn't feel…like hard work…until I stopped," Stofferson gasped.

"Speak…for your bloody self," Fryes groaned. For the first time, Stofferson saw the vicious signs of battle seared into the visible skin of the strange being. "I'll need to rest…for a month…after that," he added and patted down several tiny fires still smouldering around his clothes.

Stofferson looked around the room in which they had arrived. He found himself in space similarly shaped to Fryes' shop. Although, instead of books, a mahogany bookcase lined most of the inner circumference. And again, instead of books, shafts of clear crystal lined the shelves. In the centre of the room stood two Coleridge chairs. A small area, the segment where the hole appeared, contained a reflective surface almost like a screen

"It's exactly like a screen," Fryes said, his breath back.

"Would you mind not doing that?" Stofferson groaned. "If I have a question, I'll ask it."

"I'm only trying to help, Master Stofferson."

"I get that, but it strikes me as a little rude. And please, call me Stoffa…"

"Very well to both requests," the elongated being shrugged. "Fancy a cuppa?"

"I thought demons didn't drink?"

"I told you, I'm neither nor. A seraph can drink, and that side of me wants a bloody good cup of tea." He stood and strode towards the screen. "This serves two purposes. It will serve you virtually anything you want. With the exception of hard drugs. So, food, medical supplies, drink, stationary, etc. And it also works as a screen for entertainment. All you do is choose a crystal with whatever you want to watch or read, wave it across the screen and you have your enjoyment. You can hole yourself up in here for as long as you want. Oh, the screen will also show you the outside of the door, so your enemies can't sneak up on you. And believe me, demons grow bored very quickly, so unless you have injuries to recover from within the pocket, you won't need to stay too long before they bugger off."

"What do you mean by 'pocket'?" Stofferson asked as he followed his strange new mentor.

"A large pot of tea for two and a box of assorted biscuits, please," Fryes told the screen. "Preferably with Bourbon biscuits inside. Thanks. The pocket is this. It's a pocket in space and time that no other demon can enter. I created it with the first magician I taught to use the ley-lines. It allows only me and the appropriate humans inside."

"What pushed you to create it?" Stofferson asked.

"When I fell and didn't like the hole, I landed in. It's served me well for many centuries."

"Who was the first magician?"

"A question for another time. You may meet him one day."

"He's still alive?" Stofferson asked, exasperated.

"For now."

"Where does he live?"

"Like I said, needy baby, a question for another time."

"Okay. Did you both create the crystals and the screen?"

"I did," Fryes shrugged. "I'd seen it once in the future shortly after building this place."

"You can travel to the future in this?" Stofferson asked aghast.

"I used to be able to because the pocket it first sat on wasn't, shall we say, as stable as this."

"Surely that would be an advantage against the demons?"

"My goodness, no. The damn thing tipped back to the dinosaurs once and I nearly found myself in the belly of a mean-looking beast. It may seem fun, but I have no way of knowing what year, past or present, I would end up. Now, I can relax. I took the tech from the twenty-fourth century before rectifying the position."

"What's that time like?"

"Surprisingly dull, apart from the media tech."

And despite opening the door for the first time over twenty-five years ago, it felt like yesterday to Stofferson. Time and its swiftness scared him. He constantly thought he had so much to do and so little time to complete it that he ironically gave little actual time to enjoyment. He regarded this as his lot.

Now, as he sat in his chair, legs and head aching, counting the minutes to his next dose of painkillers, he wondered how long it would take before his body felt strong enough for him to get back out into the action. A book about counter-curses played on the screen, but his mind echoed with too many other thoughts for him to concentrate.

"Screen, show me 67a Broughton Road, please." The screen changed to a view of the front room of the flat. "Damn," Stofferson cursed. He had placed the box with the relay crystal set behind a mesh panel on the top of the ghost box near the window so he would get a good view of the lounge. However, Michael or Lydia had moved it so it faced the back of the sofa. Which meant, because they both occupied the sofa at that moment, he could hear the two talking but couldn't see them. "Well, at least I can hear they're safe," he conceded with a groan.

For a few minutes he felt like a stalker as the two spoke about some photographs Lydia had unearthed from the archives of the local library and the internet. Photographs with some link to Michael's past. Stofferson wished he could see them for himself.

"This is so frustrating," Michael said.

"For you and me both, brother," Stofferson grumbled.

"I don't recognise any of the people in the pictures," Michael added.

"Don't worry. It will come back to you," Lydia said.

"Yes, but by what Stofferson said, my remembering spells the end of my time here and The Thirteen pushing you to take my place."

"They can't push me into committing suicide," Lydia stated and wished she believed the words. Because anytime Michael raised the subject, her stomach whirled. "Besides, I still don't believe they are even real."

"It does worry you though," Michael said. "I can tell."

"Of course, it does. But that's a good thing because I can keep my guard up. And, what have I told you about reading me?"

"Sorry. It's a habit."

Stofferson heard a telephone beep a few seconds before Lydia told Michael, "I hope this is good news."

"Why? Who is it?" Michael asked.

"Harry asking me to ring her ASAP. Fingers crossed," Lydia said and then a sullen silence passed before, "Hi Harry. You okay?"

Lydia must have pressed the speaker icon because Harry's loud voice came belting out for all to hear, pleasing Stofferson. "No. Where have you been? You said you would ring."

"Sorry. I went to visit a friend in hospital."

"Well, a bad friend visited me earlier. Care to guess who?"

"Shit. Not Julia?"

"Yes, my old fruit salad, the wicked witch of the east, west, north and every damned rancid bloody point in between."

"She didn't threaten you, did she?"

"I'd kick her in the crotch so hard the blind fish she spawned from would feel it, old love. On the contrary, she arrived all sickly sweet, begging for my help to find you."

"You didn't…"

"Of course, I bloody didn't. Do you take me for a prettier Winston Smith?"

"Sorry. I know you wouldn't. I panicked and know how manipulative she can be."

"Well, her powers don't work on me, my old bag of candy floss. She stayed for about ten minutes dribbling stories of you leaving her with no word and how she's dead inside without you and other blah, blah, blahs. I told her the almost truth." Harry said with a little snigger. "I hadn't seen you for ages until you called and fired me as your agent, saying you didn't need me anymore. I was fooking fuming about that I can tell you. Well, that's what I told her, anyway. She then left and I saw her talking to some woman outside and then they both disappeared out of view."

"This might seem a little paranoid, but you didn't leave her on her own in your office at any point, did you, Harry?" Lydia asked.

"Do you think I just fell out of the funny farm, old cock-spring? I would have to trust the fetid rag-donkey to leave her on her own in my office. No. I watched her every second she stank up the place. If you're thinking bugs, then worry not, my little love-jockey."

"Thank you, Harry. I owe you."

"You owe me sod-all, my pretty petal. Scum like her are lucky I didn't rip out her beady, ferret eyes and vicious tongue. Just keep in touch more often, eh?"

"I promise this time, Harry. Sorry."

"Accepted. Now, I've got Cushty Rushdie coming in five. Must dash. Love you, kitten."

"Love you too, Harry, you angel. Speak soon."

They soon finished the call.

"What happens now?" Michael asked Lydia.

"As Harry is the only person who vaguely knows where I am, we breathe a sigh of relief," Lydia replied.

Stofferson settled back in the chair with a groan and pondered the whole of Lydia's call and wondered who the person Julia met up with was. If he'd been there, he would have pressed Harry for more information. He cast his tired eyes towards the domed ceiling and said, "I wouldn't breathe that sigh too hard, my lovely. Screen, please call Superintendent Fisher."

The image of the flat's lounge disappeared as the screen turned blank. After connecting, Fisher answered.

"Jan, it's me, Stoffa. How are you?"

"Hey up, stranger. Are you still in hospital?"

"No. I'm sort of in hiding as I get better. It's hard to explain but it wasn't an accident."

"You think someone tried to kill you?"

"Oh, I'm almost certain of it. Not that I have a scratch of proof to back it up. I doubt I ever will after the lorry driver that hit me killed himself. That's another reason why I've called. Did you ever get the transcript from Markham's Dictaphone?"

"Yes. I kept it in my drawer. Two seconds." Stofferson heard rustling and rattling before she returned. "To be honest, Stoffa, it doesn't give a lot. He mumbled on about his pills and defences for his guest. I presume he means you?" Fisher asked.

"Quite probably."

"Then he turns a little manic and repeats the words, "It's just the pills and this isn't real." We then hear crashes as if he's stumbling around a room. But, the police report states the place was tidy, and even his housekeeper, a Mrs Williams, says everything looked normal the next day."

"Hmmmm," Stofferson pondered.

"Then there's a lot more denial of something we can't hear before he begins screaming and pleading."

"What's he pleading?"

"Can't really tell until he says, "For the love of God, please open." He then must be outside because the transcript reader hears wind and rain. Markham is then heard asking why someone is doing this to him. He then cries that he didn't say anything before falling silent for exactly two minutes and thirteen seconds."

"No other voices or other noises?"

"Nope. Just the wind and rain until he tells someone who he is."

"Is he still upset?"

"The transcriber writes that Markham appears nervous at first and then calmed. He even asks, "Really? I studied it too," in an excited way. The way he's talking suggests he's conversing with a young woman."

"What gives you that idea?"

"Well, the transcriber says his tone turns a little flirty and then proud as he tells the other about how he's trying to help a chap shake up the world. He goes on to say that the chap visited and he, Markham, told him exactly what needs doing. He then goes on to say that the corrupt will rue the day."

"Sounds like our previous meeting," Stofferson conceded.

"Well, that's just about all he said until he whispered the word Ose before he jumped off the cliff."

"Ose? You sure?"

"That's what the transcript says."

"Shit," Stofferson hissed.

"What? Does that mean something?"

"Yep. It means I'm right. He didn't jump."

Chapter Thirteen

The next few weeks ambled by for Lydia. Again, without word from Stofferson, or Jenny, new doubts began to grow inside her mind.

"Do you think any of this true?" She asked Michael for at least the fourth time as the air began to chill the world outside and the leaves of the silver birch on the sidings across the road turned golden. Her laptop sat open on her knees.

"You mean Stofferson?" Michael's voice asked from the ghost box, though Lydia no longer noticed.

"Stofferson, The Thirteen, any of it. I mean, I know you're real. I'm not that mad that I've made you up. But all the rest just seems like some ridiculous drama now ridden out. I certainly don't want to kill myself, and never have. Even after Julia."

"To be honest, he had me believing in his story for a while."

"And now?"

"Like I say, it feels like nothing more than a story. I remember no more than when you moved in and, despite you still suffering nightmares, you seem happy writing. So, I just don't know."

"My nightmares?"

"Yes. Well, I think they must be nightmares. I hear you screaming every now and again."

"Do I scream anything in particular?" Lydia asked, aghast, moving the laptop to the side.

"Sometimes you say please no. Most times you just scream. It worried me at first. I used to rush up to see if anybody had broken in. But, when I arrive on the stairs leading to your room, the door's shut and I can't get close to your door." Michael said with a sigh. "Now, I'm used to the screams."

"I'm so sorry," Lydia said, embarrassed.

"Don't be silly. I have dreams where I wake screaming. It's just that you don't hear it because I turn off the box before I go to sleep."

"It's funny how I don't remember them. How regularly do I scream?"

"Oh, not half as much as you used to."

"See? If there really was some curse on this place to make me suicidal, surely I would have nightmares more often and not less."

"I suppose."

So, the days drew on towards the winter months and with it warmer clothes. And even though her new home in Yorkshire only sat a few hundred miles north of her old address, she felt much colder then when she lived in the south. She even began the day with the radiators blasting. All but the one in her bedroom worked. Every night she rushed into bed, fully clothed, and undressed under the quilt.

Of course, Michael experienced little in the way of discomfort when autumn gave way to the dead months.

"I'm going to have to call a bloody heating engineer to show me how to set this damned thing," Lydia growled as she rushed down one morning, wrapped in a heavy dressing gown, to click the thermostat into life. "This is bloody freezing."

"What does the cold feel like?"

"An interesting question," Lydia replied through chattering teeth. "Erm, I suppose it's like your body feels an unpleasant tingle from your bones out and it makes you shiver. Damn! I'm a writer and I'm struggling over that one. How about you ask me after a hot cup of tea."

He did, but by that point all but the radiator in her bedroom blasted out dry heat and she found describing the sensation even harder.

Later, with the bedroom radiator still not warming, she left the flat to buy a key to bleed it. Yet, no matter how much filthy water spurted out onto the carpet, the radiator remained cold.

"More expense," she muttered. She tightened the nut and took out the key.

"No luck?" Michael called from the stairs, his voice slightly out of sync as it floated up from the lounge.

"No. I'm gonna have to call an engineer."

This she did. Four hours later, a balding, stooped, middle-aged man appeared at the front door.

"Problem with your radiator, love?" He asked, wearing overalls bearing the name "John."

"Yes," Lydia replied, standing back. "It's the one in the bedroom."

The engineer squeezed past, lugging a large toolbox and reeking of tobacco. Well, a large toolbox for his slight frame. "Worry not," he said. "It's probably just a stuck pin in your TRV."

"That sounds painful," Lydia said as she followed him to the first floor. "Do you want a cuppa, John?"

"Oh, I'm not John. But yes, please."

"Sorry," Lydia cringed. "It says John on your overalls, so I just assumed."

"Yeah, most people do. No, John was my other half. He died three years ago," the engineer told her without looking around.

"Oh, I'm sorry to hear that."

"Thanks, but no need. You're probably wondering why I wear them?"

"To feel closer to him?"

"No. He can rot for all I care. After he died, I found out he had loads of other men. I'm only wearing them because my others have got tomato soup on them."

"Oh," Lydia replied, feeling it would by fine if the world yawned and swallowed her whole.

"But, that said, I would love a cup of coffee."

"Oh, sorry, I've only got tea."

"Then no worries." They reached the lounge and Lydia showed him up to the bedroom. "Can you make sure the heating's off for the mo'?"

"Sure," Lydia replied, turned, and headed back down to the first floor.

Not more than two minutes later, the engineer trudged down to the lounge. "I'm afraid it's not what I first thought," he told her.

"How bad?"

"Not bad, bad. It's just full of sludge and will need blasting through."

"Can you do that?"

"Yep. But not until tomorrow. I have a customer booked in for this afternoon and only jammed you in because it sounded like a quick job," the engineer explained.

"How big of a job will it be?" Lydia asked.

"Well, I'll have to take it off the wall, carry it to the back and flush it through. I can get here for nine?"

"That sounds good. Thanks."

"Right, to make it a quicker job, can you unscrew the shelf across the top of the radiator? I'll leave you a screwdriver if you haven't got one."

"That's okay. I've got a set."

"Great. I'll see you tomorrow. By the way, what is your name?"

"You better not laugh."

"I won't."

"D'artagnan. My father was a big fan of Dumas."

"That's actually quite cool."

"Thanks," D'artagnan blushed. "See you in the morning."

"Michael, you can come out now," Lydia called out as she climbed back to the first floor after seeing the engineer out. She reached the lounge without Michael appearing. "Michael?" Still nothing. "Michael?" She asked again, this time a little worried.

"Here!" Michael called out as he appeared, clutching his tape ball.

"Jesus," Lydia growled. "You scared me then."

"Sorry," Michael cringed. "Just thought I'd try my hand at playing a trick."

"Very good. You nearly gave me a heart attack, you dick. What did you think of D'artagnan?"

"Apart from seeming a little sad, he seemed nice enough. Why?"

"Just wondered. It's handy having someone around to weed out the weirdos."

"You'll miss me when I'm gone."

"You're not going anywhere," Lydia smiled.

D'artagnan, the heating engineer, arrived exactly at nine o'clock the next morning, carrying a rubber bucket in one hand and his toolbox in the other. A feat not known for most tradesmen. Lydia had grown used to nine o'clock meaning anything between nine-thirty and three in the afternoon.

"I've taken the shelf off," she declared as they made their way to the second floor. "There's a lot of rubbish stuffed down, though."

"That's probably why the lazy decorator topped it off with a shelf," D'artagnan told her.

"Probably. I tried to get most of it out with a coat hanger but could only pull out an ancient sock and lots of balls of tissues. Sorry."

"Don't you worry, love. It'll all fall out after I take the radiator off the wall. You should have seen some of the rubbish I've found over the years. Some of it would make your eyes pop out."

"What sort of stuff?"

"Anything from knives to sex aids."

"Seriously?"

"Yep."

"Mental. Ooh, I bought coffee if you want a cup?"

"Awww, bless ya. That's very kind. Thank you."

"Not a problem. You go up and I'll bring you a cup," Lydia told D'artagnan.

"That'll be super. Thanks," he replied and shuffled up the short, narrow stairs to the second floor.

A little while later, Lydia walked into her bedroom to find the engineer had laid a plastic sheet on the floor before draining the radiator. The bucket contained a centimetre of brown water in the bottom.

"Thanks," D'artagnan said as he took the steaming cup. "I hardly needed the sheet. This must be chock full of sludge. Has it ever worked?"

"I don't know. I only moved in in the summer, so have never used it."

"Makes sense. Can I ask you to keep that side level as I undo the rest of the bolts."

That she did. A whole heap of detritus fell to the floor after removing the radiator.

"Oh, my god," Lydia exclaimed. "Who stuffs that much crap behind their radiator?"

"Like I said, you'll be surprised." For a diminutive man, D'artagnan picked the radiator up as if it was nothing more than cardboard and lugged it out of the room.

"Are you okay with that?" Lydia asked, though didn't really need to as the engineer had made it halfway to the first floor without much of a sweat.

"I'm fine, thanks," he called over his shoulders.

Lydia shrugged and kicked the pile of socks, balled up tissues and a dusty notepad. "Bin bag," she muttered and trotted downstairs to the kitchen for the bin bag, and a dustpan and brush.

"He's stronger than he looks, isn't he?" an unseen Michael whispered as she passed through the lounge. "He didn't even stop for a rest."

"Never judge a book," Lydia told the empty room.

"What does that mean?" Michael asked, again in a whisper.

"I'll tell you later," Lydia whispered back and skipped up to her bedroom.

Once there, she scooped the rubbish into the opened bag. Flicking through the pad didn't occur to her until one of the pages opened to reveal a rather scruffily written poem signed by M. Parker. She bent closer to the pad. "M. Parker? Michael Parker?" she muttered, aghast. She fished the pad out of the bag, keeping her finger on the page with the poem. When free of the bag, she read, "Winter is not death, but the clearing of the fields for the renewal of all things. 2008."

Chapter Fourteen

For a while, Lydia sat on the end of the bed staring at the poem and pondering where to go from there. *Could this be the gate that opens to release all of his memories?* She thought. And then remembered she didn't believe in any of this crap anyway.

"Right," D'artagnan announced as he, without even one bead of sweat, carried the radiator back into the bedroom, "it's ready to reattach."

"Uh?" Lydia replied, before, "Oh, that was quick. Do you need any help?"

"You could slip the bolts through for me while I hold it in place, if you don't mind?"

"Not at all." This she did. The task took her mind away from the poem. For only a few minutes, though.

"Right, thanks," D'artagnan told her. "I'll take it from here."

"Do you want another coffee?"

"That'll be grand, thanks."

Lydia turned to pick up the bag of rubbish and the tatty notepad before making her way to the kitchen. The pad seemed to grow heavier the closer she came to Michael's usual perch and grew no lighter as she passed. She felt his eyes pouring over her aura and knew he would ask questions after the engineer left. *What do I say?* She thought. *I can't lie to him. He'd know. I could leave with the engineer and go for a drive. That would work.*

As the kettle bubbled to a boil, Lydia tore out the page with the poem, stuffed the pad into a drawer full of tea towels and readied herself for a quick escape. However, the engineer took another hour to complete the job, and each second passed interminably slow. Lydia stayed in the bedroom pondering her predicament as D'artagnan worked, pretending to work on her laptop. A laptop into which she hadn't even signed her password. She just wanted out. She sort of wished she could speak to Stofferson about this. *But would he just fill my head with more superstitious nonsense?* she thought.

Eventually, D'artagnan finished and tested the radiator to make sure it worked. It did, so he began packing up his gear. "You should have no more issues with the old girl," he told her, touching the now hot radiator. "If you do, just give me a call."

"Thanks," Lydia replied, jumping off the bed. "I'll walk you out. I've got to go to town." She followed him downstairs, not daring to cast a glance towards the window sill. "I'll just grab my bag and coat." She shot into the kitchen and grabbed her things before continuing behind him to the front door. "Thank you again for the great job, D'artagnan. I'll be sure to leave a glowing review."

"Glad to help."

They said their goodbyes at the door before he climbed into his van and she her car. Without a look towards the flat, she drove out of town.

"Well, that was weird," Michael said out loud after they

disappeared down the road, his tinny voice bouncing from each wall of the lounge.

Meanwhile, as the dying verges passed by, Lydia called the only person she knew who would at least offer some semblance of sane advice.

"Harry here," her only friend's voice boomed from the car's speakers. "Well, slap my rosy arse. Are you sure he wrote it?" She asked after Lydia explained her situation.

"He's called Michael Parker, and he died in 2008. I can't think who else it might be." She then went on to tell Harry the supposed curse of the flat as told by Stofferson.

"And you're still bloody living there?" Harry asked. "Jesus and his chain of mucky Marys, even if it's some exceptional fiction from a dicked-up mind, I don't think I could risk it."

"I thought you were the tough one?"

"Oh, I am. If you have flesh and you dare to piss me off, you're in for a wiener whacking, whether you have one or not. But I don't mess with the other side. Science may have proved most of it pure bollocks but physicists didn't know about quarks until the sixties, and they sound like something a broken bloody duck hollers. Why don't you buy yourself some time away from the madness and stay in a hotel for a few nights? If this bloke says they won't hurt you because you have to do it yourself inside the walls of the flat then sell the damned thing and be done."

"But, aren't you even curious?"

"I'm curious to find out what your new book is going to be about. I'm not curious to wait to find out if you've topped yourself because of some deal done with forces beyond our knowledge. Fuck that, my beautiful lunatic. And if Michael getting his memories back is the sign of your end days, why are you even considering showing him his death poem?"

"He can't live out eternity stuck in the flat," Lydia protested. "That's hardly fair."

"At the risk of losing you, he seems happy enough, doesn't he?" Harry asked. "He's not the one worrying about his past. You, for reasons way beyond sense, are. Maybe that's part of the curse. The living finds the answer for the dead and then replaces their ethereal arse. A shitty-shit deal if ever there was one, old cocker."

"Hmmmm," Lydia replied.

"You know I'm making sense, my little red jellybean."

"How come red?"

"They're my favourite, of course." A silence descended on both ends of the call before Harry's tone softened. "Listen to me, doll, for the love all things sensible and joyful, get out of that flat. The idea seemed fun to me until you just filled me in with the fricking rest. If it's bullshit, then all you stand to lose is a friendly ghost in your life. Visit him and wave at the window he sits in. If true, you lose your life and I'm not visiting your spirit in hope to swap places, I can tell you that for sweet sod-all, my pretty marigold."

"Do you have a book full of those little names for me?" Lydia asked, hoping to ease the tension.

"Nope. They just come to me. Now, promise me you'll at least book into an hotel for a few days to think this through logically."

"I promise. Has she that shall remain nameless appeared again?"

"She has a name and she is a dick," Harry spat. "And, no. I haven't seen her."

"Good."

Lydia finished the call with more promises to book into an hotel. After a U-turn in a little village by the name of Gisburn, she headed back to Burrstone, bought an evening dress, shoes and the other things a lady needs for an impromptu stay in an hotel before booking into the Bon Suite. The room offered less views than the first time she had visited but it felt comfortable as she threw herself onto the bed with a sigh, and that's all that mattered to her right then. She ran a bath and slipped into the hot soapy water. Michael smiled inside her thoughts, replacing any idea of relaxation with a nice slice of guilt.

"Stop it," she scolded herself. "He's not my problem." A sentiment she couldn't accept as they'd grown as friends. "But what if Harry's wrong?" No solid answers floated back to her. Only the constant wash of worried tones of her own inner voice replied. She groaned and climbed out of the water. "Pointless," she added.

She wrapped a towel around her body and stomped back into the bedroom. In a hope to still her whirling thoughts, she attempted to meditate. Rain spattered against the windowpane as she laid back against the pillows and chose a video called "Release Your Anxieties." A deep Australian male voice instructed her in breathing exercises with which she was more than familiar. She followed his advice, nonetheless. She may have expressed surprise as her thoughts slowed to the sound of his calm voice. Lydia, though, felt too relaxed to notice. Sleep soon took her hand. She dreamt of a boarded-up hotel. She and three friends long since lost danced from the dusty bar to a gleaming ballroom at the rear of the building. Streamers and banners declaring the wedding of Jason and Connie hung from the walls. Lydia then woke up wondering who the hell the bride and groom were, as she knew nobody by their names.

"Dreams are weird," she yawned, feeling calmer than earlier.

Later, dressed for dinner, she made a mental note to call Harry to thank her for her splendid idea. Because, despite Michael edging into her thoughts now and again, she had never felt more optimistic. She decided to sell the flat, with the promise to fill her life with more peace. She had gone from living persecution to ghostly insanity without recuperating properly from the latter.

"I'm a madness magnet," she told herself as she touched up her make-up. "That's what I am. Time to change. I should get a house near the beach. And a puppy."

She had always wanted a puppy. Julia, of course didn't want, in her words, "Some shedding piss-monster crapping around the house, stinking up the carpets." So, as always, Lydia acquiesced. Better compliance than another broken bone.

"Now," she told herself, "I can have what I bloody well want." She pulled back her shoulders and strode, as free as the air, out of the room and down the hall to the lift. Once there, she dropped one floor to the dining room. The room already tinkled with many diners. This time, as opposed to her first stay, Lydia felt no anxiety about eating on her own. She even smiled at those she passed as the tall maître d' with the tight black trousers showed her to a table. She wondered how on earth he managed to fit them over his shapely rear. She also speculated on her chances of tearing them off him.

"Can I get you a drink, madam?" the maître d' asked as Lydia sat.

"And your number if you're giving it away?" Lydia asked, shocked at her sudden salaciousness but hiding it with a smile.

"I wish I could," the maître d' bowed, obviously used to such advances, "but, hotel policy."

"Shame," Lydia conceded, "I could do with the company."

"My apologies. I'll fetch your waitress." The maître d' bowed again, with a glint in his eyes, and left Lydia to her thoughts.

Her thoughts were less than clean. She fought hard to suppress a giggle. This new version of herself surprised and pleased her. An older man with a not-so-neat combover, sitting at an opposite table caught her attention with a rather slimy smile. As if to say, "I heard that. Any chance?"

In your dreams, Lydia thought and turned her eyes to the menu.

Later, after returning to her room, stomach content but not full, Lydia sniggered to see *Bridget Jones Diary* beginning on the first television channel on which she clicked.

"All I need now is a bottle of gin and my life is complete," she told herself as she slipped out of her dress and into her night clothes. She climbed into bed and grimaced as something scratched her neck. She slipped back out if bed, removed the nightie, pulled off the tag, and reversed the procedure.

An hour into the film, Lydia frowned as someone tapped on her door. The frown turned to excitement as she peeked through the peephole in the door and saw the maître d' standing on the other side holding a bottle of wine.

"I thought it wasn't hotel policy?" She asked with a grin after opening.

"Well, it's against hotel policy to give my number out during service. I've meticulously combed through the rules and found nothing against me visiting a guest with a bottle of wine, though."

"Then I suppose you better come on in."

He did, and Lydia found his tight trousers came off easier than she thought. Along with the rest of his clothes.

Chapter Fifteen

Lydia awoke at nine the next day with a smile pasted across her face and a new sense of positivity she hadn't experienced in so long it unnerved her. The maître d', who turned out to be called Marcus, left around five-thirty as he had the breakfast shift. She vaguely remembered saying thanks as he shuffled out of her door.

I can't believe I just picked up a guy like that, she thought with a sigh. Sure, she'd done similar things when she was younger but never thought it would happen again after her life took a rather large detour into a dragon's lair and then on through the afterlife less-than-amusement arcade. The evening of fun and many frolics cemented her plan to sell the flat and live anew. *I have to start thinking of me,* she thought, as much as leaving Michael saddened her.

With this spring of new beginnings creating a bounce in her step, Lydia hopped out of bed, fulfilled her ablutions, dressed and skipped down to the next floor for breakfast. Marcus greeted her at the door with the naughtiest of smiles, addressed her as "Madam," and led her to a nice table with a view of the canal and passing colourful barges. *The perks of stringless sex,* Lydia surmised.

"Would you like a tea or coffee?" Marcus asked, maintaining a complete air of professionalism.

"Tea, please."

"I will arrange that for you," he replied after making a note on his pad. "Your waitress will be here in just a moment for your breakfast order."

"Aren't you going to ask me my room number?" Lydia inquired with a coy grin.

"No need, Madam. I remember it from last night," Markus replied, struggling to keep his mask in place.

"Last night?" Lydia asked in mock innocence.

"Yes, Madam. You gave it before dinner last night."

"You have a good memory."

"Thank you. One always tries to remember the nicer customers," Marcus said with a slight bow and an even slighter wink. "Have a lovely day."

"If yesterday is anything to go by, it shouldn't be hard. Thank you."

Marcus smiled again and left Lydia to watch his packed trousers stride away.

After breakfast, she trawled the local area for another estate agent. Not risking alerting Stofferson's Thirteen by going back to Daniel and company. She soon decided on an agency situated in the next main town to Burrstone; Keighley. The company sounded innocuous enough. It went by the name of Spencer & Co. She tapped their number into her telephone and waited. A strong, gruff Yorkshire accent answered.

"Spencer and company," the man said.

Lydia explained that she needed to sell her flat as fast as possible as she had found a job abroad. A lie, but plausible.

"I'm surprised you've come to me. There's other agencies over Burrstone way," Spencer said.

"I bumped into a man in Keighley on a night out who recommended you highly."

"Did he give his name?" Spencer asked. "It sounds like he's owed a little commission." He then laughed a throaty, heavy smoker's laugh.

"I think he said his name was Carl," Lydia said, amazed how fast the lie shot on to her tongue.

"Hmmmm. I can't think who that might be. Anyway, I can be over today at three to look at the property. If that's not too quick?"

"That's ideal. Can I ask you to come in a plain car? My neighbours are very nosy, and I'd rather tell them I'm moving when everything is finalised. They'll want to throw a party and I'm not one for that."

"Sure, no worries. Nosy neighbours are the worst, aren't they?"

Lydia soon ended the call before ordering a taxi for two-forty-five. Deciding to leave her car for obvious reasons. She then relaxed into the day.

Later, after a simple lunch in the bar of steak and ale pie and chips, she waited outside the front for the taxi. The taxi arrived on time, though the new, sullen face didn't say much as they sped through the town and down Broughton Road. The driver came to a stop in front of a rather dilapidated Ford Focus. The front bumper barely clung to the body of the car with the help of a lot of duct tape. As Lydia paid and exited the taxi, a rotund man with little hair and a suit that had seen better days climbed out the Focus, coughing as he did, carrying a clipboard and well-chewed pencil.

"Miss Richardson?" He asked after the racking subsided.

"Yes?"

"Malcolm Spencer. We spoke on the phone."

"Ah, yes. Nice to meet you."

"Is the car plain enough for you?" He asked, moving closer. The wave of tobacco blowing from his cracked lips nearly knocked Lydia sick.

"Perfect," Lydia replied, taking a step back. "Shall I show you around?"

"Sounds like a plan."

"Obviously, this is the main door," she said and opened the door with her key. "This leads to my two-storey upper-floor flat."

"Who lives downstairs?"

"Nobody. Apparently, it's used for storage."

"Hmmm," Spencer grunted and made a note.

Lydia opened the flat door, "So, everything has been recently painted and it has a lovely new bathroom."

"You ever need a job in the estate agency business, you just give me a call," Spencer quipped. "You're a natural."

"Sorry. I thought I'd save you some questions."

"No need. If you don't mind, I'll walk through the flat, take some measurements and piccies, and if I have any questions, I'll ask," Spencer said without any malice.

"Sure. Do you want a drink or anything?"

"No, thanks. I won't be that long."

As good as his word, he flashed through every room in minutes. With a quick measure here and a photo there. While upstairs, Michael appeared for a brief moment and offered an excited but confused wave to Lydia. She smiled as wide as she could muster and waved back.

"Right," an out of breath Spencer began as he returned to the lounge from the second floor. "All we need now is a copy of the deeds to make sure all is super."

"No problem. I have them here," Lydia told him and turned to a little oak chest of drawers. She pulled open the top drawer and removed a large, brown envelope. She passed it to Spencer.

He opened the envelope and flicked through the stapled pages he pulled from inside. His eyes moved at impressive speed. Every now and then he made funny little acknowledging grunts in his throat. Until he reached a page where his expression dropped and his groan sounded more defeatist.

"I'm afraid I can't sell this property for you, Miss Richardson. Sorry."

"Why not," Lydia frowned.

"Because, there's a lovely little clause in the small print that states you signed an agreement that if the flat is to be sold within ten years of purchase, Greyson, Sutcliffe and Milner would then get first refusal over any other party. Ergo, not me."

"There must be something I can do?"

"Not as far as I can see," Spencer shrugged. "Maybe see a solicitor for advice, but it looks a bit cut and dried to me. You have my details if anything changes."

"Well, I'm sorry to waste your time."

"Think nowt of it. These things are sent to test us, aren't they?"

"Seems so. Are you heading back to Keighley?"

"Yep."

"I couldn't be cheeky and grab a lift to Bon Suite, could I, please?"

"I can hardly refuse a lady in distress, can I?"

Lydia dare not look behind her in case Michael made a quick and sad appearance as she and Spencer left the flat and stepped out into what was once a sunny day but now reflected her mood, with heavy clouds and the beginning of rain.

"The passenger door doesn't open from the outside," Spencer told her. "I have to push from the inside. Won't be a mo'." Lydia watched, with puzzled amusement, as Spencer squeezed into the driver's side and then leaned across to the passenger and began pushing from inside. After the third push, it flew open, nearly taking her legs. "There we go," he called, slightly out of breath.

Lydia slipped into the passenger seat and fought the urge to clamp her nose. The car stank of cigarettes, sweat, and desperation. She turned to pull the safety belt around her, but it wouldn't move.

"Ah. The bloody thing's temperamental," Spencer told her. "You have to tug it gently a couple of times and then it'll release." Lydia smiled through the stench and did as Spencer told her. It worked on the fourth tug. "Do you mind me asking why not just sell back to the Greyson lot?"

"I had a few issues with them and now you've shown me the clause, I suppose my concern was justified."

"Well, to be fair, it's sneaky, but bloody clever. Though, I have to wonder why?"

"What do you mean?" Lydia asked.

"Well, an agent sells a house and moves on to another," Spencer began. "No one expects a new owner to sell within ten years. Not unless they know something the owner doesn't."

"So, it's not something estate agents do?"

"Not as far as I know."

"Could it be illegal?"

"I doubt it. Though, I hope so for my sake," Spencer sniggered. "Just be careful which solicitor you take it to."

"What do you mean?"

"Well, to what I hear, you kick one person from Burrstone and others feel it," Spencer said.

"What does that mean?" Lydia asked.

"If they're not all related in some way, they know someone who is, is all I'm saying." Spencer pulled into Bon

Suite's car park. "Well, I hope to hear from you again. If not, good luck." He held out a pillow-like hand.

Lydia shook it, amazed how dry it felt. "Well, sorry again for wasting your time and thank you for the lift." She tried the door, forgetting the difficulty Spencer had. The door didn't move.

"You have to give it a bit of welly," Spencer advised.

Lydia gave it a heavier shove. Still nothing.

"Do you want me to try?" Spencer asked.

The thought of Spencer pressing his body against her filled Lydia with no joy and gave her a greater incentive to exit the vehicle. She almost threw herself against the door. A searing pain shot from her still healing ribs as the door flew open. "Thank you again," she said through clenched teeth.

"My pleasure. All the best," Spencer said and pulled the door closed from inside. He waved from the driver's side as he skidded out of the car park.

Lydia, holding her now-throbbing ribs, stood as tall as possible and entered the hotel, cursing inside. *Bloody typical. First time I've felt any pain in ages.*

She reached her room and ran a bath, emptying a complimentary bath soap bottle under the tap. When it was full, she slid carefully into the hot, soapy water and sighed. "And the day started with such promise."

Chapter Sixteen

Michael watched Lydia ride away with her strange companion, in shock. "She's leaving me," he said aloud and felt an unusual ache. "But why isn't she happy? Is it the supposed Thirteen?" He wandered around the lounge like he used to do before his new friend arrived to eradicate the solitude. "She was fine before the engineer came to fix the radiator. Maybe he said something." This traipsing the room while asking himself questions went on for quite a while. Until he stopped and frowned. "She came down with a notepad. I wonder if that has something to do with it."

Michael rushed to the kitchen. He recalled Lydia scurrying into that room and then returning without the pad. Now adept at gripping and moving common objects, Michael looked through the cupboards and the drawers. When he reached the towel drawer he lifted the tea-towels inside to see if she had placed the pad underneath. That's when he found it. He pulled it out and walked back to the living room, flicking through the pages as he went. He then stopped. His mouth dropped open. He arrived at a page that began with, "Dear Michael, please read this carefully..." As he shuffled on to the window sill, he began reading a testimony from someone called Mary who confirmed everything Stofferson had told them.

As he read, Michael reeled forward as if his whole spirit had received a whack. He staggered to his left and slid through the sofa, dropping the pad. “ARRGGHH!” he screamed as a whir of old memories with his pretty former housemate punctured his thoughts. Images of his parents, one moment bed-ridden and then next walking, sliced his mind. He rolled back through the sofa to ball up, screaming with inner pain. He saw their funerals and him moving from the family home. He witnessed his first meeting with Mary. He felt a wave of love for her. He experienced the drudgery of life working in the local supermarket and the anger of ridicule. He remembered amusing chats with Mr K. The only thing he couldn’t recall was how he ended up replacing Mary. The barrage of images went on for so long, the sun set around him before they stopped. Childhood, school-life, first girlfriends, football, music, fear, fun and every tiny ineffectual emotion and experience in between. Yet, he could only recall memories from his life running up to his plan of suicide. Everything afterwards seemed to hide behind a sullen dark cloud.

Michael stopped and simply said, “The pad.” He stood and staggered around to the back of the sofa, where the pad lay.

Chapter Seventeen

After the bath and three paracetamols, Lydia meditated on the bed. By the time she cleared her thoughts, the pain had subsided a little, leaving a dull ache to hum in its place. Her stomach rumbling as she dressed took her mind to Marcus and away from the dull throbbing.

"There's no way I'm up for his kind of loving tonight," she mumbled to her reflection in the mirror. *Unless he's gonna take full control,* she added inside her mind. Such thinking pushed the flat and its problems to the back of her mind.

She left the room sometime later, feeling a little lighter, and headed towards the lift. She looked forward to a little flirting with Mr Tight-trow. Further up the hall, a tall blonde, with her back to Lydia, heading into her own room, almost stopped Lydia's heart.

"It can't be," Lydia whispered, a sudden weight on her chest hindering her breath. "It can't." The lift pinging open startled her. She shot into the empty car and clung to a chrome handrail. The inside swam before her. The doors closed but Lydia found herself unable to move. All of her previous colour had flushed from her face in the reflection from a mirror to the side. "I've done this before. It can't be her. I'm imagining it," she told herself over and over. She took a deep inhalation before releasing a longer breath to slow down her heart. This did little to help. Until her third attempt. "I'm stressed and overthinking. That's all. And you can fuck off," she scowled to her image. She took several inhalations before calming enough to decide to ride down to the reception before having dinner. Surely the receptionist could tell her if anyone called Julia Gardner had checked in.

"Yes," the dark-haired receptionist with far too much filler in her lips told her with what must have been a smile.

Lydia felt her knees buckle.

"Are you okay, love?" The receptionist asked.

Lydia nodded and turned to head back to the lift as steadily as her shaking legs would allow. *Fuck. She's found me. She's fucking found me.* Her first instinct was to get in the car and find another hotel but her keys and cards sat on the dressing table in the room down the corridor from her abusive ex's. She fell into the lift as soon as the doors slid open, knowing she had only one option. "You've got to do it," she told her reflection. "You've no choice." She hoped Julia had returned to her room after eating and wouldn't leave. "She must've. She likes to eat early." The lift pinged to announce its arrival on her floor and the doors opened. The elderly couple waiting on the other side startled Lydia.

"Sorry, love," the gentleman said. "Didn't mean to make you jump."

"That's okay," Lydia replied in a whisper. "I'm tired."

Squeezing past them, Lydia skittered towards her room; her wide eyes fixed on the door she had seen Julia enter. She fumbled with her key card, panic rising as she dropped it and then couldn't get it to work in the door.

"Come on," she muttered. "Come on. Idiot." Lydia realised she attempted to enter the door one down from her room and rushed forward. This time the key slipped into the door and Lydia fell into her room. She collected her things in under five minutes, the fear and anxiety fighting with the will to escape. When she was ready, she pulled open the door inch by inch, and then peered down the hall. No sign of Julia. Lydia bolted to the lift, pressed the call button and waited. And waited.

"Come on," she told the lift, panic threatening to supersede any other feeling. "Come on."

The lift pinged before opening. A large lady and her much more diminutive male colleague, holding hands, smiled as they exited the lift car. Lydia did her best to return the smile before shooting inside and pressing the ground floor button. The doors stayed open. She pressed again. And again. And… the doors closed. Lydia almost vomited with relief. On arrival at the required floor, she bolted towards the reception desk.

"I'm sorry, I have to leave. An emergency. I'm paid up for another day, but it doesn't matter. Here's my key card."

She all but threw the key card at the frowning receptionist. "I'm sorry you have to leave. I hope everything is fine. Can I just get you to sign…"

The lift pinged behind her. Lydia shot her head in its direction. Her wide eyes and pickled brain expected Julia to rush out to confront Lydia. "Haven't got time." She turned and ran through the main doors and towards her car. She again fumbled with the keys, but this time didn't miss the keyhole. A sudden banging caused her to turn back to the hotel. Julia stood framed in a first-floor window, slamming her palms against the glass. Lydia's heart fell out of her rear as Julia began pleading for Lydia to wait for her to come down. She then left the window. Lydia knew why. She opened the driver's door, threw her things across to the passenger seat and sped out of the hotel car park, her tyres screaming as she went.

Lydia travelled no more than half a mile down Burrstone bypass before she stopped in a lay-by, leaned out of the car, and emptied her stomach across the oil-stained tarmac. After three explosions from her torn throat, she added to her pain by screaming into the darkness beyond. "WHYYYYYYY?" She sobbed.

Hearing an oncoming vehicle approaching, and seeing its headlights, stopped any answers. She wiped her eyes on her sleeves, swung back behind the wheel, spun out of the lay-by and headed back along the by-pass, tapping her telephone in between changing gears. Soon enough, Lydia found the number she needed and tapped the call icon.

"Hiya, doll-face," Harry answered.

"She's found me, Harry. Bloody found me. What am I gonna do? I don't even know how. What do I do?"

"Hey. Calm, my sugar plum. Is she near you now?"

"No, I've left the hotel. She could be following me for all I know."

"You've lived up there for a while now, and she won't know the area. Do you know any B-roads that she won't?"

"I think so." Lydia came to a roundabout. She took the road to Broughton, but instead of turning left down Broughton Road, she carried on and took a right down a narrow road to a village called Gargrave she'd found some weeks back.

"Is anyone following you?" Harry asked.

Lydia checked the rear-view mirror, for the umpteenth time, but saw no other vehicles trailing her. "I don't think so."

"Good. Now take a deep breath and tell me everything." As Lydia arrived in Gargrave, she took a left after a small humpback bridge that spanned a narrow stream and explained everything to Harry. Even the dalliance with Marcus. "First of all: You slut. You know I was next in line." Lydia smiled for the first time. "Secondly, she can't have known you were staying down the corridor from her or she would have belted your door down."

"Is that good?" Lydia asked, confused.

"Damn right," Harry replied. "It means nobody's following you. And when I mean nobody, she must have been tipped off about your whereabouts from someone. I'm guessing whoever met her outside my office."

"Maybe."

"Maybe? Who else? Because, even I didn't know at what hotel you were staying. For all I know, there could be hundreds. So, she must presume you were at the flat. Which also means, she must have only just arrived."

"You sure?"

"Occam's Razor, my old honey spoon."

"Occam's what?"

"The simplest explanation is normally the correct one."

"Oh. Yes, I suppose."

"No supposing. Now, can you get out of the country?"

"My passport's in the flat."

"Damn. You can't stay in a local hotel tonight. That would be too risky. What town is closest but far enough away that they won't look?"

"I don't know… erm… Harrogate?"

"Do you want me to find you a good hotel there while you drive? There's no messing then. You stay the night there, hire a different car, rush over, get your passport and sod the sod off."

"But what if she's waiting?" Lydia asked, too stung to see any positives.

"Then stay a couple of days in Harrogate. See the sights, eat the food and then go over. Maybe even stay in two different hotels. Actually, what in the bells of flaming, fiery hell are we worried about?" As long as you get in the flat unscathed, surely your guardian-fricking-ghostie will defend you. He did against the burglars, didn't he? You call the local coppers. Tell them your psycho ex is trying to find you and kill you and then you get in and out. Simple."

"I don't really trust anyone local. Spencer said if you kicked one, they all felt it. I don't know if they have someone in the local police."

"Shit the bed, doll-face. I know she and this Stofferson have done a number on you, but the cops can't be in on it."

"I can't know that for sure, and don't want to risk it.

"I could ask around. Someone may know someone in private security."

"You could, but that might take a while. I want away as soon as possible. I would be grateful if you can find me a decent hotel and I'll sneak over tomorrow. If I can get in, Michael might help me."

"Good girl. I'm on it. I'll give you a bell when I've found one. Drive carefully, my chocolate raisin."

"I will. Thank you, Harry."

"Hush. Love ya!"

"Love you too," Lydia replied, just before the line became dead.

Lydia swung the car around at the first convenient junction and headed back down the A59 to the spa town of Harrogate. Only once did her heart batter her ribs, as she passed Menwith Hill American Air Base and heard a siren behind her. Nerves jangling, she pulled to the side. She then breathed a sigh of relief as the screaming police car shot past her and on down the road.

The phone rang through the speakers a short time after.

"Right, my lovely gumtree, I've booked you into The Majestic. It looks grand enough for my favourite jam-pie," Harry told her after they exchanged pleasantries.

"Thanks, Harry. You're a gem."

"Kindly remember that when you're cavorting with the bell boy of this hotel."

"You want me to remember you if I have sex with the bell boy?"

"Always. Whoever it is. My supple lines should be at the forefront of your mind when slipping between the sheets with anyone, my old sex kitten."

Chapter Eighteen

Michael picked up the notepad, strewn behind the sofa, with all the care of a bomb disposal operative. He didn't want another flood of emotion. He merely wanted answers. He shuffled over to the window but didn't risk sitting on the sill for fear of falling off. Instead, Michael sat crossed-legged under the sill before opening the pad at the page that began;

"Dear Michael, I beg you, please read this carefully and break the chain. I now know, there is a curse upon this building dating back hundreds of years by demon-worshippers calling themselves The Thirteen. I was told this when I took over from the previous spirit occupant. As his predecessor told him. However, each time, the new occupier somehow loses any grasp to their past and the warning given until it is time for them to move on. I suppose it is part of the curse, though, I don't know why this happened to so many innocent souls. All I do know from what I was told is that The Thirteen prey on people who carry a heavy burden of sadness in their heart and are good people. The words, "pure of soul" has been passed down but I can't see myself as such if I do not leave this warning. I can only hope it reaches you, or at least

somebody next in line to take over from you when your time as occupier comes to an end. This has to stop. Please make sure the next person leaves this flat before the urge to commit suicide grows too much for them.

Wherever we end up, I hope to see you again.

All my love,

Mary"

Michael stared at the letter for a long time. Every now and then, his gaze saddened as it rested on the name, Mary. He recalled his love for the woman after he first saw her warm eyes illuminating the air around her with kindness, as she stood framed in the bathroom door. After all those many years of loneliness, looking after his elderly, ailing parents in the family home, before the emotional move to his new flat, it staggered him to find it already occupied by such a wonderful soul. He remembered the initial nervous uncertainty he felt before they met, due to the rumours of Mary having committing suicide in his bedroom. The trepidation evaporated soon afterwards when he realised she had looked after him since he almost boiled his first pan of potatoes dry, and nearly flooded the bathroom by forgetting to turn off the tap before visiting Mr K's shop. The addition of the bubbles frothing in the warm bath water on rushing back in a panic told him she possessed no malevolent tendencies towards him. Her appearance days later then stunned him with her beauty. Their friendship grew from there. Although, poor Mary didn't have the luxury of a ghost box in which to communicate. She utilised copious notepads. Michael smiled at the memory. His smile soon faded as he longed to speak to her and find out what fresh things she had learned to pass on to him in these new uncertain times.

As the light of day faded to black outside and still he stared at the letter without seeing the words, Michael heard a rattle of a key in first the main door and then the flat. He stood in a panic, yet rested Mary's final testimonial on the sill with care. *I have to warn her,* he thought. Lydia being the "her" he expected to walk up the stairs. The bright bulb illuminating the house outside the lounge just before long blonde locks strode on to the landing and into the kitchen soon clamped his mouth. With this new actor out of view, Michael picked up the letter and slid it under the couch. He then rushed to the kitchen. However, the blonde woman stepped out as he entered and passed through him, showing him everything about the human body he no longer needed in all its horrific vividness, causing him to gag. He groaned and stopped, with wide, fearful eyes as his groan also came from the ghost box now tucked by the side of the sofa.

"Hello?" The lady called, switching on the room's light. "Is there anybody there? Lyd? Is that you?"

How does she know about Lydia? Michael thought as he skirted around the woman and the furniture to flick the off button on the ghost box. The switch made a click.

"Hello?" the woman called again. "If there's someone there, come out. I won't hurt you, I promise. I've changed, Lyd. I really have. I can't bear to live without you. Please come home."

"So, you're Julia," Michael said, free to talk without her hearing him. He strode closer to her. Despite her obvious good looks, Michael saw much more darkness from her aura. "Thank goodness Lydia isn't here. I dread to think what you'd do."

Julia's piercing eyes scanned the room before she trotted up to the second floor and turned on more lights as she checked for life. Michael sat near the top step and watched her rummage through Lydia's drawers. Every few seconds he heard her mutter incoherent words. Her aura showed signs of jealousy, anger and sardonic amusement. He watched as she fished a book from Lydia's nightstand and sat down on the bed to read the pages therein.

"You bitch," she spat after flicking through the book for a few moments. "That whore will regret lying to me."

Julia carried on reading intermittent passages of what Michael reasoned must be Lydia's diary, the anger building with each passing second. Until she screamed in rage and tore the book to shreds. Her outburst shocked Michael, who had never seen such unchained fury. Alive, she would have scared him witless.

"Unfortunately for you, I'm not alive," Michael grinned, remembering the burglars. He then frowned as Julia began sniffing Lydia's quilt cover and pillowcases and making noises that quite frankly disturbed him. The kind of noises he recalled from his living childhood that filtered through the wall between his bedroom and his parents' early on most Sunday mornings when they carried the energy and will. Michael sidled down to the lounge and left the blonde weirdo to her strange and, quite frankly, disturbing behaviour.

Chapter Nineteen

Meanwhile, Lydia endured no less of a puzzling evening. After checking in at the huge and, from the outside, impressive hotel overlooking the outskirts of the spa town, she headed to her room. A high-ceilinged room sadly underwhelmed by the dated décor.

"As long as she doesn't pop out of the next room, I don't care," she told her reflection and then gasped as a series of heavy raps struck the door. "Who is it?" She called, trying to keep the nerves from her tone.

"Room service," replied a male voice, she recognised through the terrible falsetto disguise.

"Where the hell have you been?" She snapped as she whipped open the door to reveal Stofferson leaning against a walking stick. "And more to the point, how the hell did you know where I was?"

Stofferson grinned and pulled a clear crystal on a short gold chain from his coat pocket. "I scried you."

"Oh, like in *Charmed* where you dangle it over a map?"

"Goodness me, no. I might try that next time, though."

"So, how do you do it?" Lydia asked and motioned for Stofferson to enter her room.

"I place the chain over my third eye and then I can get a fleeting glimpse of your whereabouts," he told her as he entered and took a seat opposite the bed. Lydia perched on the end of the bed.

"Third eye? That's not some pervy sex magick thing, is it?" Lydia asked, disgusted.

"No," Stofferson protested. "It's here in the middle of my forehead." He tapped the spot.

"Oh, sorry," Lydia cringed. "A long and tiring day. I'll ask again, though, where have you been?"

"I visited one of the magickal healing spots, or demon doors as we call them. I also studied the curses on your flat and think I've figured a way of reversing them. So, I'm guessing you're here because you're starting to believe?"

Lydia updated Stofferson on all the events since he disappeared from the hospital.

"Was there anything else in the pad?" He asked after she finished.

"I don't know. I didn't have time to look."

"Why didn't you take the whole pad and not just the poem?"

"I don't know. I panicked. Okay?" She spat.

"Alright, Lydia. No need to get testy. I'm just curious. It may have contained more clues."

"It's been a rough day. Sorry."

"Accepted. I'm sorry too. I'm sure seeing she who shall remain nameless hit you hard."

"She's not Voldemort, Stofferson. But, yes, very hard. Do you think The Thirteen have anything to do with her arrival?"

"Hmmm," Stofferson mused. "Possibly. Seeing as though you and Michael saw through their first try with Jenny, they may think Julia's presence might push you into taking your own life. If so, they've played their hand too soon. Or, they didn't expect you to bump into her. Either way, the best move for us is to sleep here and then go back tomorrow and reverse the curses."

"I've got to be honest with you, Stofferson," Lydia began, "I don't give a stuff about your curses anymore. I just want my passport and then I'm off."

"But…"

"But, nothing. I don't need this shit in my life anymore, Stofferson." Lydia felt every suppressed emotion building to explode from the top of her head. "I'm done. Do you hear me?"

"Okay. Calm down."

"Calm down nothing. I can't take any more of this nonsense. This is your world and you're welcome to it." She stood, tears building in her eyes to fog her vision, and rushed into the bathroom before slamming the door and locking it. Within the tiled room, she felt safe. Bathrooms always gave her some security since childhood. As she sat on the downturned toilet seat, the tears flowed without witness or judgement. She sobbed without abandon for the years wasted, for the beatings Julia sent her way, for her lost friends, and, lastly, for Michael.

An hour later, Stofferson tapped lightly on the other side of the door. "Lydia, I'm sorry if I upset you. I can act without thought for others sometimes."

She stood, washed the dry tears from her face and opened the door. "It's not just you. It's everything. I'm spent and just need to get away for a while.

"I get that," Stofferson replied, before doing something he never did. He opened his arms. Lydia all but fell into his embrace, heavy with the burden of the past few years.

"I need to sleep," she said into his chest.

With no words spoken, they moved to the bed and slipped under the covers. There, they hugged again. Just two floating souls needing an anchor for a short time as the storm raged around them.

"One thing I don't get," Lydia began, one foot in sleep land. "Why doesn't The Thirteen just send that madness demon to climb inside my head and push me over the edge?"

"The curse and the deal with Clauneck require a willing participant. One not pushed by outside forces," Stofferson mumbled.

"Oh."

Moments later, she heard his breathing change as he slipped from consciousness. A light snoring soon followed.

Lydia floated in and out of sleep. Dreams of a snarling Julia pounced intermittently to make her gasp. This went on until she heard movement in the corridor beyond. Nothing dramatic. Just room doors closing and patrons shuffling towards the lift for breakfast. Stofferson, by this time, had disengaged from their embrace and lay sleeping on the other side of the bed. Neither had undressed. This made it easier for Lydia to slip from her side of the bed, pick up her keys and bag, with care, and leave the room without waking him.

Lydia knew what she needed to do and Stofferson didn't fall into her plans, as grateful as she was for their night together. On arrival at the reception, she asked, "Is it all possible if you can box up a breakfast? I woke a little late and have a long day ahead."

"I think that should be possible," the cheery receptionist replied. "If you pop into the restaurant, I'll get the kitchen to send you a box."

Ten minutes later, Lydia pointed the car back to Burrstone. Less than an hour after that, with little incident on the road over the moors, barring a rising tension in her chest that hindered her breathing somewhat, she pulled up outside the flat. Her palms slipped from the wheel, drenched in sweat. Her eyes shot from the front to the side mirrors. Everything appeared normal. Mr K appeared from his shop and waved. She offered a tentative wave back. His presence offered Lydia a little security. *There's no way Julia will attack me with him around,* she thought and opened the driver's door.

"Hello to you," Mr K called. "You look tired."

"I am. How are you?"

"I am, as the young person's say, rocking."

"You haven't noticed anyone hanging around the flat, have you?" Lydia asked.

"Nope. Just old K moving stock in and then out. Why? Men stalk you?"

"Not a man. A woman."

"Ooh, women no stalk."

"You'd be surprised."

"I would. Now, men, they are sick. Women are the fairest. Take my Mrs K. She is like a rose with me as her thorn," he said and then laughed his booming laugh.

"Well, if you see a blonde-haired woman hanging around, could you tell me?"

"Of course."

"Thank you, Mr K. You're a good one," Lydia smiled and headed for the door.

"My wife would love you. You must promise to have the tea, eh?" Mr K asked as Lydia slid the key into the lock.

"It would be my pleasure." Lydia smiled and closed the door. The silence of the house didn't please her as it should. She had one job to do and then get out.

She opened the door to the flat and skipped up the stairs, hoping Michael didn't ask too many questions. *I don't want to lie to him,* she told herself. Michael's worried presence on the landing, looking down and imploring her to turn back, startled her. "What is it?" she whispered. "Just talk to me," she added as he continued to mime peril. He pointed to the kitchen with frustration. Lydia followed. Her heart now thrashing in her chest. "What is it?" she asked again, once inside. Michael did not need to answer. Lydia felt the bottom of her stomach fall out and she let out an involuntary squeal as Chopin's Marche Funèbre played from somewhere in the flat. She threw herself into the corner of the room and wedged herself between a wall and the cupboards before sliding down to a crouch, shaking. Michael, worried, dropped the ball and disappeared. Lydia felt utterly alone.

"Did you think for one tiny second that you could move away from me and I wouldn't find you?" the deranged voice of Lydia's worst nightmare called.

Lydia's bladder opened and released its warmth between her legs to pool on the linoleum.

"You ungrateful little bitch. I'm going to make you pay for the months of upset you've caused me." Lydia whimpered as Julia's voice grew ever closer. "I am going to make you suffer for hours. Every hour will equate to every week. And if there is anything of you left, I will…"

"You will do nothing of the sort, you evil woman," Michael's voice boomed from the ghost box. "You will leave my friend and this flat forever."

"Show yourself," Julia replied, with no fear in her tone, "you coward." Lydia assumed, through the fog of fear, Michael must have shown himself, because Julia soon added, "What kind of trick is this?"

"It's not a trick," Michael said with a sneer.

Lydia heard a crash, as if one of them threw something at the other. "It's a hologram," Julia cackled. "You think you can stop me with a hologram?"

"I've no idea what a hologram is, but I'm not one, watch," Michael said before Lydia heard another crash. Michael fighting back gave her new confidence.

Lydia wiped the snot and tears with the back of her hand, stood as tall as her fear allowed, and inched towards the room as more crashing rang out.

"How are you doing this?" Julia screamed as Lydia's huge Writer's Handbook whacked the wall above Julia's head. "And there she is," she sneered as Lydia appeared and the music stopped.

"Lydia, stay in the kitchen," Michael told her.

"N-no," Lydia replied. "I w-will no longer hide from her."

"You will wish you had," Julia growled and lunged towards her.

Instinctively, Lydia raised her arms to protect herself and crouched. Michael shot across the room and shoulder-barged the attacker, sending her flailing against the wall. Her head connected with a sickening smack and Julia slipped to the floor.

"Is she dead?" Michael asked, hands to his mouth.

Lydia just stared, open-mouthed. Lost.

"Lydia? Is she dead?"" Michael asked again. Still nothing. "Lydia?"

"Hmmm," Lydia mumbled. "Yes. Yes." She poked Julia's crumpled body with her foot. Her ex didn't move. Slowly, as if approaching a sleeping lioness, she reached down and touched her neck. "She's still alive," she muttered after feeling her pulse.

"Thank goodness for that. What do we do now? Call for help?"

"I'm not helping her. I'm gonna do what I came to do."

"What was that?"

"Just keep an eye on her, will you? I need to get changed." She stumbled up to her bedroom, hardly noticing the state Julia had made with scissors and rage, and removed her wet clothes. She then dabbed herself with baby wipes and dressed in the only clothes Julia hadn't cut up. The colours didn't match but she cared little for such things. She then pulled open her sock drawer and felt underneath before pulling her passport free of the scotch tape holding it in place. Without another glance, she headed back down to the lounge, where Julia still lay, unconscious. Lydia resisted the urge to boot her in the face. "How did she get in?"

"She has a set of keys," Michael replied.

"Make sure she doesn't move," Lydia told him as she searched Julia's pockets. She found them. "Do we have anything I can write on, Michael?"

"I still have the pad you hid in the kitchen. Why?"

His words seemed to knock her from her trance. "I'm sorry about that, Michael. I found your poem and didn't know what to do. That's why I left."

"What poem?"

"Oh yes. Wait here a minute," Lydia said and walked back to the kitchen and fished into the bag she'd dropped on the floor. She pulled out a folded piece of paper and returned to the lounge, "I think you wrote this before you…erm… died."

Michael took the paper and read. His jaw flopped. Without a word, he turned and pulled the pad out from under the couch. He passed it to Lydia. "This was also in the pad."

"Mary? Is this the lady of your dreams?"

"Much more. I remember everything, Lydia."

"Everything?"

"Everything," Michael shrugged. "My life with my

parents, moving in here, meeting Mary, my feelings for her. And my suicide. It all came to me over the last few days."

"Oh my God. I'm so sorry."

"I'm not. Maybe I'll see her again. Well, I hope, anyway."

Lydia slumped on to the arm of the couch. "I've been so selfish. So bloody selfish. All I thought about was me."

"There's nothing wrong with that," Michael told her. "I've had my life. You've still got yours. And you don't want to commit suicide. With what she put you through," he said, tipping his head in disgust towards Julia, "You've every right to want to, but you don't want to. You want to live. You're a fighter, Lydia. If Mary and Stofferson are right, I want you to get whatever you need and say goodbye with a smile for the good times we've shared." He smiled at her, and she thought he looked like an angel. Tears formed in her eyes and rolled down her quivering cheeks.

"I'm so sorry, Michael," she sobbed.

"You have nothing to be sorry for, Lydia. I promise," Michael told her. "You must..." A heavy knocking on the front door stopped both of them. "I'll go check." Michael dropped his ball and a moment later said, "It's Stofferson."

"He said he could reverse the curse," Lydia said, excited. "Maybe he can help you. I'll let him in." She bolted down to the ground floor and yanked the main door open. "Quick," she hissed and rushed back up the stairs. Michael leaned over the banister with a hopeful smile to greet both.

"What's happening?" Stofferson asked.

"You'll see," Lydia told him almost out of breath. They reached the top. Michael flattened himself against the wall to avoid the horror of witnessing their innards. Lydia stopped dead. Her stomach reeled. The lounge door was closed. "Michael," she whispered. "Please open the door." The living moved aside as the spirit inched towards the door and pushed. Julia no longer lay on the floor. "No, no, no," Lydia whimpered softly.

"Don't worry," Stofferson whispered, "Michael and I won't let her hurt you. I promise. Right, Michael?"

"I knocked her out once. I'll do it again," he said, his voice hardly a whisper as it came from the ghost box.

"I'M NOT SCARED OF YOU," Julia screeched from the second floor. "YOU'RE JUST A TRICK."

"Well, Mrs Gardner," Stofferson called up, "If Michael is the trick, I'm the magician. You may as well come down now."

"Oh, little scaredy Lydia has a boyfriend, eh?" Julia called back, the pain in her voice evident for all.

Stofferson placed his finger to his lips as he looked at Lydia. "Yes, she has a loving boyfriend. We are to marry when her divorce against you comes through. So, you may as well leave quietly. Nobody will get in your way."

"I'LL NEVER DIVORCE YOU," Julia howled. "YOU WILL ALWAYS LOVE ME, AND ME ALONE."

"She never loved you, Julia. And you will give her a divorce if you want your career intact. Otherwise, we will go to every press agency and expose you for the depraved monster you are. Do you hear?"

"NEVER," Julia screeched, "IF LYDIA DOESN'T COME UP HERE IN FIVE SECONDS, I WILL KILL MYSELF AND MY BLOOD WILL BE ON BOTH OF YOU. DO YOU HEAR ME?"

"I hear you, Julia," Lydia said and then whispered to Stofferson, "I'm okay." She turned and walked to the foot of the second-floor stairs. "I hear you, Julia, but guess what?"

"What?" Julia asked, a little calmer.

"I don't give one tiny shit if you kill yourself because you've killed any love I ever had for you over the years of abuse. So, kill yourself or don't. I don't give a damn." A strange silence floated down to the lounge. "Do you hear me now, Julia?" Lydia asked, her voice colder than nitrogen.

A few moments of deathly silence later, they all heard Julia plead, "Please, help me."

"I'm not coming up, Julia. I'm not falling for your crap ever again."

"Please. I'm serious. Please," Julia pleaded once again.

"I'll go," Stofferson told Lydia.

"It's just one of her games, Stofferson. She's probably waiting behind the door with a knife or scissors in her hands. "Don't trust her."

"I'm on the bed," Julia, her voice almost too faint to hear, called. "Please, help me."

"I'll just poke my head upstairs," Stofferson insisted. "I won't go all the way up until I know where she is."

"Do what you want," Lydia shrugged. She then said. "Please, be careful."

Stofferson crept up the narrow stairs. Lydia watched as he slowly poked his head around the door. "OH, MY GOD," he hollered. "LYDIA, SHE'S NOT KIDDING. I NEED YOUR HELP. BRING TOWELS."

Lydia stood, confused for a moment, until the urgency within and around Stofferson's words hit her. She then rushed into the kitchen and emptied the towel drawer before bolting up to her bedroom. What she saw widened her eyes. Because Julia lay, ashen against the flow of crimson on her bed, her wrists slashed beyond healing.

"Do you have any belts or ties for a tourniquet?" Stofferson asked.

"Look in the wardrobe," Lydia replied.

"Please, help me," Julia's voice sounded like it came from a long tube.

"You idiot," Lydia whispered as she wrapped her wounds. However, the blood soon seeped through. First in flowers then in floods.

Stofferson tied her arms with two thin leather belts. Moved away to call for an ambulance, cringing down at Lydia, as if to say, they'll be too late.

"Lyd, I'm c-cold," Julia stuttered, her lips all but devoid of colour. Lydia pulled the quilt, now heavy with the stench of copper, across Julia. "I'm s-sorry," Julia whispered.

"Hush," Lydia told her. "Save your strength. The ambulance will soon be here." She looked up to hear Stofferson talking to the emergency services.

"I need to tell you…how…" Julia began, but lost consciousness.

"Stay with me, Jules," Lydia said and shook her ex.

"Is there anything I can do to help?" Michael asked, appearing behind Lydia.

"We need to keep her awake," Lydia replied, shaking Julia with a little more force.

"The ambulance is on its way. But, I'm guessing we may be too late, Lydia. I'm sorry," Stofferson told her.

"Don't say that," Lydia snapped.

"I'm not saying it. Michael standing in this room is telling you. I'm so sorry."

Chapter Twenty

The ambulance arrived merely to take the body of Julia Gardner away in a bag. The police followed to take statements. Lydia remained coldly calm throughout. She answered their questions as honestly as possible.

"Yes, we were estranged," she told the male and female. "Yes, I have changed my name." "No, I didn't know she was in the flat when I arrived home." "No, I don't know where she acquired the keys." The questions kept on coming and she felt no need to lie. Her hell could now pass. Her life could begin again. Lies only hampered her progression.

The police took away the bloody towels and the scissors and taped up her bedroom, telling her not to go in until the forensics team had arrived to take prints. They then advised her to stay at a hotel and then questioned Stofferson. The third witness remained silent.

"Right, we need to hurry," Stofferson told them both after the police left. "We need to set up protection spells and then reverse the curses before our next visitor."

"Next visitor?" Lydia asked.

"I'm guessing Clauneck is the demon to settle our dear departed into her new role. So, I need you to follow me and both repeat these chants." He pulled out several sheets of paper, stapled in the corner, and handed them to Lydia.

"Is this dangerous?" She asked.

"Only if we don't hurry."

The three swept from room to room repeating the same, as far as Lydia and Michael were concerned, gobbledygook. They even slipped under the tape to Lydia's blood-covered bedroom, gagged at the stench and recited the spell. The last room proved the strangest.

"We can't break into someone else's property," Lydia hissed as the three stood before the door to the downstairs flat. Michael, smiling, just enjoyed the new freedom he had acquired from nowhere.

"Allow me to quickly ask you if this supposed storage area has ever had a visitor?"

"Actually," an excited Michael began, "I've seen several people come and go at least twice."

"When?" Lydia asked.

"And how many is several?" Stofferson added.

"Before you moved in. And, in fact, a day or so ago. And I counted at least twelve to…"

"Thirteen?" Stofferson cut in with a knowing look towards Lydia.

"Now I come to think about it, yes," Michael replied.

"And I'm guessing they chanted for a while and then left?" Stofferson asked.

"I'm not sure if they actually chanted. I just heard a lot of mumbling before they left."

"But, they didn't stay long?" Stofferson asked Michael.

"I wasn't good with time before Lydia came, but it didn't seem long."

"My guess is, behind this door is their altar to open the gates for the next victim."

"And if you're wrong?" Lydia asked.

"I doubt I am," Stofferson told Lydia. "So, why don't we get our ethereal friend here to poke his fine head through the door and report what he sees. If it's what I suspect, then we bash the door down and finish the rituals before dear Mr Clauneck arrives to rip out our innards. Or much worse."

Michael shrugged, took a breath he didn't need and pushed his head through the painted wood of the door. After a couple of seconds, he returned with a stunned expression.

"I don't know much about altars, Stofferson, but they have a table with a large crystal in the middle, and a red and a black candle on either side. There's also a huge painting with a goat man in the middle of a star," Michael told them.

"Satisfied?" Stofferson asked.

"Let's just get on with it," Lydia growled.

"Michael, would you mind bashing the door down?"

Michael shrugged before throwing himself at the door. He then bounced back to land, embarrassed, on the floor in front of them. "That hurt," he grumbled.

"How can that hurt you?" Lydia asked the stricken ghost.

"Another damned curse. Well, I came prepared. Stand back, please." Stofferson told them.

Lydia and Michael frowned at one another and did as asked.

Stofferson pulled out another sheet of paper from his long coat and began chanting a different incantation, the words hardly audible to the other two. After a few moments of repeating the chant, a red glow appeared around the door frame. Faint at first, then brighter and brighter until looking at it hurt Lydia's eyes. The light then reached its peak of illumination before fading once more.

"That should do it," Stofferson told them, looking a little

tired form his efforts. "Now, when we get in, be prepared for an attack."

"What kind of attack?" Lydia asked, not liking the sound of things.

"I can't be sure, but these are no amateurs," Stofferson warned. "They are bound to have left some kind of defence. You may feel an unseen fear. Or you may see monsters that strike you with fear. Michael should be safe. Lydia, put this around your neck." Stofferson pulled a pale blue crystal on a white gold chain from his bottomless coat pocket and handed it to her. "This should protect you."

"Should?"

"Sorry. Poor choice of words. It will protect you."

Lydia gave Stofferson a look that suggested his life depended on it working before dropping the chain over her head.

"Right," Stofferson began, "if you'd like to do the honours, Michael."

"Honours?"

"Yes, as in knock the bloody door in," Stofferson said. "Time is of the essence, my friend."

"Oh, okay." Michael took a step back, cringed at Lydia, ran headlong toward the door and smashed straight through, leaving precious little to show it had once functioned as a door.

Stofferson thanked him and stepped inside, followed by a tentative Lydia. The room sat exactly as Michael described it. "We must act fast," Stofferson warned them. "Remember, nothing can harm you if we stick together and don't remove the crystal."

Michael and Lydia nodded. Stofferson began the chanting. The other two joined in.

The lack of threat relieved Lydia. For a moment. Until

the one piece of music that could pull her to her shaking knees erupted from unseen speakers.

"Ignore it, Lydia," Stofferson called over the music. "It's an illusion designed to work on your worst fears. Any minute now, we'll be standing on a high precipice. My fear. BRING IT ON!" He hollered. "You can't scare us." He regretted those words for a second as the room dissolved to reveal clouds and sky around them…and nothing but air as far as the eye could see. A fierce wind built around them, buffeting their bodies. "I HAD TO OPEN MY BIG GOB," he called above the howling wind. He and Lydia clung to one another. Michael stood to the side and carried on chanting. "IT'S JUST AN ILLUSION," Stofferson called out in defiance. "WHAT ELSE YOU GOT?" He returned to chanting, closing his eyes as he did so. Lydia saw this and followed suit.

For what felt like hours but was only minutes, voices tempted them to open their eyes. Former lovers promised activities of the flesh most countries of the world find illegal. Lost parents begged and cried for their children to come to them. Members of the law demanded they cease this nonsense or face imprisonment. Michael screamed in pain and fear. Well, he did until the real one told them both to ignore it. They heard babies crying, animals whining in fear, and finally silence. Both feared one last attack.

"I think it's finished," Michael said in hushed tones.

"Everybody read the chant one last time. For luck," Stofferson requested. The other two joined in as peace hummed around them. "Right," he sighed, "Let's go back upstairs. I need a cuppa."

"I need something much stronger," Lydia replied, her insides in bits.

They all made their way upstairs. Lydia broke off at the kitchen to put the kettle on.

"I've got honey this time," she called out as she filled the kettle from the tap in the sink.

"I suspect we may need a third cup, Lydia," Stofferson called back.

Lydia plugged in the full kettle and flicked the switch. "Why's that?" she asked as she made her way to the lounge. Stofferson didn't need to answer. A tall, ridiculously handsome man, dressed in the finest-cut cloth, sat cross-legged on Michael's perch.

"Lydia, I presume," the man stated. "I've heard so much about you, I feel as if I already know you."

"I know little about you," she replied, scared but too damn sick of the bullshit to show it.

"I'm Lord Clauneck. I'd like to say it is a pleasure to meet you."

Chapter Twenty-one

"Come. Sit," Clauneck ordered Lydia, though added a friendly pat on the sill.

"I'm okay standing, thanks," Lydia replied. She looked from Michael to Stofferson. Neither seemed unduly worried by this new arrival. Though, they did appear less than comfortable in his presence.

"That wasn't a request, my dear."

"Your threats won't work here, Clauneck," Stofferson warned.

"Really? Let us put that to the test, shall we?" He raised his hand, a flicker of flame appeared, growing into a flaming ball that gave his face a ghoulish look. He grinned a grin that would make a rhino pause for thought, pulled back his hand and flung the ball at Stofferson. Lydia's eyes widened as the ball screamed and shot towards its target. Yet, much to the annoyance of the demon, it faded the closer it got, until it fizzled out by Stofferson's feet. "You've reversed my charms. You naughty boy. You've triggered the curse and messed with my charms. You may well decide never to leave this flat, young man. For your own protection."

"You've tried to kill me several times before, remember? And as recently as weeks ago," Stofferson said. "Didn't work then."

"We obviously didn't pick the right lorry driver," Clauneck sneered. "Well, that's by the by. Are you ready to say goodbye to your little fleshy friends, young man?" he asked Michael.

"Where are you taking me?" Michael asked.

"Oh, I'm not taking you anywhere. My boring counterpart of light will take you. You may even get to see your parents again."

"And Mary?" Michael asked, eager.

"I neither know nor care. My attention is firmly fixed on the one who replaced the dear intended who cares not to sit."

"Who's that?" Lydia asked, hoping it wasn't who she thought. The notion of spending her time in the flat with her former torturer made her feel sick.

"You should know. You watched her bleed out."

Lydia shot a glance towards Stofferson. He offered her a slight shake of the head she hoped meant the demon lied.

"Ohhhh, Julia!" Clauneck called out in a sing-song voice, looking past Lydia and on to the landing behind her. "Your presence is required. I trust your charms won't prevent me summoning my next guest?" He asked Stofferson.

"It shouldn't," Stofferson replied.

"Good. I fear she will at this moment be struggling to get out of the bath. The silly lamb," the demon said before raising his hand.

Lydia turned to face the same direction in which Clauneck crooked his finger and gasped as Julia appeared in the bathroom doorframe. Rather than the furious expression Lydia had become used to, Julia looked nothing more than benignly puzzled as she floated towards her new master. "Where am I?" she asked as she entered the lounge.

"It is of no consequence as you are no good to man nor beast," Clauneck snarled.

"Is she not going to take over from Michael?" Lydia asked.

"I'm guessing she isn't part of the usual deal," Stofferson told her.

"Most perceptive of you, occultist. She isn't the kind of soul accepted upstairs, I'm afraid. Thanks to you." His eyes narrowed as he looked at Lydia. She fought the shiver running up and down her spine.

"What? Because I'm not willing to kill myself for your pleasure, this is my fault?"

"You get it," Clauneck sneered.

"There's one thing I don't get," Stofferson cut in.

"I'm sure there's much you don't get," Clauneck began with a grin, "But, go on."

"How the hell did you engineer all this? I mean, Lydia lives hundreds of miles away. She kept her relationship and unhappiness a secret. How many other innocents passed up on the opportunity of buying this place before you found her? There are too many coincidences for me."

Clauneck leaned back against the lounge window and preened himself with a wide, self-satisfied grin growing ever wider across his face. "Silly mortal. There are no coincidences at play. Nothing is left to chance. It is all by fabulous design. Coincidence," he then cackled at the stupidity. "I have more covens than just The Thirteen, spanning the entire globe. I took you for more than a naïve fool, Irving. Tut-tut. Let's just say, in this case, many covens interacted. One of my personal favourite pawns in this game came from a coven in the capital of your country."

Stofferson cast a glance towards Lydia. She however appeared too deep in fearful thought to return anything.

"My father?" She asked with nervous anticipation of his deceit. He hated her lifestyle after all. And, "he's a member of the Masons."

"The Masons are nothing more than man-children who crave a little power and perversion," Clauneck laughed. "Try again, child."

"I would have said Julia before she turned out to be too unstable for such games."

"Bingo," Clauneck said. "Who else?"

Lydia trawled her mind through exes and former friends but found nobody who even vaguely met the credentials. Yes, some of her old friends floated a little close to flaky, but none into witchcraft. Well, as far as she knew.

"You're thinking too hard, girl. Who knew more than most that you suffered at the hand of this dreadful creature?"

"Who me?" Julia asked, still puzzled. "I've never met her before."

"Oh, hush, you," Clauneck growled and mimicked clamping his lips.

"Not…Harry?" Lydia asked, the colour draining from her face.

"The same," Clauneck grinned. "After you started pumping your residual cheques into another account, dearest Harriet, she of the Regent's Chapter, put the feelers out. She had colleagues in the NHS check your records. They worked out that your past injuries rang alarm bells you were too scared to listen to."

"But Stofferson's book? She didn't know about that or that I would become interested in the flat," Lydia protested, fearing this was nothing more than a trick because Harry was her friend.

"In that little bookshop you visit with remarkable regularity? Yes, that was sooooo difficult to plant that dreadful book on a shelf for you to see and find too ridiculous not to wonder about."

"Why didn't you just get rid of me before now?" Stofferson asked. "You may have saved yourself a lot of time and error. A little sloppy, don't you think?"

"Watch your mouth, dabbler," Clauneck snarled. "We tried. Remember? It appears you have had your own friends along the way. The imp, for one. Though, he won't be around forever. Remember that too," the demon growled and turned back to Lydia. The smile reappearing, "Unfortunately for me, The Thirteen aren't as bright as they once were. The temptress was all breasts and no brains. They are beginning to bore me. And whomever came up with the plan of sending this thing up here to push you over the edge will suffer."

"Including Harry?" Lydia asked.

"Most definitely if she had any part in this creature appearing here. I'm sorry, my dear, you may have to find new representation as she might just become absent for the foreseeable future if she orchestrated this idiocy," Clauneck shrugged.

"I don't believe it. She's my friend. She's the only one who…"

"Allow me to stem any histrionics, my dear. They have no effect on me. Yet, if you still don't believe me, listen." He pulled a silver mobile device from the inside of his suit jacket and flicked a number. "See, she's on speed dial," Clauneck sniggered. "Oh, and no screaming out threats until I've established the facts. I'll point to you when I'm ready for your snot and recriminations."

After a moment, the one voice Lydia wished did not answer the call answered the call. On hearing the voice, Lydia shuffled over to a chair and collapsed heavily into it, her face devoid of colour. Tears had already formed in the corner of her eyes, which amused Clauneck. Stofferson shuffled over to offer comfort, but she barely noticed him.

"Your lordship. This is an unexpected call. I'm hon…" Harry simpered.

"Yes, yes, lah-dee-dah. Tell me, my child, who made the decision to send dear old Julia up to Yorkshire?" His tone softer than at any time he had entered the flat.

"I really don't know, your lordship. Definitely not from my order."

"When was the last time you saw her?"

"She came to my office, ranting and sobbing several weeks back. I sent her packing and then saw her on the street with a woman who appeared to offer her hope."

"The woman? Describe her to me."

"Bottle blonde. Way too much make-up, your lordship. Trying too hard to be classy but not pulling it off."

"Hmmmm," Clauneck mused. "Interesting. One more thing before I go. Our friend in Yorkshire found out you're not really her friend in London, after all. Go ahead," he told Lydia.

"Why, Harry?" Lydia asked, broken.

"Lyd?" Harry asked, all reverence dropping from her voice. A nervousness Lydia had never heard before replaced it. "I'm sorry. I was just…"

"You said you were there for me," Lydia cried.

"I was more than there for you for many years, Lyd. You knew that and trod all over the torch I carried. I thought it might change after that night at my place years ago, but you woke up and claimed not to remember. Then you met her and shut us all out until you needed something."

"I didn't tread on anything, Harry. I was drunk," Lydia yelled through a wash of tears and pain. "Too drunk to remember even leaving the pub never mind anything else. I swear I would never hurt you on purpose. But you, for that one night, planned for me to kill myself in this flat! What kind of fucking love is that? I came to you as soon as I got myself free from Julia and you pretended you knew nothing, you psychotic bitch!" She hollered and fell into Stofferson's arms.

"Put yourself in my shoes, Lydia. Just for once stop thinking of only yourself."

"WHAT?" Lydia screamed.

"Okay, okay," Clauneck interceded. "I've little time for these girly rants. I'll speak to you later, Harriet." He cut the call. "Right, I must go."

"What happens now?" Stofferson asked.

"Oh, I presume a blinding light will call this young man to the bosom of pathetic love, and you better look over your shoulder. Just another day for you, eh?" Clauneck smiled. "As for this place, the gig is done. So, any future stories will be moot. Shame though. I made some good money from the old place. All good things and all that, eh?"

"What about me?" Lydia asked, wiping her nose on her sleeve and leaving a mark only a giant snail would make.

"I'm going to have to think about that," Clauneck grinned. "I'm obviously kidding. You can neither hurt me nor earn for me, so go free. I'm feeling charitable today. Maybe not so much tomorrow. But, today, I am. Come on, wretched creature." He snatched Julia by the hair and disappeared.

Chapter Twenty-two

A dark cloud of nervousness hung over and around the cowled heads of The Thirteen as they summoned their lord. Diana sat slightly in front of the others, as their custom decreed for centuries, yet felt little of its usual honour. This time she knew the others sat further back to separate themselves from the unholy mess Broughton Road had become.

Daniel had called her earlier with the dreadful news.

"Are you certain the barrister is the one who killed herself?" She asked Daniel.

"Certain," Daniel replied. His voice carried no triumph. Only worry.

"But, how? Aren't the charms supposed to push the other woman into suicide?"

"Yep."

"Then, what went wrong?"

"We don't know yet."

"So, what is it we do goddamned know?"

"She came to the agency the afternoon before she killed herself, ranting and somehow knowing we had sold Lydia the flat and why. She threatened to expose everything so, to shut her up, I gave her a copy of the flat's keys."

"You did what? Are you that stupid, Daniel?"

"Did you hear me? She threatened to expose everything she knew."

"What more did she know than her estranged wife lived in a flat we sold her?" Diana asked, furious. "Hardly damning evidence, Daniel."

"Well, she said she knew about The Thirteen," Daniel told her.

"How, Daniel? How could she possibly know anything about us? Jesus."

"What was I supposed to do, Diana? This woman is a well-respected barrister in London. The fallout if she exposed us would end us all."

"That would be a scratch on our cheeks compared to what Lord Clauneck will do, you brainless, gutless fool. You will explain this to our lord. Because I'm damned sure he will want someone to explain things, and I'm not going up in flames like your little dolly bird, Daniel. Do you hear me?"

"I'll see you at the manor," was all that Daniel replied before he cut the call.

On arriving at the manor, Diana found that Daniel wasn't as stupid as he made out. She sensed the alienation from the moment she arrived. The other twelve, Daniel included, didn't give her the due respect she deserved as leader. Not one bowed, another custom spanning the years.

"It would seem, I'm to be the sacrificial lamb, eh?" She snarled at the others waiting in the entrance hall.

"You are being paranoid, Diana," Daniel told her. "We are merely nervous. We stand behind you as our leader."

"Is that so?" She asked and looked from one downturned expression to another. They mumbled their loyalty without casting a single glance. "Gutless," she growled to hide her fear before sweeping down the corridor to the summoning room.

And now, as the smoke began to billow from the mirror, she would face Lord Clauneck and throw them all into the oncoming violence. Yet, Lord Clauneck didn't arrive first. Before he stepped through the looking glass, he launched a silently sobbing and battered Julia. She landed before the shocked Thirteen and curled herself into a tight ball. Clauneck waited the required amount of time to cement the fear before he stepped through to stand, emotionless, in front of them. He appeared to tower above them more than usual. His eyes rested for an horrific moment on each head.

"Remove your cowls," he growled. They did as Clauneck demanded with shaking hands. "Do any of you recognise this stinking ball of offal?"

"Daniel might," Diana told her lord.

"Is that so? And you do not?" Clauneck asked, his eyes stripping away her mortality.

"No, my lord. I have never met her."

"Truth, woman," Clauneck snapped.

"I swear, my lord," Diana whimpered, "I have never seen her before this day."

"And you never visited London and talked with her during the last weeks?"

"No, my lord. Well, I have visited London, my lord, but that was on other business."

Clauneck stepped forward and tore Diana from the ground by her throat. "Do you remember seeing her now?" He asked, his eyes turning red.

"I swear, my lord," Diana gargled in reply.

Clauneck dropped her to the floor with a bump. "We will come back to this. How did she end up in the flat, Daniel?" His eyes never flickered from Diana as he asked.

"M-my Lord, I-I…"

"Am I your first girlfriend, Daniel?" Clauneck asked, turning his fearsome gaze to the frightened former leader.

"No, My Lord."

"Then talk to me without stammering."

"Yes, my lord. I, I mean, she visited the agency yesterday. She was in a state, screaming about exposing us if I didn't give her a key to the flat. She's a famous barrister and I..."

"I know exactly what she was, Daniel. Why did you not get rid of her and come to me for help? This sack of shit would not need to raise scissors to her wrists if you had."

"But..."

"DID I GIVE YOU PERMISSION TO SPEAK?"

"No, My Lord," Daniel squeaked.

"Then you listen when I speak. Why did you not come to me?"

"I...erm..."

"You panicked like a coward and an imbecile. Have I not removed any threat to The Thirteen for centuries?" Daniel nodded his head and cast his eyes to the ground.

Diana fought to keep the smile from her lips.

"Have I not kept you in the finery of wealth and the security it offers? Even during your world's so-called depressions and wars?" Daniel nodded again. "Answer me," Clauneck snarled.

"Yes, My Lord."

"And, yet, through those years of decadence, The Thirteen has become fatuous and weak. Your forefathers and mothers would cringe at the sight of all of you. The shame of the seed they sowed and the sacrifices they made would destroy them. What am I supposed to do with this vile abomination?" He pointed at the still-balled-up Julia.

"Will the white lighters not take her, My Lord?" Daniel asked.

"What is the condition of my deal with the Seraph, you inane dullard?"

"The soul must be pure?"

"Are you asking me?"

"No, My Lord. Sorry."

"And is this thing pure?"

"I only know through intelligence that she abused the occupier of Broughton Road, My Lord."

"So, in your mind, that is purity at its finest, Daniel?"

"Well, no, My Lord."

"Then you have answered your own ridiculous question, haven't you? This thing," he pointed again at Julia, "may bring me a few laughs from my Lord, but nothing from the seraph." He snarled and raised his hand. A ball of blue flame shot out and engulfed a silently screaming Julia. She vanished in seconds, though the horrific image played on the retinas of The Thirteen for a few moments. They may have wished it played longer. Because as the image faded, a new red fire engulfed all but Diana. She screamed in fear as the bodies of her former coven spat as they burned.

"Do shut up," Clauneck told her. "Your time may or may not come, depending on the following outcome." He then reached out, grabbed her by the scruff of her neck and dragged her into the mirror.

Mere seconds later, Diana felt Clauneck shove her into an unknown room, landing on her knees upon a sheepskin rug. The flames of her former coven still crackled behind her eyes, so it took a moment for her to see her new surroundings.

"Wakey-wakey!" Clauneck ordered to someone in the room.

Diana blinked a few times to clear her vision and then realised she sat on the white, fluffy rug of someone's bedroom. A four-poster bed stood inches from where she landed. She thanked her stars she didn't hit it. The pillars were carved oak and thick. The impact would surely have concussed her at best.

"I said, wake up!" Clauneck bellowed. "Don't make me shout again."

"My Lord," a nervous female voice said. "Please forgive me. I didn't know you would visit."

"Well, I am here now, woman. Diana, stand," Clauneck spat. Diana didn't wait for him to ask again. She shot to her feet. "Is this the woman you say you saw with the barrister?" He asked the woman Diana now recognised as Harriet Breeden-Soames of the Regent's Chapter. A coven not as old, nor as distinguished, as her own.

"It is sire," Harriet said.

"She's lying, my lord," Diana pleaded. "I swear on everything unholy; I have only met this woman once and never the barrister. I swear it."

"She's lying, my lord. I saw her," Harriet replied, as quick as a photon. "She met the woman outside my office."

"I've never been to your office. I've only met you once, years ago, when you came to visit my coven."

"No, you were…" Harriet began.

"ENOUGH," Clauneck barked. "I will settle this via an old friend. Ose," he called out. A moment later, a monstrosity of a creature slithered out of the full-length mirror from which Diana fell. Harriet backed up the bed's headboard, eyes wide, as she stared into so many dead eyes circling a head that looked freshly scorched black. Several rows of jagged teeth protruded at all angles from its wide and frightening, lipless mouth. One or two even seemed to have punctured its cheek to continue growing. It appeared to have no neck, yet a barrel chest grew from underneath its head. Diana gasped as she made out its heart pumping between charred ribs. Ose didn't have a stomach to keep its innards in place, so its entrails hung, cancerous and puss-ridden, down its tree-trunk thighs. Some even reached just above its ankles. Ankles that each contained a spike pointing backwards like macabre spurs. Despite this horror, Ose didn't leave a mark on the white fur rug. "Ose, be a pal and reach into the minds of these miserable bitches and tell me who actually met the barrister. Thanks."

Both women tried to back away in horror, however two slimy tendrils shot from separate points to shoot up each woman's nostril. Both made a noise nobody makes twice.

"The one in the bed," Ose growled. "She seemed to think she has a claim for leadership of The Thirteen."

"Thanks, my friend. You may remove the probes," Clauneck said and shook his head in dismay. "These silly humans."

Ose removed the tendrils. Diana collapsed unconscious to the rug, still breathing but ragged. Harriet fell back against her pillows, in a similar condition but at least awake. Though, she soon wished otherwise.

"You dare consider your own paltry ambitions over mine?" Clauneck snarled down at Harriet.

"No, My Lord," Harriet croaked. "I thought I could revive The Thirteen for you. They are full of fools."

"Then, why not speak to me about your audacious plan? Is it because you are no less foolish?"

"But…"

"But, nothing."

"Please don't kill me, My Lord. I can help you."

"Oh, I don't think I will do something so final, my lovely. I am going to allow your misplaced ambition to haunt you deeper before I see you next. Ose?"

"Please, My Lord, pleeeease!" Were the last coherent words Harriet Breeden-Soames would say out loud for quite some torturous time.

Chapter Twenty-three

Lydia spent the next few days staggering between floods of tears, staring at the wall in a trance, and white-hot anger. The tears sprung from two diametrically opposed wells. One erupted as soon as Michael left for the other side. Whatever that meant. One moment he stood before Stofferson and herself, wishing them well and thanking them for all they had done. The next he smiled like a benign monk as he grew brighter and fainter at the same time.

"It's beautiful," he said, his voice no longer emanating from the ghost box, before he disappeared with a small wave of his right hand.

Lydia missed him more than she thought possible after only a short time in his presence. She hoped he found all he wanted wherever he materialised.

The other tears, mixed with anger and guilt, fell for Julia. Lydia never once, even as she heard her bones break all those times under Julia's control, wished her dead. And to see her bleed out brought forth such conflicting emotions, Lydia felt like a caseicultureist had rammed her head in their press and repeatedly tightened and released the pressure every odd hour.

One moment she felt furious and the next boulder-heavy with pity and regret.

Stofferson tried his best to help her, but he couldn't really relate. He stayed on the couch and said little. Other than, "I'm here for you, Lydia."

"I don't bloody need you here for me. I need you to tell me how this even happened."

"They fed on your sorrow. That's what leeches like those do."

Even after hearing about The Thirteen's manor house burning to the ground and the disappearance of so many local figures Stofferson said were attached to the coven, the turmoil boiling inside her did not ease.

Another reason for her rage came from Harry.

"I can do something about her," she told Stofferson, wiping her salty eyes on the fourth morning after Michael had gone. "Because I bloody need answers, or I will expose the traitorous bitch to the world."

"Maybe you should speak with her when you are a little calmer," Stofferson advised. "You'll get little from her angry."

"I am calm," Lydia spat.

"Show me your hands."

"What?"

"Show me your hands."

Lydia shrugged and raised both hands. They almost flapped with the anxiety running along her veins. "I'm just tired," she lied.

"Then have a lie down before you call her."

"I can't sleep, for God's sake."

"I didn't mean for you to sleep. I meant meditate. Though, now you mention it, have you had any sleep since the hotel?"

"Have you?"

"My point. Neither of us have. If you want, we'll both meditate. We could do with it."

After more persistence form Stofferson, Lydia eventually agreed to try and meditate. They lined the floor with sofa cushions, because, despite not entering the bedroom since cleansing it and being told by the police they were satisfied no foul play was involved in Julia's death, she hadn't entered the room since.

Stofferson found some soothing music on YouTube and they both lay down next to one another. Lydia found shutting her mind to all the horrors she had witnessed difficult at first. She then tried concentrating on counting. She reached ten several times before Julia's ashen face juxtaposed with the scarlet of her blood jumped into her thoughts. She shuffled on the cushions. Her hand brushed Stofferson's. Something she hadn't felt for a long time kept her from moving it away. Something alive with energy, yet something peaceful. She pressed a little harder. Stofferson must have felt it too because he opened his hand. Almost an invite. Slowly, slowly, like teenagers on a first date, their hands clasped. The energy she initially experienced became more intense, creating a flush of giddiness. It bubbled and popped through her hand, up her arm, into her head, and down her entire body. She opened her eyes and turned her head. Stofferson turned to her. An unspeakable attraction drew their lips together. Again, slowly at first. Sensual. Light touches from her lips to his. She cupped his face with her free hand and the kissing entered a new gear. Whether by design, he allowed her to dictate the pace, but not in a shy way. Oh, quite the reverse. Soon, they lay naked and explored one another as if they had both seen each other's maps and knew the special places each liked to visit. Yet, they only popped into each place for a snack before sliding away to another. Sometimes, they re-visited. Sometimes they stayed for a full meal. And, when they reached climax, together, they appeared to transcend the room, the town, and the world in which they lived. They soared a universe of their own making before resting in one another's arms.

"Is that calm enough for you?" Lydia asked with a sassy smile after turning to him.

"I'd ask to see your hands but I'm too relaxed to let them go," Stofferson replied, his flushed face bathed in happy sweat.

"Why don't we find a hotel for a few nights?" Stofferson asked. "You need a good sleep in a comfortable bed and a grand meal."

"Can we order room service?" Lydia asked. "The thought of sitting in a heaving dining room does not thrill me at all."

"Absolutely."

"But, what about that demon?"

"What about him? He said you're safe."

"I'm talking about your safety, Stoffa. He said he'd get you."

"He said to look over my shoulder. Not a new thing for me. If it makes you feel better, I'll cleanse the car and then the room when we get there."

"I'd feel less anxious," Lydia admitted.

So, Stofferson made a show of cleansing the car before they left.

"Where do you fancy going?" Stofferson asked after Lydia packed a few things.

"Anywhere where there's sea."

So, they decided on Scarborough. That way they could drop in on Stofferson's mum on the way. They set off across the moors towards Harrogate as a small dusting of snow fell from the sky. Despite feeling calmer than she'd felt for quite some time, she needed to speak to Harry. She needed closure.

She pulled out her telephone. However, the cell service was limited that far into the wilds.

"You okay?" Stofferson asked.

"I am." She smiled and clasped the hand he rested on the gearstick.

"Do you want some music on?"

"Actually, no thanks. Unless you do."

"I'm easy," Stofferson replied, though the glance he cast her appeared full of concern.

"Seriously. I'm good. I am thinking about ringing Harriet, but I'm not seething. So, don't worry." She smiled before turning her gaze to the outside. Fields with few or no animals passed her eyes. After driving around for the last few months, she missed watching the world go by.

"I've never noticed them," she told Stofferson as the humungous golf ball-shaped spy equipment loomed ahead.

"Ah, good old Menwith Hill," Stofferson sniggered. "One of my teachers used to picket it during the eighties when it was all the rage. Well, I say one of my teachers. She soon lost her job when the heads saw her protesting, shall we say, without clothes."

"Seriously?"

"Seriously. She appeared on the news."

"I bet you liked that," Lydia sniggered.

"What?" Stofferson asked. "Because she was starkers? God, no. She was about sixty and not in good nick."

"Have you ever been in?"

"To Menwith? No. Doesn't interest me. Does it you?"

"A little. We don't have any American bases where I'm from, but a friend of mine from uni' who lived near one said they make proper, little American towns inside, with bowling alleys and malls. I'd like to see if it's true." She looked at her telephone. "Ah, signal. Do you mind if I ring her now? Just for closure."

"Of course not. Just..."

"I will," Lydia answered, knowing he would caution calm. She took a deep breath before tapping the number adjacent to Harry's name. The telephone rang...and rang...and rang. Lydia's nerves soon jangled. "I bet she's ignoring me, the..."

"Hello?" A nervous voice Lydia vaguely recognised as Harry's assistant asked.

"Hi, is that Sara? It's Lydia, a client of Harry's. Is she there?"

"Oh my God, you've not heard. Erm, Harry's, erm, in hospital."

"Oh, is she ill?"

"Yes, but not a...erm, regular hospital."

"What do you mean?"

"She's in a...erm, mental hospital," Sara explained. "She, erm...literally isn't talking to anyone."

Chapter Twenty-four

Lydia did not reach Scarborough. Nor even as far as Stofferson's mum's. She arrived in Harrogate with her decision made.

"I have to go back, Stoffa, I'm sorry," she said.

"To Burrstone?" Stofferson asked as he stopped the car at a red light outside Harrogate Conference Centre.

"No. Down south. I need to see her. I've also got to sort Julia's estate out. I'm sorry. I can't just plod off to the seaside. I don't know what I've been thinking."

"You've been in shock."

"And now I need to sort myself out. Can you drop me at the train station, please? There's bound to be a train to Leeds from there."

"Are you coming back?" Stofferson asked quietly, as if fearing the answer.

"Of course." She touched his hand as he pulled away from the traffic lights.

They said nothing more until they reached the station. Even then it was little more than a few words of comfort and luck before embracing. She pulled out her luggage and watched him pull away with a little wave.

It took little time for a train to Leeds to arrive. She climbed aboard and took a seat, thinking about the last time she took a train. The fear and the joy of freedom flushed her system. This time she had precious little to fear if the demon stuck to his word, but still felt the chill of anxiety rush up her spine. She was going home to her prison and the guard no longer lived there.

I should be over the moon. What the hell is wrong with me? She thought.

She opened her handbag and rummaged inside before pulling out a set of keys, one of which looked like a car key. Julia's keys. Lydia had fished them from Julia's handbag before the police arrived. She didn't know why. Maybe some kind of keepsake. She gave no thought to using them at the time. Now, circumstances called for her to use them.

The train clattered on through picturesque fields and over bridges, however, the sun dropping down the sky soon hid the scenes. They arrived in Leeds without incident. She departed the train, though to many riot police officers patrolling the station. Lydia sensed they appeared ready for some kind of battle, so asked a passing guard what was going on.

"Bloody Millwall are playing Leeds tonight, love. Them Londoners always bring trouble," the balding guard shrugged.

"I see," Lydia replied, hoping she might miss them coming the other way. "What time are they coming in?"

"Oh, they come in dribs and drabs all day, but the main rabble will be here on the six-thirty train."

Lydia looked at her telephone. 17:10. "What time is the next train to London, please?"

"Twenty minutes on platform one, love."

Lydia thanked him, looked for the direction to platform one and headed for the platform. Many business suits already waited for the same train when she arrived. She shuffled through them to a free space to wait.

"Lydia, darling," a familiar voice chimed, sending freezing shards into her heart. "Worry not. I don't think I'm here to harm you," Clauneck whispered into her ear.

"You don't think you are? That's comforting. Then what do you want?" Lydia asked, trying to keep her fear in check. She knew running would do her no good.

"I'm here as a travelling companion. The journey can bore the pants of the most imaginative people, after all." Lydia heard a loud train horn blast further down the line, startling her. "You're not nervous, are you?"

"No," she said and turned to look the demon in his startlingly disarming brown eyes.

"You're a terrible liar," Clauneck chided as the train pulled up in front of them. "Not a bad thing. Believe me."

Lydia turned back to watch the doors and windows filled with faces pass by before it stopped with a door full of Burberry-wearing Millwall fans leering out at her. She stepped back to allow them to exit as the door slid open. Clauneck held his ground.

"Hello, hello," the largest of the group began with a leering grin. "You're a sort, ain't you, darling? You fancy a bit?"

"The lady's with me," Clauneck said with no notable malice.

"I couldn't give the first f…" The thug stopped after looking directly into Clauneck's eyes. His back-up looked ready to fill their underpants.

"Yet, I could," Clauneck replied, with much more of a sinister tone. "Now go. Before I burn the rotten hearts out of you and your pathetic pals."

The group, all blood drained from their faces, rushed out of the train and away.

"You didn't need to do that," Lydia said as she followed the demon on to the train.

"Oh, but I did, my dear. It's fun. Come, join me at this table. I assure you we won't suffer any more disturbances as we chat." Clauneck held out his hand to allow the lady to sit first. Lydia felt she had little choice, so shuffled into a seat behind the table. Clauneck cast a grin around the carriage as others took seats. "You all look sleepy," he called out when all the passengers looked settled. Each lowered their heads and slept. Clauneck turned back to Lydia and asked, "I take it you've ditched ghost boy?"

"No," Lydia replied. "I have things to attend to in London. That's all."

"Anything I can help with?"

"No, thanks. I need to deal with Julia's estate, as we were still technically married."

"Ah, the screamer," Clauneck grinned.

"Pardon."

"The barrister. She's a screamer. Seems she doesn't like it when the power's taken from her."

"Sorry, but I'd rather not know that."

"I thought you of all people would revel in the joy of knowing your abuser is…shall we say, less than comfortable."

"I watched her die," Lydia replied trying to keep her fractured emotions in check. "I no longer hold any ill-will towards her."

"How charitable of you. Are you religious?"

"Not really."

"Are you going to tell me you're not religious, but you are spiritual?"

"No. Despite sitting with a demon…" Lydia began.

"We prefer to go by the fallen," Clauneck told her.

"My apologies. Despite sitting with one of the fallen, I'm struggling to understand why a just god or angel would allow the things I've seen to happen. And not just to me. For instance, how can any god create a parasite that eats through a person's eye?"

"Ah, the acanthamoeba. A personal favourite. And I know the fallen who created it."

"That wasn't God?"

"Nope. But don't allow that fact to stop you wondering how he can permit a roof to collapse onto a full church of his own believers. Another thing he didn't do but failed to prevent."

"Did you do it?"

"Heavens, no. Kill a load of potential customers? No. I merely provide a service that makes many rich. Including myself."

"Look, don't think me rude, but why are you here?"

"Visiting with you?"

"Yes."

"I merely wanted to see how you're doing."

"You came to see if I'm going to expose things I know nothing about."

"Oh, you know more than nothing, my dear. Let's not be coy."

"Okay, I know of your dealings with The Thirteen," Lydia began. "I've heard of your deal with an unknown angel for souls. I don't know which one and, quite frankly, I don't care."

"How can you not care?" Clauneck asked, puzzled.

"Because it has nothing to do with me."

"Ah, but it does. Do you think the seraph will just shrug

his bony shoulders and find another way of appeasing his boss? And do you think the coven to which Harriet belonged will forgive you for the loss of their leader?"

"The seraph as you call it will have to forgive me. It's in his nature. And I had nothing to do with Harry. Though, I'm guessing her going mad is something to do with you."

"I don't have the ability to make others insane."

"Yes, but you know a demon, I mean a fallen, who does. Ose or someone."

"See? You do know much about my business."

"Yes, and like I said, I don't care. So, you needn't worry."

"Oh, I'm not worried, dearest Lydia. I see an opportunity for a deal between you and I."

"What kind of a deal? Actually, scratch that. I don't care."

"I'm going to be frank with you. I'm bored. I was becoming bored with the deal with the seraph. You, Stofferson and Harriet, in a way, did me a small favour in destroying The Thirteen."

"Then why send Harriet insane?"

"She's not technically insane," Clauneck grinned. "Ose just reprogrammed certain areas of her brain to make it seem like she's lost the plot. Inside, she knows everything that's going on. One day, I will release her. But for now, she needs to pay penance for her over-reaching ambition."

"Sorry?" Lydia asked. "That's a pretty extreme punishment."

"It may seem so from a human perspective. However, it's nothing in my world. Or even in the seraph's."

"They're good, aren't they?"

"There's that naïveté shining through again, Lydia, darling. The seraphim want you to think them just and kind. But did they forgive us when my boss wanted a piece of the action? Not one ounce. We were cast down lower than humans. No offence, by the way, but that is the exact opposite of forgiving, wouldn't you say?"

"So, you're telling me that you are fine with me, but an angel might just get revenge for me shutting down his spirit-acquiring scheme."

"That's exactly what I'm telling you."

"And, because you're bored, you just popped up to warn me to watch my back from an angel?"

"No. I'm also bored of doing deals with petty fools and backward thinking occultists. Harriet had some progressive ideas before she became greedy. When she's done her penance, we may just revisit them. But, for now, I have a deal to make with you. If you're in?"

"You must think I have a death wish. I've had enough of all this crap. I just want an easy life," Lydia hissed.

"You will have an easy life, Lydia," Clauneck replied with a smile that almost looked kind. "My deal with you will require nothing illegal nor immoral. You'll be helping many beings, the fallen and others whose only desire is to come in from the cold."

"Don't you mean from the hot?"

"Don't believe everything you read, Lydia, darling. The flames of hell was a metaphor the Nazarene cooked up when he saw the burning pyre outside Jerusalem."

"Whatever. Like I said, I want nothing more than to go home, sort out Julia's estate and potter in my garden for a while."

"I'll give you a week to mull it over in your garden. Oh, and I will also tell you something juicy about Harry if you agree. FYI, she didn't want you dead, after all. She actually wanted you safe and lied to you on the phone for reasons I will divulge later. Tatty-bye." And with a little grin,

Clauneck disappeared.

The people seated around the carriage yawned as if waking.

"Well, this gets better and better," Lydia told the passing view outside. "Out of the frying pan and into a metaphor." She picked up her telephone and looked up Stofferson's number. Her finger wavered over the call icon. "Maybe later," she sighed and closed her eyes. The first dreamless sleep for quite some time took her in its gentle arms and carried her to a place where decisions could wait.

The end…for now.

Other Books by C. A. Middleton

The Custodian Circle of Sorrow: One socially inept man lost in the past and looking for love. One nameless lady ghost lost in the present and trapped inside his new home. One shared connection neither understand until it's too late. Will either break the circle of sorrows?

Dexter Booth and the Last Dragon: Most grandchildren go swimming or enjoy a burger when visiting their grandparents. Dexter helps his grandparents, alongside a clan of wood faeries, save the last dragon from evil as old as time during his weekend visit. Written under the name: Prof. Carrot-Phwack

The Custodian
Breaking the Circle

In the Custodian: Circle of Sorrow we find out who the Custodian is. Now we find out why 67A Broughton Road has trapped souls within its walls for almost three centuries. Can the newest occupant, Lydia, a woman in hiding from spousal abuse by a barrister specializing in spousal abuse, and ghosthunter, Irving Stofferson, break the circle and end the misery surrounding the house? And what do the Pendle Witches, the demon of wealth and a rogue seraphim have to do with the place? Open the book and find out. It will not disappoint.

Author Bio

Me? I am just a loony Yorkshire dude, proud father, and Pop-pop, with many voices in my skull screaming for time on a page. To paraphrase the words of Jim Morrison, I have lived a life you could make a movie on. I've worked as a chef, drilled for oil in the raging North Sea, and worked in tv and film. However, I did have to decline work as an escort some years back. No judgement. Just not me. True story.

These days, I'm a gym rat in between trying to find homes for three other books I've scribbled. When your cholesterol's eleven, you have little choice than to dump that lazy life in order pick things up and put them back down again and again...

Lightning Source UK Ltd.
Milton Keynes UK
UKHW010814181222
414088UK00003B/42

9 781958 000021